About the Author

Cat Hogan was born into a home of bookworms and within spitting distance of the sea. Her father, Pat, a lightship man, instilled in her a love of the sea and the stars. Her mother, Mag, taught her how to read before she could walk. Writing, storytelling and a wild imagination is part of her DNA.

The beautiful County Wexford is home to Cat, her musician partner Dave, two beautiful sons Joey and Arthur, and her tomcat Jim Hawkins. There they live a life of storytelling, song and adventure.

When she is not bringing imaginary friends to life, she runs a professional writing service for businesses. She can also be found in an Order of Malta Ambulance Corps uniform, volunteering in the local community.

The other love of Cat's life is food. A self-professed foodie, there is nothing she loves more than feeding a houseful of friends round her kitchen table.

They All Fall Down is Cat's debut novel.

Acknowledgements

'Let us be grateful to people who make us happy; they are the charming gardeners who make our souls blossom'– **Marcel Proust**

For me, getting the elusive book deal was the stuff that dreams are made of and it's something I don't take for granted – not for a second. 'No man is an island' as they say and I certainly didn't get here on my own.

So many people, knowingly or otherwise, have helped me. I would go so far as to say a few bent over backwards for me. I'll never forget that, and it's a thought that gladdens my heart every day.

Wexford is a magic little place indeed, a little pocket in the south-east corner of Ireland where dreams and creativity are embraced. Not every newbie author can claim to be made of the same stuff as the literary giants Colm Tóibín, Billy Roche, and Peter Murphy. We are all Yellow Bellies and that's good enough for me.

My own writing dreams would have remained just that if it was not for three amazing women taking a chance and believing in me. They are: my beautiful agent Tracy Brennan, my formidable publisher Paula Campbell and my genius editor Gaye Shortland. In the short time I have known these wonderful professionals, I have learned so much. Thanks for believing in me, ladies.

Back to Wexford and amazing author friends, of which there

are also three. I am blessed to be able to call Eoin Colfer a friend. He was the one who threw me up on the horse a few years ago and has been a constant friend and mentor since.

Then there is the absolute legend that is Paul O'Brien: playwright, author, film-maker and hustler. He is keeping a seat at the table for me.

Carmel Harrington. I could write a book of thanks to this author. I had the good fortune of signing up to her creative writing course a couple of years ago. From day one we clicked and she is now a dear friend. Without Carmel's gentle encouragement and sometimes stern words, this book would still be under my bed.

I have met some wonderful writers and authors in the last year who are so generous with their time and encouragement: Louise Phillips, Joan Brady, Lorna Sixsmith, Tara Sparling and Carolann Copland to name but a few. Thanks so much, ladies, for your kindness and advice.

Thanks to my lovely friend Caroline Busher, a wonderful author, and to Paul O'Reilly, author and playwright. Paul and Caroline assured me it is totally normal to have conversations with the voices in your head – preferably out loud!

To Brian Byrne – my pal and fellow scone-lover. Thanks for all the chats, your good taste, and for being an all-round decent human.

A word of thanks to the stunning Victoria Mary Clarke who taught me miracles can be manifested, and to her wonderful partner Shane McGowan who so generously allowed me to quote his beautiful lyrics.

Thanks to all the beautiful women in #WIN – Women's Inspire Network – the women who build each other up and support each other always on the good days, but especially on the bad days. I won't name all of you for fear of forgetting one – you know who you are.

Thanks to Susan Murphy for her legal advice, and to Diarmuid Sinnott for his medical advice. Massive thanks to Brian 'Molly' Molloy for being my reader and to Tony Parle for being my fisherman's friend. Thanks to all in the Jukebox Gypsy family for gently teaching me I am a much better writer than singer/piano player. To all my pals on Facebook – your words of praise and encouragement are always appreciated – some days they're the only thing that keeps me going. Kenny Ruttledge, magician photographer, thanks for making me look like a purdy human.

Sabia Barron – my constant friend, the most inspirational and the strongest woman I know. Thanks for always being my sounding board, thanks for the Maltesers and thanks for letting me use your four-legged baby in the book. I can report, the real Butch is even more full of life and mischief than his namesake.

Sharon Messitt – thanks for being the friend I go to when I need the absolute truth, for always being there and for making me buckets of tea in The Little Cotton Shack. One day we will ramble around that mansion together. And, thanks for letting me name a character after you.

Melrona Doyle – thanks for just being fabulous and keeping me up to date in the world of glitz, glamour and travel. You are my go-to girl in all things fabliss, darhling.

My family – without you, I would be nothing. I love you all so very much. Dave, Joey and Arthur, you are the reason I get up in the morning and have a smile on my face every day. Mam, Fidelma, Paraic, Sas and Leslie Ann – thanks for always loving me anyway, even if I was always the dreamer. To my extended family in Newcastle – thanks for making me one of your own. Howay the Toon!

Dad – you will always be my lighthouse.

For Dad x

He that will not sail till all dangers are over must never put to sea.
Thomas Fuller

PRELUDE

At that exact moment she knew she was going to die. It was the same moment she stopped feeling terror. Nothing mattered any more – her time had come.

The wind battered her bare arms and whipped the hair back from her face. The sound of the waves crashing below drummed a beat in time with her retiring heart. Time slowed as her feet reluctantly shuffled towards the edge of the high cliff. Despair hung heavy in the air like fog and even the comforting glow of the lighthouse beam couldn't compete with the darkness surrounding her. Death had been invited, and now it had arrived.

For the briefest moment she was suspended in mid-air – like a dancer. Then, resembling a puppet whose strings have been cut, she fell free . . . limbs pirouetting on the wind. Her thoughts were of those she loved, wrapping her in a comforting hug as she sailed down through the abyss.

She could hear music but couldn't tell if it was in her head or rolling in on the sea. It was the tune to a childhood rhyme – she remembered it from her playground days. The words formed in her head.

Ring-a-ring o' Roses,
A pocket full of posies,
A-tishoo! A-tishoo!
We all fall down!

She hit the surface and her last breath hurtled from her lungs. Her broken body sank down into the icy black water. Time stopped, just like her – it had no relevance here any more.

Chapter 1

'Why are ya crying, Mam?'

'Ah, I'm just a little bit sad, Danny. I miss her today.' Jen bent over and planted a big kiss on her son's head.

There they stood, hand in hand, in front of the home Pat had lived in for most of her seventy years. The house that Jen now owned.

Today was the day. They were moving in. As per Aunty Pat's explicit instructions, they had been down several times in the preceding weeks to clear bits and pieces from the house.

'Good old Aunty Pat,' Jen murmured.

Pat had been like a second mother to Jen. She had passed away from cancer in January and had left the house and a sum of money to them.

'Right, Dan. Let's get on with it. No point in standing here, staring at the door. Your dad and Sal will be here soon with the last of the boxes. Bring Butch in as well – he could probably do with a drink.'

She didn't have to ask him to bring the Jack Russell in – they went everywhere together anyway.

Danny unlocked his hand from hers, and scampered in through the front door, his four-legged friend at his heels. Jen followed.

Danny grabbed a bowl and filled it with water for Butch. 'Mam, I'm thirsty too.'

'OK, I'm coming – gimme a second, will you? We'll have some tea and a sambo before your dad arrives.'

Jen dumped the shopping bags on the table and filled the kettle.

'Dammit!' She shook her head as she looked into the fridge. 'I forgot about the bad weather, and *him*. He must be down in the harbour – they won't have taken the boat out.'

There was a snag with the inheritance. Jen had also inherited a lodger. A fisherman named Andy McCleane, Pat's best friend's son. He had lodged with Pat since she had a break-in last year. Jen knew him from growing up around here but, as he was a few years older, she had never hung out with him. The arrangement was only until the end of the year, but it was a real inconvenience to her.

'It'll be grand, Mam. I think he's cool anyway. And the last time he was here he gave me chewing gum and let me help him fix the puncture on his car. And he likes *X-Men*.'

Wise words from an eight-year-old, she thought.

'Danny, you're right. I'm sure he's cool.' She turned from cobbling together ingredients for a snack and faced Danny. 'He'll be around at some stage today. Just be polite, and stay out of his room.'

Despite the sadness in her heart, she was beginning to feel excited. The little house was beautiful, and now they had the security she had craved for so long.

The kitchen was Jen's favourite room. The French doors opened out onto decking which led down to a large sloping garden, behind that the orchard. Farther on from that, a little lane led down to Stony Strand.

The phone rang as Danny raced out to the garden with Butch.

'Hi, Dad.'

'Hello, my love! How's it all going down there?'

'Ah, we're good now, thanks. Will is on the way down, and your boy is in the garden. I'm just about to make some lunch.'

'Good, good. I just rang to tell you we won't be over tonight. Get yourself settled, love, and we'll come over on Sunday instead. Also, dear, I was speaking to Andy. He's having awful trouble with the trawler. Engine is giving him hell. But he told me he'll stay with his parents for a few nights, just to give you and Danny a bit of a chance to find your feet.'

'Oh, thank feck for that!' she sighed in relief.

'He's a good lad, Jen, and he's been through the mill. He was very good to your Aunty Pat. Be nice to him.'

'I know, Dad, I will,' she said. 'Oh! I can hear the cars pulling up now – I'll let you go. See ya, Dad. Love to Mam.'

'Bye, bye, bye, bye, love.'

Jen laughed as she threw the mobile back in her handbag. Her dad always finished a phone conversation with about ten byes.

Will appeared, laden with boxes – Sal behind him, boxless. According to his earlier phone call, their mutual pal had declared she was only coming over to drink tea and watch them do all the hard work.

Danny raced down the hall and straight into his daddy's arms.

'Come up to my room, Dad! Mam got me new Lego! Come up and see it, will you?'

'Slow down there, boyo. Let me get the boxes in, and then I will, OK?'

Will was a good man and a great dad, and Jen often wished she could fancy him but it just wasn't there. They had tried of course, but it was never on the cards. Lifelong friends who have drunken flings don't make marriage material.

Jen was relieved that she and Sal had spent so much time boxing and labelling her belongings the previous week. It made the task of getting them from the cars to the right rooms much easier.

The house had come alive with a flurry of excitement and activity, Jen the conductor sending boxes with humans attached in one direction or another. Butch had come back in to see what all the excitement was about and it wasn't too long before he nearly tripped Will up as he was bringing in a box.

Twenty minutes later, Jen's whole life was now in neat boxes under her roof and they needed a cuppa. Sal had come armed with Maltesers and shortbread biscuits as usual.

The girls went outside with a tray. Will and Danny had disappeared somewhere, probably down to the strand.

The weather was warm for April, still windy but pleasant in the sheltered garden. There were lavender and tea-rose plants everywhere, along with all sorts of bushes and other plants Jen would eventually learn the names of.

She smiled to herself as she poured the tea. 'I feel happy and sad at the same time, if you get me, Sal.' She was quiet for a moment, collecting her thoughts. 'I want this to be the start of something a bit more positive, you know? Not that there is anything wrong. My life is just a bit bland. I'm a bit bland. Look at you and Tess, everything going for you, and here I am, plain old Jen. I hate that poxy job in the restaurant, and I've wasted that bloody degree. This is the year, Sal. I'm going to get my act together.'

'You go, girl! That's the spirit. It's about fecking time. You're a great mam but you're stuck in a big fat rut, and let's face it – you *are* a little bit boring. We need to get you out there. You need a life!' Sal whooped and did a chair dance.

'Thanks a lot, Sal! That's great to hear from my best friend.' Jen laughed and bit into a Malteser.

Danny and Will finally emerged from the orchard and Danny handed his mam a little selection of shells he had picked up on the beach for her.

'Danny, my little champ, I have to go,' Will said, lifting him up into the air. 'Mam wants you at home this weekend to get settled into the house, but you can come over before the holidays are finished, OK?'

'That's OK, Dad. I want to stay here with Mam until she's not sad any more,' he whispered into Will's ear.

Will just hugged him.

'Oh Jen, it's half six! I'd better get going.' Sal stood up and flung on her scarf. 'Don't tell Mam I was here – I haven't time to drop down to them.'

She hugged all of them and scarpered.

The rest of Jen's evening was spent with Danny unpacking boxes and finding new homes for all of their possessions. Eventually, exhausted from the excitement, he passed out in the front room on the couch in front of the television. He was wrapped up in his favourite little blanket and Butch was snoring at his feet.

Jen gently roused him – long gone were the days where she could carry him up the stairs. She navigated him through a sea of Lego and, as soon as his head hit the pillow, he was fast asleep again. Butch snuck up behind her. He knew that he wasn't allowed in the bedrooms.

'Oh, go on, you little mutt – hop up there with him! Just for tonight.'

If Butch were human, she would have sworn he had smiled at her. In moments, he was asleep too.

As she lay in her own bed, her thoughts turned again to the lodger. How would she cope living with a man under her roof? Would he be a nightmare? Would Danny be OK with him in the house? It was going to be a massive adjustment for both of them. What kind of mental state was the poor man in?

Then, as the beams of the lighthouse bathed the curtain in the soft familiar glow, she thought no more of Andy McCleane and fell asleep.

Andy woke with a fright, confused and disorientated. The sight of the large *Lord of the Rings* poster reminded him where he was. Home, in his own childhood bed. He had fallen asleep with the lamp on and had suddenly woken up, the old familiar feeling of fear hanging heavy over him. It was just a dream, he told himself, as he reached out for the pint of water on the nightstand. 3:30 the clock told him. Seven bells. Middle watch. Safe navigation.

His thoughts turned to Aunty Pat. He missed her and her stories. He had really enjoyed his time lodging with her. What a broad, he thought. He should have moved out when she passed, but who would break a promise to a dying friend? Aunty Pat – she was never known by another name to anyone in the village. He would keep his promise, and then he would be gone.

He thought about Sharon as he switched off the light. The love of his life. The dream was always the same, and he always felt like shit when he woke. If only he had gone after her that night, it would all be so different.

Chapter 2

He smelt the tobacco smoke before he saw her, followed by the sweet scent of her Chanel. She wore her evening gown of deep purple with amazing grace, the colour enhancing her dark beauty. She was striking, her presence a force of nature, and she appeared far taller than she was. He knew she had been there for some time, just watching, trying to understand him, but ultimately not caring.

She leaned against the door frame as she held the cigarette in a gloved hand. Those familiar dark eyes bore into him and he made no attempt to hide his nakedness. He turned from the mirror and met her stare, while the bile rose in his throat. Playing the game, he hid his emotions well and managed a smile that never reached his eyes.

So many times, he had tried to look at that face with love, but there was no love there. He wondered what it would feel like to punch her really hard and watch the blood flow from her perfect nose, down her chest and all over her designer dress. He imagined how her manicured nails and diamond rings would cope with the gush of blood.

He wondered how quickly the thick carpet would soak up the blood and how swiftly a feather pillow over her face would stop her breathing and eventually stop her heart. A heart as cold as forgotten coffee.

But he knew it was just a fleeting thought. He wouldn't do any of those things. She was right, he was spineless. He could never harm her. He was a silly little boy.

'Scottie, darling, do hurry up.' She exhaled the last of the smoke. 'The guests will be arriving shortly and I expect you downstairs beside me to greet them.'

Years of elocution had just about buried the Italian accent. Years of elocution at Father's expense.

'Yes, Mother,' he said without emotion.

'Chop chop, darling!' She clicked her fingers at him and walked away.

Mother now held the reins – and the whip. She didn't deserve that grand title, she was never mother material. An embittered, neurotic, once-famous opera singer, who amused herself by sleeping with everyone from the stable hand to the president of the Rotary Club.

Father was dead. He hanged himself at the height of the recession.

Scott returned to the ensuite and retrieved his wallet from the pocket of his abandoned trousers. He licked his lips and his heart quickened as he poured the little heap of white powder onto the vanity unit. With deft hands and a sense of purpose, the crystalline powder was sniffed away from sight.

He lay down on the bed and waited. Minutes later, the familiar numb feeling in the back of his throat arrived and his rage subsided.

Mother and her garden parties, he thought – yet another

pretentious gathering on the grounds of Weybridge estate. Another excuse for the cream of society to lavish bullshit and false compliments on them. He wished he was back in his apartment in Dublin, but he had to be here. It was his duty.

He snapped out of his reverie and dressed in front of the mirror. The sounds and smells wafted up from below. He did not have to look behind the heavy drapes to picture the scene unfolding in the walled garden. He had seen it often enough.

The quartet would be there, reverently removing instruments from cases, and warming up with the sweet sounds of Haydn's 'Sun Quartets', the bass notes bouncing and dancing on the walls of the garden. Staff drafted in for the high-brow occasion would be scurrying around in black, like an army of ants, darting in and out of the marquee, never speaking. The maître d', with an accent as fake as his watch, barking orders. They would lay picture-perfect tables. They would fold napkins the same colour as the floral centrepieces. Lint from the perfect white tablecloths would dance in the air.

Chafing dishes of polished silver would be laid out on the buffet tables beside case upon case of champagne. Dozens of candles would be lit at the last minute before the staff lined up and stood to attention. He wondered about the lowly catering staff, and came to the conclusion they were all uneducated foreigners or single parents. Meagre, insignificant insects. Working for minimum wage. Scraping the plates of the guests tonight would be the closest they ever got to Culture. Rats, every one of them. The only staff member he had ever tolerated was Mr Jenkins. He used to be the resident gardener and the only person who took an interest in him growing up.

He hated it here, but he knew he could never live without the lifestyle, and the eventual inheritance. He gazed in the mirror at the stunning man there who had inherited his mother's striking, dark good looks – and he smiled. Undoubtedly, the upper echelons of society present for the meal and recital would throw

11

their daughters at him. He was a catch. Or was he?

He remembered the last time he was close to a woman. Oh, how he had hurt her! But maybe the bitch deserved it, all things considered. They were all money-grabbing whores, each and every one of them.

The sound of his mother summoning him brought his thoughts back to the present.

Everything about her, him and this evening was a cliché. That thought amused him. Pretentious bastards. He wanted out from his history, his family, and from this pantomime. But, much like his love for cocaine, wealth and status were his addictions. Any other life would not be good enough. He needed her.

He followed her down the stairs and out to the lawn like an obedient dog.

Showtime.

Chapter 3

The sight of a strange car in her drive annoyed Jen when she arrived home. Patience was a virtue she did not possess at the best of times, but today was Monday. It was the first day back to school after the Easter holidays and she was wrecked after a busy weekend in work. Danny had gone to school, amidst tears and tantrums, and all she wanted was a coffee and peace and quiet.

No doubt it's a friend of Andy's, she thought, as the tyres crunched over the gravel. He had come back to the house on Friday. The trawler was still tied up because of a problem with the engine and he would be around all week. Her clapped-out Saab came to a halt beside the sleek Lexus and let out a groan of envy as it shuddered to a stop. Maybe it's a girlfriend, she suddenly thought. The idea of dealing with a well-dressed, all-cheekbones-and-Botox type in her living room made her crave a cigarette. She had given up in January and every day was a fight not to go to the shop and buy a pack. She felt like the wreck of the *Hesperus*. She had stepped back into the clothes she had been wearing yesterday, and her wavy hair stood on end. Yummy Mummy, my arse. As she fumbled out of the car, she stuck her hand into her bag and grabbed a lip gloss. She quickly applied it, ran her fingers through her hair, pinched her cheeks and braced herself for an audience with Andy and his model girlfriend.

Oh for Jesus' sake, Jen, will you cop on to yourself? Cheekbones and Botox – where did that come out of? It's probably a fecking salesman trying to flog internet.

She thought about dashing upstairs and changing, as she came through the front door, but was pipped at the post by Andy. He was standing in the hallway between the kitchen and the front door.

'Oh hi, Jen! How are you? The kettle is just on if you would like a cuppa.' He smiled at her as he held the kitchen door open.

He was taller than she remembered and so very handsome. She wondered how he had got the scar over his left eyebrow. As she nervously stepped past him, smoothing her hair, she could see that he too was feeling ill at ease. A degree in psychology and a lifetime of working in the catering industry meant that she was a natural at reading people. He was fidgeting and kept shifting his weight from one foot to the other.

'Jen, I'd like to introduce you to a really good friend of mine. This is Scott.'

She felt his presence before she even looked in his direction. The room felt as though the air had been sucked out of it, and her hand went straight to the crystal hanging around her neck. He stood up and extended his hand to her. His smile was mesmerising and she felt completely inferior standing before him. He was so striking and she recognised him instantly. He didn't recognise her, oblivious to their last encounter – the faceless waitress being spoken to like a piece of shit by the snob. She noticed his suit, charcoal grey and obviously made to measure. This exchange all happened in a matter of seconds but Jen's legs felt unsteady.

'Jennifer, it's such a pleasure to make your acquaintance.' His manner was easy and relaxed as he shook her hand. 'What a lovely quaint little home you have here. Very charming.'

Jen had lost the ability to speak. She came back to the present when the whistle of the kettle broke the silence.

'Would anyone like a coffee?' she asked in a high-pitched voice.

'Mug of tea for me please, Jen,' Andy replied, before Scott enquired as to whether the coffee was filter or instant.

The men sat at the table and made small talk while Jen took cups and plates down from the press.

Luckily, she had some Lavazza filter coffee and a cafetière in the house; she had bought them for her dad. Her parents had been around for lunch yesterday and he loved a nice coffee after a roast. She watched the coffee swirl in the water before taking yesterday's dessert out of the treat cupboard. Chocolate Cola Cake, Danny's favourite. She cut three wedges and put them on the plates. Refreshments served, she sat at the table beside Andy.

'Do you have a napkin or a fork, Jennifer?' Scott said as he examined the plate before him.

'You can call me Jen. I'll get you some kitchen paper.' He was beginning to get on her nerves, but Andy seemed completely oblivious to his bad manners. I'll stick the fork in his eye in a minute, she thought, as she returned to the table.

Then again, maybe it was just her being a bit of a cow; she was tired and a bit frazzled. He couldn't be that much of a pig if he was a good pal of Andy's. She stirred sugar into her tea and took a deep breath.

She decided to make a bit of an effort and they all made small talk as they ate. She began to warm to him when the conversation turned to music. Andy filled her in about how they had met in a music club in university. They had got into a dispute over the original band members in Cream, and who exactly Crosby, Stills and Nash had played with before they got together. They shared a love of music and followed the scene in Dublin.

She could see why Scott liked Andy so much – he was lovely, easy company. He had a gentle charisma about him, almost melancholic, in stark contrast to Scott's daunting presence. An odd pairing as friends but who was she to judge? The nerves were beginning to subside about her new housemate. It mightn't be so awkward after all.

'Jennifer – sorry – Jen!' said Scott. 'You have the most amazing vinyl collection. I'm really impressed. It's rare to see such taste in music.'

'I have my mam and my Aunty Pat to thank for my eclectic taste, Scott. How could I get out of it really? Thanks to my mother's lifelong obsession with one particular artist, I was christened Jennifer Juniper – years after the song was released I hasten to add.'

'Donovan!' the men said together and laughed.

Scott made the large kitchen-cum-dining-room look tiny as he stood up. He sauntered around, fingering the vinyl and picking up random pictures. She couldn't figure him out and he made her feel on edge. Maybe it was just because of the night in the restaurant – he certainly had a swagger about him.

Andy turned his attention to Jen.

'I hope you didn't mind about my bedroom door being locked, Jen. There's a lot of fishing lures up there. I didn't have time to pack them away safely and I didn't want Danny getting at them. And my old hunting knife is there too – I have a new one I use on the boat now. I meant to text you and explain but the time ran away with me.'

'Ah, that's OK, Andy. Don't worry, we will respect your privacy. Danny knows better than to nose about in your room. He's a good little boy and won't cause you any bother – he spends all his time outside with Butch or upstairs with his Lego.'

THEY ALL FALL DOWN

'I didn't mean it like that – I was afraid he might hurt himself. We'll get along fine. He's a character.'

'I know he is!'

'Are you settling in OK? It must be strange for you in a way?'

'It's weird not having Pat here. I miss her, but I can certainly feel her around. Anyway, I'd better get cracking and get some stuff done. Nice to meet you, Scott.'

Jen left the room and went upstairs.

'She's an odd one, Andy. Pretty, but odd,' Scott mused as he looked at a picture of Jen and Danny. 'She does go on a bit, don't you think? The rug rat looks like her. What's the situation there? Was it a one-night stand or is there a man on the scene? I don't envy you – what was that old bat thinking about, forcing you to stay here with them? There's plenty of room in my apartment. You don't have to be here. If money is an issue?'

'Stop, Scott. Jen is OK and her son, Danny, is a great kid. There is a dad on the scene, but they're not together any more. The "old bat" you referred to was my friend. I'm here until January and then I'm heading off. I don't want to be stuck in this small village either, but I'm past the madness that goes with your lifestyle. I've moved on, man, bigger fish to fry.'

Andy picked the dishes up from the table and dropped them in the sink. He had forgotten how arrogant Scott could be.

'Easy there, Andy. I'm simply making an observation. Don't try to bed her is my advice. I must dash, meeting scheduled for twelve, then back to Dublin. I'll be in touch. *Ciao ciao.*'

Upstairs, Jen heard him leave and breathed a sigh of relief.

Andy's voice floated up the stairs. 'I'm heading down to the boat for a while, Jen. See you later.'

'All right. Have a good day, Andy,' she called to the closing door.

Finally, a bit of peace! She looked at her lovely bed and her novel sitting on the locker. It was tempting but it was nearly eleven and she had a mountain of things to do before the school run. I'll be back to you soon, Mr. Lamb, she thought and headed for the shower.

He was incandescent with rage. He thumped his hands repeatedly on the steering wheel, before punching the radio into silence. When the speedometer hovered at ninety, he figured he had better calm down. The last thing he needed was the local police sniffing around his car. The trip he had made to the harbour before dawn was not one for sightseeing, and not one he had told Andy about. Slowing his driving also slowed his breathing.

He pulled into a lay-by and poured two lines of the early morning delivery onto a CD case. He rolled the note and the lines disappeared up his nose. He sat and waited for the torpid feeling to come.

His mind flashed back to the first time he had met 'Aunty Pat' as they all called her. She was a very sharp old woman, and after twenty minutes she had the measure of him. She didn't hide her disdain for him and his welcome was short-lived. She had practically thrown him out.

In the time he had spent in Jen's kitchen that morning, the realisation had dawned on him as to why dear old batty Pat had insisted Andy lodge with her niece and the brat. In short, she was matchmaking from beyond the grave. They would make a good couple, he thought with disgust. There was easiness between them and it would only be a matter of time before they got down and dirty. Andy had been quick to defend her. Scott had seen that before – with that damn Sharon. Women – they were all the same. They wanted the handsome man to swoop in and save them, before screwing him around and leaving him broken, just like his mother had done with his father.

Andy reminded Scott so much of his father. He wasn't able to protect his father from his wife but with Andy, his best friend, it would be different. He would protect him, and no bitch would ever come between them again.

Aunty Pat had tried to come between them. He knew it, even though his Andy had never said it outright. Andy had told him about the cancer. He was devastated that she was refusing treatment. She wouldn't sit back and wait for the disease to consume her. She was going to get her affairs in order, she told him, and then when she was ready she would slip away into the night, on her own terms with a free heart and soul.

Scott thought of her sitting there the evening he had visited her – so frail, yet her eyes were bright and clear. He could still hear her voice in his head, louder and clearer today. His plan that night was to teach her a lesson. How dare she imply that Andy was too nice to be friends with him? He told her what he had done to come between Andy and Sharon. Her response was tears. 'How could you do that to your best friend and his wife?' she had asked. 'You will answer to your God, and you will have to live with your decisions and actions until your own life ends.' When he shrugged she went on, real strength in her voice: 'I am an old woman. I have seen so much, I have lived so much. Neither you nor your black heart can scare me. Do as you will now, or be gone. I am at peace. My advice to you, young man, is to face your demons, make things right and save your own soul. Do you believe that the soul lives on? Do you believe that a spirit can come back and wreak vengeance on those who have wronged them in this life? You should consider that question before you hurt me. Having the capacity to intimidate a dying woman tells me that your soul is more ravaged by sickness than my old body. What has blackened your heart so much, Scott? Why is there nothing but anger in it? Who hurt you so much that you have no happiness or love in your life?'

He remembered that last line so well, and her question floored him. No one had ever recognised that before. He wanted to tell her everything, he wanted to sit there and tell her all about his twisted life and the twisted urges that consumed his mind and frightened him. Was she threatening to come back and haunt him? Something told him that she might just have the ability. The tormentor had become the tormented. Stupid, silly little boy. He couldn't go through with it, whatever *it* was? Was he going to stuff pills down her throat until they made her heave? Was he going to smother her, bludgeon her to death with a blunt object? What the fuck was he going to do? He was frightened of this old witch. He had said too much, and now there was no going back, but he couldn't do it. Damn it. So he played the only trump card he had left. He told her that he would spare her life, but she would also spare his. A life for a life. A trade-off, so to speak. She would take to the grave what he had told her and the arrangement for Andy to remain in the house would not change. He would never know that Scott had visited her – otherwise her 'little hurricane' as she called him would simply disappear one day. His little body would be found washed up on the beach just beside his new home and his mother Jen would probably kill herself in grief.

When the last of the colour had drained from her face, he stood up, shook her hand, wished her well on her impending journey and left.

The sound of a car horn blasted him back to the present. He rolled the car back on to the main road. He had a meeting to get to for midday, and then he was headed back to Dublin. A good night out was needed and he had in mind exactly who he would be spending it with.

Chapter 4

Banging on the front door of a public house at half ten in the morning made Jen feel uncomfortable and she wished Tess would hurry up. She had her back to the wind – which by now had abated to a boisterous breeze, strong enough to stir the ropes and make the poles whistle. It was a beautiful morning and, this early, little could be heard except the chug of an engine from down at the pier. The swallows observed her from their perch on the telephone wires. Like sentries, they watched. Nothing would disturb them there, bar the screech of a gull. Summer was on the way, the sight of the little birds a welcome reminder. The thatched rooftops all around her were drinking in the morning sun, glowing golden and bright. The village was really stunning, like a movie set. The heavy door opened with a groan.

'Morning,' Tess chirped as she extended her arms for a hug.

She looked tired and Jen was alarmed to see that she had been crying.

'Morning, Tess.' Her eyes tried to adjust to the light as she closed the door behind her. 'Doc gave me the message to come down. Is everything OK?'

'Yes, fine, Jen. It's just that my mobile phone is on the blink. I was hoping he would catch you in the school yard. Sit down, the coffee machine is on.'

The blinds were still down in The Gale Public House. The hum of a fan and the morning news report were the only sounds coming from the kitchen. Something smelled good – baking bread – and Jen wished she had got up in time to have breakfast. All but one of the stools rested upside down on the counter, the lack of life giving the bar a very different feel.

Tess and Doc Martin were the couple that everyone aspired to be like. They ran the pub together. Tess had taken it over when her dad retired and Doc was the in-house entertainment – a musician and one of the most amazing singers Jen had ever heard. They had been together forever and had a little boy the same age as Danny.

Tess steamed milk at the coffee machine while Jen pulled down a companion to the one stool on the floor. Before long, the smell of freshly ground coffee replaced the smell of the baking bread.

'So, Jen, tell me all. How goes it with the lodger? Your own personal fisherman!'

Jen noticed Tess had a glint in her eye as she passed the latte over the bar.

'It's fine actually. He's genuinely a nice guy and it's not as awkward as I thought it was going to be. He was around a fair bit last week, as there was some problem with water pumps or something, but he hopes to have it fixed in the next few days.'

'And how is the wee man of the house settling in? Are they getting on all right?'

Jen stirred a little mountain of sugar into the coffee and took a sip.

'Ah, that's a good coffee, Tess! Yeah, Danny seems to really like him. They get on great in fact.'

'He's a lovely guy, Jen. He comes in the odd night for a couple of pints. I've always liked him. He's very good-looking too, don't you think?'

'I suppose he is, Tess.'

Jen stood up to take off her coat. When she sat back down, Tess had the same glint in her eye.

'"Suppose", my eye, Jen! Come on, woman, spill the beans! You have thought about it, haven't you? I bet you're trying to get a look at him every time he comes out of the shower. I know I would!' She laughed as she dipped a biscuit into her coffee.

Jen laughed with her. He was gorgeous. She thought about Scott.

'Did you ever meet a friend of his called Scott? Was he ever in here with a tall guy, really well-dressed? Black hair and absolutely fecking hot?'

'Aha, so you have met the elusive Scott Carluccio Randall then! What a name, eh? Yeah, he has been down quite a few times over the last couple of years. He's fond of his 18-year-old Jameson and craft beers. Rather posh, daah'ling. The women in here go a bit mad when he's around. Very charming.'

This all sounded hilarious coming from Tess. Doc was the best catch in the village, and he adored her.

'On a serious note, mind, he's a snob. Always very lovely to me, but the lads here don't like him. It seems he's above making small talk with staff. Fond of the pretty girls too, but strangely quite taken with Andy. I can't figure that relationship out at all. I know they were in college together and all that, but it's a bit weird. Chalk and cheese. I quite like him apart from that.'

'Well, I agree on the snob part. He was in work one night with a group from the Opera Society. He gave one of the girls an awful time and then had the cheek to slip her a business card on the way out the door. She's Swedish. Tall and beautiful, but she's only nineteen. He's such a charmer – even though he'd treated her like shit, she went around for the rest of the night with a smile on her face and his card in her apron. He was up in my house one morning last week. I don't know, there's something about him that makes me feel really uneasy. It's none of my business though – he's Andy's friend. He's entitled to have his friends in the house.'

'Jen, my duck, the best way to find out the dirt on someone is good old Facebook! No time like the present!' Tess opened her laptop which was sitting on the bar beside the paperwork. 'Here, log in and find him.'

'Ah, Tess, I don't know about this. Facebook-stalking, first thing in the morning?' Jen was reluctant.

'Come on! If you don't, I will.'

Tess was grinning now. She was a great character and knew everything about everyone in the village, but was never one for idle gossip. She simply liked to stay informed and the bar was the perfect place to do that. She knew more than the local Guards.

Curiosity had now got the better of Jen as well. Andy didn't have a Facebook account. He barely had a phone so she would just have to search for Scott's name and hope for the best.

The first tab she opened was Facebook. Facebook prompted her to search for people, places and things. She ignored the little red notifications and entered his name. There he was and they had three mutual friends. Interesting. Two of the friends were bands she liked; the third was an acquaintance of hers who had gone to Trinity. Really getting into the swing of things, Jen hoped his profile wasn't private. She wanted to have a snoop in his photos, but checked the 'about' page first.

No schools/universities to show. No places to show. No relationship info to show. Nothing. Photos next: Scott at weddings, dinner parties, shows, awards. Everyone with saccharine smiles, all in tuxedos and ball gowns. Everyone looked amazing and wealthy. Always surrounded by beautiful people. Not a bad selfie in there, not a single shot of him in a local pub or in a casual setting. Trawling through his timeline wasn't helpful either. All pseudo-intellectual posts and the odd music video. Nothing personal. No banter. No craic.

'That's weird, Tess. There's nothing light-hearted or really personal in his profile.'

She then went to Google. He had a profile on Linkedin, he was on Twitter and there were some images from newspapers. More award ceremonies. An article about his honorary membership on the board of The Opera Society. She was about to click out of Google and nearly missed it. His father had died in 2008. A full write-up in the paper about the circumstances, funeral, the family, their history and the sprawling estate he came from. A family portrait. They were all stunning. He had his father's height and build, but was an absolute dead ringer for his mother. They had an identical smile; it didn't reach their eyes.

'My goodness, Jen, that's a creepy picture. The poor man. Suicide, that's really sad. Just be careful on this one. He and Andy are good pals so keep your mouth shut. Scott's a very strong character, so leave well enough alone. I wouldn't like to get on his bad side.'

Then, without warning, Tess burst into tears.

'Tess, honey, what's wrong? Why are you crying?' Jen closed the laptop and faced her friend. Worried they would be overheard, she hopped off the stool and closed the door to the kitchen.

'Don't worry about them, Jen – the cleaner doesn't have a lot of English and that bitch of a cook doesn't come near me. She only works part-time and, I swear, if she wasn't so good I'd let her go.' This prompted more tears. 'It's all gone to pieces, and I don't know what to do.'

'What has gone to pieces, Tess? What are you talking about?'

'I had the bank on the landline, just before you came in.'

Between the sobs, the story came out. The business was

really struggling. EU quotas and restrictions on fishermen didn't just affect the fishermen themselves. Every business in a small community like theirs depended on the others. To add insult to injury, the weather had been atrocious for months and the only busy times were school holidays and the tourist season. Taxes, rates and VAT were crippling. Tess had to let two of her staff go and now she was picking up the slack, working crazy hours. She had no time to spend with Doc other than in work and little Hugh was a permanent fixture over in his grandmother's house. Doc was working in the pub during the week and around the country at weekends, doing gigs to make extra money. They were working opposite shifts seven days a week and she couldn't remember the last time they had all sat down together for dinner. Hugh was feeling the strain and giving her a really hard time. He was acting up all the time, at home and in school.

'Things have been really bad with me and Doc as well. We are constantly arguing, as we are both running on empty. We have no down time and when he gets back from the gigs at the weekend it just pisses me off. He bangs on about the great fun he's had, with all these amazing people and I'm just here scrubbing and cleaning. When I'm not slogging in the pub, I'm slogging at home. I can't do it any more.'

Even though Tess was a good six inches taller than Jen, she looked small on the stool. Jen studied her friend. She looked vulnerable, with dark circles around her eyes.

'We're stuck with the place and it's like a noose around our necks. We bought in the good times, just after we got married. We can't sell as we'd be worse off – penniless and jobless.' Her body shook with sobs and she was grey in the face with stress.

Jen hugged her and her heart went out to her friend. Little do we know, she thought. From the outside they looked like they had it all. Jen had known real money struggles, but not on this scale.

'You're not telling me everything, Tess, are you?' Jen looked her friend in the eye, knowing by her that she was holding something back.

Tess played with the stack of envelopes beside her on the bar and stared into her cup.

'Jen, I think I'm pregnant. And, just to put the icing on the cake, I think Doc is having a fucking affair.'

'Pregnant! Sure that's not the worst thing in the world – a little baby? Bad timing perhaps? Doc'll be over the moon with another child. And there's no way he would be stupid enough to do the dirt on you again, Tess. He learned his lesson the hard way that time. And that was a long time ago – he's a different person now. You are stressed and worn out and you've got the wrong end of the stick somehow. Come on, Tess, you've always said that you'd both put that behind you and you trust him. What makes you think that he's having an affair?'

'Because he is different with me, Jen – secretive almost. He's so distant and he's not interested in spending any time with me. All we talk about is Hugh and stupid small talk about bills. He has completely disconnected from me, and I just don't have the energy to try and reconnect with him any more. It's so infuriating listening to him waffle on about the great bloody time he has at the gigs, and all the interesting people he meets. I'm sure they're all lovely, but to him I'm invisible. I don't matter any more. He has pigeonholed me into cook, cleaner and mother, and has completely forgotten who I am. I'm completely fed up with the whole shit situation.'

'In fairness to Doc, he's out doing gigs to make money that you desperately need, it seems. It's not all fun and parties.'

Tess didn't respond. She rounded the bar and put on another brew.

'Tess, how late are you? Maybe it's stress that has you late, and all the running around? You need to just take a breath here for a minute. First things first: *do a fecking test.* You need to tell him.

And, you know, things can't be that terrible between you if you're still having sex.'

Jen was in a bit of a panic herself. Tess was always so together, taking everything in her stride, but here she was, falling apart in front of her eyes.

'We hadn't been, for months. We were here after lock-up a few weeks ago and had way too much to drink. Hugh was with his gran so we were in no rush to get home. I was worried that he didn't love me any more and I practically threw myself at him. He loved it of course – one thing led to another and we got it on in here. On the bar counter, to be exact.'

In spite of the situation, they dissolved into fits of laughter. The thought of Tess, a respected businesswoman, humping on the bar counter cracked both of them up.

'Tess, that's hilarious!'

'Things were good for a few days after that, Jen, then he went away for the weekend working and we were back to square one. He was supposed to be home for Sunday lunch with Mam and Dad – they were coming here – and he didn't get back until after nine. His phone was off as per usual. When his phone is on, it's stuck to him. He gets strange calls and texts late at night.' The tears returned. 'OK, I'll do a test and figure out my next step from there.'

'Do you want me to go to the chemist's and get you one?'

Tess nodded. She looked scared. 'Will you stay here with me while I do it?'

No answer was needed.

Jen grabbed her bag and shot out the door.

Tess sat at the counter and cried again. Jen was a good friend. She could rely on her. It should have been Doc here this morning with her, but he was in town and would not be back until after school pick-up.

Jen was back before long with the little paper bombshell. The pub did not open until twelve, and thankfully none of the usual suspects had knocked on the door to be let in. They had time. She sat the bag on the bar counter and went to the coffee machine.

Tess was on the phone with what sounded like an irate supplier looking for payment.

Jen did not ask her if she wanted a decaffeinated coffee – it was too soon for that. She had nearly bought a box of cigarettes on the way back from the chemist's as well. Tess was also a former smoker, and had encouraged Jen to quit. The cigarette machine stood proud in the corner of the bar winking at her. Gosh, poor Tess was a mess. A cigarette would be lovely now.

'Sorry about that, Jen. Did you get it?' She spotted the paper bag on the counter and grabbed it. 'Right, it's now or never.'

Her hands shook as she removed the packaging from the little stick that could change her life for good.

'I'll be back in a minute.'

Jen's hand now shook in solidarity with her friend. She remembered the day she had done the same thing. It said three minutes, always three minutes, but it never took that long. The fate of one's future boiled down to peeing on a plastic stick. Two years she had stayed with Will, playing at happy families. That's all it was: playing. Tess and Doc were different. They were good together. Yes, they had their ups and downs, but she found it hard to believe he had the capacity to behave so treacherously again, to take everything they had and throw it away. Maybe the stress was making Tess see things that just weren't there ... but, then again, he had cheated on her before.

The bereft look on Tess's face as she returned replaced the need for conversation. Jen just hugged her and they cried together. The tiny screen on the fancy digital test had told her that she was 3+ Weeks.

'So that's that. Now I know for sure. Please don't breathe a word to anyone, Jen.'

'You need to speak to Doc. He needs to know that he's going

to be a dad again. You can't keep this from him.'

'I will tell him. Now, I need to get organised. I have to open in ten minutes.'

She put on her professional face and unlocked the front door.

Chapter 5

Doc was in the kitchen when Tess arrived home. She stood inside the front door, listening to the sound of his singing. His beautiful voice ricocheted around the big hall and seemed to bounce off the marble floor. Something smelled good too, and she felt hungry. A quick glance in the mirror revealed that the make-up was keeping her secret. No red eyes, no patchy marks on her cheeks.

'Evening, my darling,' he said as he came around the breakfast bar and swept her up into a hug.

He was a big strong man, and she used to feel so protected and safe in his arms.

'How was your day?' he asked. 'I've made dinner, and the fire is lit.'

'My, my, you have been busy. Well done, you,' she replied.

He ignored the sarcasm. 'I picked up a bottle of wine as well. I thought we could chill out in front of the fire for the night. Watch a movie maybe?'

She couldn't speak, she didn't trust herself. She needed to be strong. She made her way to the kettle – something to do. She needed something to hold on to. Her hands shook. Everything looked as it had this morning, but everything had changed.

'Are you OK, Tess? You look distracted.'

'I'm fine, Doc. Just tired.' She couldn't bring herself to turn around and look at him.

Her palms were sweating and she was panicking, her gut screaming at her to ask the dreaded question. Maybe she should just ignore it, brush it under the carpet. Let it all slip into the abyss and carry on as though she had no suspicion of any foul play. She loved him so much. Seventeen years together and he was her one and only love. Surely he wouldn't throw that away? But she had to know. The seed of doubt had planted itself in her heart, the blossoming weeds strangling her. She had to consider the little life inside her. Would she be better off just pleading ignorance to her fear? But then she would never know. Maybe it was all in her imagination. Her Doc, he loved her. He wouldn't betray her and his little boy. Last time, it was different – he wasn't a dad then.

The high-pitched whistle from the kettle was a welcome break to the silence. The kettle, the peacemaker. In times of crisis, make tea.

'Tea or coffee?' she asked, as though she were addressing a punter in work.

'I don't want tea or coffee, Tess. I want to know why you are such a moody cow! Did something happen in work?'

So here it was. The elephant in the room, and the point where it all came to a head. The moment she would look back on as the one that changed everything. She sat down at the table, without answering his question.

He suggested dinner, she nodded her assent and the ghost of what should have been said hung heavy in the air. Looking around the kitchen, she nearly laughed. Her home, their home. A place they had spent the last decade together.

'Tess, talk to me. What's going on with you?'

'I've already told you I'm fine, Doc. I'm tired. What do you want me to do? Dance a jig for you as I come in the door?'

'Jesus Christ, Tess, I only asked you was everything OK. No need to bite my head off.'

He was on the defensive now. She knew he was right of course – she was being a cow. She slumped down at the table and didn't even say thanks as he put dinner in front of her.

If he was having an affair, what would it matter? She knew she wouldn't leave him. How could she? It would break little Hugh's heart. He thought his daddy was Superman. A mother's love for her child is the most powerful thing in the world. She would stay for the sake of Hugh and the unborn child. She felt as though she was observing herself from across the room. They sat at the table together in silence. The cannelloni sat beside the breads and green salad. She felt like throwing them against the wall but the dutiful wife sat there and ate.

'Doc, have you slept with someone else?'

The pounding of blood through her ears made her feel faint. It was said, out of nowhere, and there was no going back now. Every fibre of her being begged for a *no* in reply.

'What! Tess, where the hell is this coming from?' He laid down his knife and fork and looked at her in amazement.

'Answer the question, Doc. Are you sleeping with someone or not?'

'What the hell has got into you lately? Jesus Christ! I'm working myself to the bone for this family, and just because I have a fucking laugh at the weekends, you're accusing me of all sorts of shit!'

He stood up and snatched the plate from under her nose.

The sound of plates breaking in the sink was a metaphor for her frame of mind. The sadness lifted and she stood up as an observer, a witness to the unfolding calamity.

He was pacing now, hands in his hair, muttering something

about doing everything for the family and how she was irrational and neurotic. Was it any wonder he stayed away at the weekends just for a bit of peace? All this nagging was driving him crazy.

He turned away from the sink to face her. He was furious.

'Just answer the question,' she deadpanned.

He was still pacing, but his demeanour had changed. Here it comes. His face had aged in minutes and he looked as though his world was just about to fall asunder.

'No, I haven't been sleeping with someone for Chrissake! You are deluded, Tess. I'm getting pretty sick of this crap. I knew there was some fucking thing you were brooding about! Have you any idea what it's like? You've been moping around the place like you resent every move I make, and now you come out with shite like this!'

'Get down off your high horse, Doc. I am working non-stop and I'm completely tired of never going anywhere or seeing anyone and, to top it all off, you're like fucking Peter Pan. You take no responsibility for anything.'

'Fuck off, Tess! You are full of it! I do my best to help here when I'm here. But I have to do the gigs. You know that. It's always the same with you. I do the gigs you have a problem, I don't do the gigs and there's a problem. What do you want me to do?'

'You clean up and cook dinner once in a while and expect me to be fucking grateful? Don't give me that bullshit. *You fucking never listen to how I feel!*' She was screaming at him now, and it felt good to her. He was right about the money – they couldn't survive without it – but she didn't care.

He was taken aback by her swearing. She rarely swore.

'Please, Tess. I hate all this fighting. I am not doing the dirt on you, and I love you. Can we please just sit down and have a talk? We don't talk at all any more.'

Doc was crying now – the weeks of tension had come to a head. Tess said nothing.

'Tess, oh my God, where is all this coming from?' He came around the breakfast bar and took her hands. 'Do you think we have a choice when it comes to me being away gigging at the weekend? No, we don't, we need the money. Please, for fuck sake, will you calm down and listen to me?'

'*Calm down?*' she roared, snatching away her hands. 'Don't you tell me to calm down! Answer me! You have done it before, after all!'

'Ah, here we go! Drag all that up again why don't you? It was ten years ago, and I promised you it would never happen again. And it hasn't. Tess, you are my whole life. You and Hugh. We're both stressed and worn out. I love you. I don't want us to fight like this. We're both wrecked. Maybe we just need a bit of time out together?'

Doc had always been the peacemaker. They argued like any couple but at the end of it they always compromised and found some kind of solution. This felt different.

She let him speak about promises and love and making time for each other and Hugh. All she could think about was when she was home tucked into bed with her son, he was out partying. She didn't trust him any more. And when trust is broken, it can never be fixed.

'Doc, I know you better than anyone. Something is going on and I can feel it. We could have worked on anything and we have done in the past. But not this. You are lying to me. The gigs are not about the money to you – it's all about what goes with it. The lifestyle.'

She was calmer now. The clarity in her tone surprised her, and frightened Doc.

'You don't give a toss about me and my son,' she said. 'You live for getting away at the weekends and partying on with your amazing friends. I'd love to know how many of them are married with children. None, I'd imagine.'

'Tess, for feck sake, I don't know why you have cooked up this ridiculous idea. I do gigs all over the country to make extra money for this family. I work in the pub all week, and do gigs here on top of that for fucking nothing! What more do you bloody want from me? And by the way, he's *our* son. Not *your* son.'

The mention of Hugh reminded her of her news.

It was getting petty now. And all her energy was gone. Maybe she had been wrong about him sleeping with someone, but she was so unsure. She mustn't soften to him. She needed to be certain. She felt as though she was having some sort of breakdown. Was she imagining all the secrecy? Was she wrong in thinking he never came home after gigs because he simply didn't want to? Not because he didn't want to drive through the night? Her head hurt.

He sensed the fight go out of her. He knew what he had to do. If he called her bluff, she would back down.

'Tess, I think we need a couple of days away from each other. I can't take this atmosphere any more, and now you're accusing me of all kinds of shit. I love you and Hugh. We need to fix this for all our sakes, but it's not going to happen tonight.'

'Whatever suits you,' she replied.

'Oh, for Chrissake! It doesn't suit me, but I'm going. I can't take this and you need to have a good think about what you want as well. Enough is enough.'

'OK, that's fair enough. If you want to go, you can go. It can't be easy on you, as you said. Being accused of all kinds of shit. But before you go, I have a favour to ask you.'

He didn't like the sudden change in direction and it threw him. 'Go on, Tess?'

'Show me your phone.'

'What the fuck, Tess? No! This is absolute bullshit. How dare you try to invade my privacy because of a psychotic whim that you've cooked up today? No doubt your buddy Jen was fanning the flames.'

She said nothing and didn't move a muscle. In her head she repeated the mantra 'please don't cry' over and over and over. She felt sick. She just wanted to hug him and tell him everything would be OK. But she couldn't.

He eventually went upstairs and she crumpled. She was so confused. She sobbed big heaving sobs. She didn't know what to do. She didn't know if he was packing a bag or hiding out up in their room until she calmed down. Her own bag was on the floor beside her. She crouched down, opened it and took out the stick. It still read 3+ Weeks. She turned it over in her hand before putting it back in her bag.

'Tess, what's that in your hand?'

She hadn't heard him coming back downstairs. The joys of carpeted stairs, she thought. She could see the overnight bag by the door, and wondered how on earth he had packed so quickly.

'Where will you go, Doc?' she enquired as though she were asking a stranger for the time.

She pulled herself and her bag up off the floor in one swift movement, while stuffing the test behind the torn lining. She composed herself and headed straight for the kettle. It's a crisis. Hit the kettle, make a cup of tea. Her mind was swimming, and her gait was unsteady. She loved him so much – should she really let him walk? What effect would it have on Hugh, what about the baby? How can I tell him now?

Disaster. Disaster. Disaster.

'Tess, I asked you what you had in your hand.'

'It's a pen, Doc. I'm going to write my fucking memoirs as an old and bitter divorced spinster.' She made the cup of tea, slopping it on the counter. She lifted the cup and held on to it, like it was a life raft. She felt normal for a minute, until she heard the contents of her handbag being spilled out onto the breakfast bar.

'What the fuck are you doing? You have some cheek talking about privacy!' She dived across the kitchen to conceal the evidence – but the hiding place hadn't let her down.

He was holding her pen in his hand. He opened his mouth to say something, but closed it without comment.

She didn't want to tell him, not like this.

The dam burst again. She was so exhausted from everything, not just this news. She loved her husband and her son, but life was really difficult. She grabbed her pen from his hand and stuffed it and her belongings back into the bag, her secret safe for now.

'Just leave, Doc.'

'Ah, Tess, please. You're wrong. I love you. Can we talk properly, like adults?'

He took her in his arms and she let him. She let him hug her tight, his familiarity enveloping her. At that moment she knew that everything had changed. At that moment he repulsed her. He was her only love, together since they were eighteen, a lifetime to some. No matter what life had thrown at her in the past, she could always rely on Doc to fix it, to be there for her, to be the voice of reason. Not now. He was hiding something, and she knew in her heart that she could never get over it, not this time. She was completely alone.

She pulled away. 'Doc, I don't want to talk any more. We will not talk about this now. I'm too tired to even think right now but I know you're hiding something. So just go.'

She spoke in a monotone, and hid her shaking hands by wrapping them around the cup in front of her. She wanted to know the truth, but couldn't really handle hearing it.

'This is crazy – it's all in your imagination. I can't believe you're going to go through with letting me go. I wasn't serious when I went upstairs and threw stuff in a bag. Tess, please, this is madness.'

'*I don't care where you go, but I can't be near you now!*'

The venom in her scream, coupled with the sound of her teacup smashing off the back wall, frightened them both.

'Just go, Doc. Be back here by the time Hugh gets home from school tomorrow. I don't care where you go, but make sure you invent a good excuse. I don't want anyone knowing about our business.'

She grabbed her handbag and walked out of the room. She texted Jen on the way up the stairs.

Doc felt a wave of panic set in. He had never seen her like this before and didn't know how to respond. He knew he had fucked up. He loved Tess and Hugh more than anything. He had no choice but to go. He grabbed his phone from the counter to send a text. He hesitated – then sent one.

He cleared up the mess from the teacup, before making his way out to the car. There was no point in arguing further.

Tess lay on the bed and listened to the sound of the engine starting in the drive. She was so confused and terrified. She loved him and was worried about where he would stay. She knew he wouldn't get in touch with Andy, for obvious reasons, and he couldn't go to his parents' place. He had seemed genuine when he denied it. Maybe it was all in her head, but why look so worried when she asked about the phone? Had she totally misread the situation? Maybe she was just neurotic like he said? Maybe the pregnancy hormones were making her crazy? She got up, ran down the stairs and out the front door. He was gone.

Doc's phone lit up and he pulled over to read the message.

Hey, baby, what a lovely surprise. I'm jumping in the shower but the back door is open! XX

He typed a big '**X**' in reply and turned off his phone.

Chapter 6

Andy, Danny and Butch were already in the kitchen when Jen got up. All three seemed to have already had breakfast and, as far as she could judge, Danny was instructing Andy on the proper way to cut his sandwich for his school lunch.

'Morning, guys! What's going on here?'

'Mammy, we didn't want to wake you. Andy told me you were up really, really late last night and he was going to bring me to school.'

Jen smiled at Andy as he put tea and toast on the table for her and pulled out a chair for her to sit.

'This is really kind of the pair of you! Thank you!'

'You're welcome, Mam,' Danny said with a big grin as he rushed out to go brush his teeth.

Jen looked at Andy who was drinking tea, standing against the counter.

'Thanks for minding Danny last night, Andy.'

41

'It was no problem at all, Jen – anytime I'm here it's no trouble to help you out. How was she?'

'She's in absolute pieces. She's so confused.'

'Ah man, the poor woman! What has got into them? They need to sit down and talk all this out.'

'I probably shouldn't have opened my mouth, Andy. Don't breathe a word to either of them if you see them. Jesus, look at the time – I have to get dressed!'

'Jen, relax there. I've promised Danny I'll drop him to school. I'm ready to go. I'll be down on the pier till lunch and I'll be back then. Have a nap and I'll give you a shout when I get back.'

She didn't know what to say. It felt weird not doing her usual thing and being told what to do with her morning. The cheek of him! Then again, how many times had she wished someone would do just that for her?

Before she could even reply, Danny was back in the kitchen. He was ready to leave – a miracle. Butch was hopping round with excitement. He could sense a change in the air and wanted to be in on the action. Danny gave him the usual hugs and kisses, part of the morning ritual, and something he never forgot to do.

'Let's go, Andy. Bye, I love you, Mam!' He was gone out the door in a flash.

Andy just laughed and followed him.

Butch disconsolately settled down on the mat inside the door.

Jen basked in the pure silence and the freedom for a moment. It felt wonderful. She made herself another cup of tea and wandered back up the stairs. She was in the middle of a great novel – Wally Lamb's *I Know This Much is True* – but it had lain neglected over the last few weeks. This was her chance to play catch-up. She was curled up in the bed with her cup of tea when her thoughts turned to Andy. He was such a gentleman, and bloody gorgeous. Don't go there, Jen, she admonished herself. Keep life simple. Her hand had gone automatically to her chest area, her own secret, and the reason behind every handleless cooking pot in the house.

Her mind drifted back to that morning. She was only a child and was home from school ill. The memory was hazy at best but she lived with the consequences every day. Her mother was making something and it smelled delicious. Mammy was out on the doorstep with the postman, and Daddy was in work. Mammy had always told her to stay away from the stove but she would show her what a big girl she was. She went to the Aga, and reached for the handle to lift the pot down. The whole pot tipped down on top of her. By a miracle, the liquid missed her face, but her whole chest and torso took the wave. Doctors later said she was lucky to be alive, but she had done irreparable damage to her chest area, was scarred for life and her body would never develop normally. She was revolted by the look of her body as a teenager and in her early twenties. Never had a boyfriend. Well, apart from Will. He knew all about the scary scars. She knew that she had to get over this, or at least speak to someone about it. She was also obsessive-compulsive about safety with Danny, hence the no handles, and the escape drills and the fire drills. She was getting better but it was still an issue. She and Sal argued all the time about it.

She could never let Andy see her naked.

Jesus Christ, Jen! You're thinking about your housemate seeing you naked. What the hell has got into you? She kicked any thought of Andy and her scars out of her head, and picked up her book again.

The trill of the phone woke her up. She felt groggy, mid-morning naps a thing alien to her usual routine. She grappled for her phone and squinted at the screen. It was Sal.

'Hey, Sal!'

'Good morning, Miss Harper. Have I got news for you!'

'Please let it be of the good variety,' she said, untangling herself from the blankets.

'Are you at home? I'll come down.'

'Yep.'

'Don't sound so enthusiastic about your friend coming over. Hit the kettle, I'm at Mam's. I'll be there in five.'

She hung up. Jen thought about Tess. There was no point in calling down to her at lunchtime – she would have no time to talk. She fired off a quick text asking how she was.

The kettle had boiled when Sal came through the back door, with the usual box of Maltesers and shortbread biscuits in hand. She smacked of sea air, linseed oil and turpentine and her skirt-tails left a trail of damp sand on the kitchen floor. She had been down to visit her mam, and had taken the short cut to Jen's across Stony Strand.

Greeting Jen with a hug, she sat down at the table.

'Right, hit me, Sal – what's your news?'

'Well. Where do I start? As you know I got turned down for the bursary with the Arts Council. Such a pain in the arse. If I'd got that, I could have afforded to give up the part-time work and paint full time – but anyway, maybe next year.'

'But you're managing for money with the classes and stuff, aren't you? I've never heard you complain before.'

'Oh yeah, I'm all right for money, and I'm getting busier. Anything to make ends meet, eh?' She was talking at a rate of knots. 'Anyway, enough about that boring money stuff, Jen. I'm too excited to get side-tracked!'

'Sorry, my fault. Tell me your news.'

'Drumroll, please, Jennifer Juniper!'

'Spit it out, woman! I'm dying to know!'

'You are looking at the next Irish Exhibitor in the Oscar Gallery in Dublin! This place is only a step away from the big nationals and, because they are giving me representation, it increases my chances of exhibiting all over the country. This is massive, Jen. I am so fricking excited. Do you remember that series of portraits I did? The ones you reckoned would make great album covers? They're the ones.'

'Sal, that's fantastic news! I remember you talking about that gallery back in our schooldays. Holy Moly, how did that come about? How does it work like?'

She jumped up out of her seat to hug her friend, and sat down again grinning. This really was amazing news, and something that Sal had been working towards for a lifetime.

Sal munched on a few Maltesers but, even eating, couldn't suppress the smile.

'The Mecca for me has always been the National Modern Art Gallery. I'm a step closer to that now, and maybe even the Turner Prize. There will be no stopping me. Jen, you have no idea how difficult it is to get in there. I am an absolute nobody in the Art world, but this is an opportunity to get out there and really get a name for myself.'

Sal really deserved a lucky break – she was a gifted artist. She had run a really successful exhibition the previous year during the Opera Festival and had featured in a couple of national magazines. It was only a matter of time before she really got it out there.

'So what happens now, Sal? When will the exhibition be on?'

'It takes a few weeks to get everything into place, and then there will be a little launch. Because the Oscar Gallery is now representing me, they will look after all the PR stuff. All my paperwork is in order, and I'm sure contracts will be involved.'

Sal had the added gift of being a really savvy businesswoman. She had a good logical brain for business, a very effective system of work, and didn't fit into the stereotypical idea of an airy-fairy artist.

'Sal, I'm so chuffed for you and your news has just made my day. Let's celebrate with lunch. We can save the Prosecco for the launch!'

Jen made her way to the fridge to see what she could put together. She had plenty in the fridge, and it was soon decided that a warm chicken salad with crusty soda bread would be perfect.

They chatted on about the exhibition but, when they settled down to eat, Sal said: 'Well, Jen, that's all my news. What's the story with you?'

'Ah, all is good with me, hon. Just trying to settle in here, and I'm still working part-time in La Mer. I've been so busy over the past couple of weeks. I haven't really had a chance to catch up with anyone – sorry I haven't really been in touch. Andy has been great – he's a pleasure to share the house with, and looks after all the man stuff. He even dropped Danny to school for me this morning.'

'Jennifer Juniper Harper! I know that tone of voice, and that face! You fancy him, don't you?'

'Don't be daft, Sal – he's my housemate! It would be too messy. Remember you and your fella in college? No, thanks.'

'Jen, stop making excuses – you're as red as a tomato there! Look at you! You fancy him. No point in lying to Sally Pally Pee here: I know you too well.'

Jen didn't answer. Her brain was too busy catching up with what Sal had just said. She fancied the pants off her housemate. How could she not fancy him? He was what every woman wanted in a man.

'Aha, Jen, has the penny finally dropped? Why do you think Aunty Pat went to such great lengths to ensure you two would be under the same roof? I love it. Aunty Pat is still a legend. Matchmaking from the spirit world.'

'Ah, Sal, will you stop! The fumes from the turps is frying your brain. I'm going to the bathroom – your artistic brain needs a rest.'

Jen looked at herself in the bathroom mirror. Sal had hit the nail on the head. That was Aunty Pat's plan. So typical of her, she thought. How did I not guess myself? Oh no. This is not going to go anywhere. He's a nice man, but I don't have time for a relationship and especially one with a live-in housemate. Too complicated and I have to think of Danny.

'There's no point in standing in there talking to yourself in the mirror, Jen!' Sal shouted up the stairs. 'Come back down here!'

When Jen returned to the kitchen, she took one look at Sal and they started to laugh. They had an almost telepathic understanding of each other.

'Sal, you open your mouth to Andy and I will never speak to you again,' she said as she sat down. 'This would be way too messy, especially with Danny and anyway he has enough of his own baggage. And he's leaving the country in a few months for good, so it's pointless.'

Sal didn't believe in the softly softly approach in any area of her life, and she was known for her straight talking. Some would call it a lack of tact – Sal called it good sense. No point in wasting precious time, she would say – grab the bull by the horns and just go for it.

'Sal, I mean it. Keep your mouth firmly closed. I have Danny to think about.'

'OK, OK, Jen. I won't interfere. But seriously, don't let this one pass you by. You have done that too many times in the past. I know you are a great mam, and you always put Danny first. But you deserve to have a bit of a life that extends outside of him and work. You have no life apart from that.'

'Jesus, thanks a bunch, Sal. You make me sound like such a bland person.' Jen was hurt by the last comment, partly because she knew it was true.

'You are bland, Jen, and your life is pretty bland at the moment. Inject a bit of colour and passion into it. You deserve a bit of fun, and you deserve a good man in your life.'

Sal knew Jen. She also knew that Jen would listen to her. She had devoted herself completely to Danny but there would come a time where Danny would grow up and fly the nest. Jen knew that too but she had put her life on hold. She needed to start living, now.

'Jen, are you listening?'

'I am, and you're right. It drives me nuts how well you know me sometimes, Sal. Yes, I fancy my housemate.'

The two of them sat there in silence, finishing the last of the lunch.

'Sal, what am I going to do?'

'Jen, my darling, you are going to seduce your housemate the next night Danny is with his dad.'

'Stop it, woman! I wouldn't know what to do with him, and anyway, he would get sick if he saw my scars. He could have any woman he wanted in the village but, because of Sharon, he has shut down.'

Jen heard the van in the drive before Sal did.

'*Shhhh,* Sal, he's back. Don't say a fecking word. *I mean it.*'

When Andy walked into the kitchen, he was greeted by Sal laughing and Jen looking flustered.

'Hi, ladies!' He raised an eyebrow at them. Women – they were a strange breed.

'How are things with you, Sal? I haven't seen you in ages. Are you hanging on the walls of the Louvre yet?'

Sal proceeded to fill Andy in on her good news and he was thrilled for her. He too knew how gifted she was, and couldn't have been happier for her.

'You girls should go out to celebrate. I won't be going back out fishing until Monday, Jen, so if you want a night out, I'll sit with Danny.'

Before Jen could say a word, Sal had a plan formulated.

'Sure Danny is going to Will at the weekend. Why don't we all go out? Maybe Tess and Doc would come as well, Jen? That sounds like a plan. Friday night, in the Gale. What do you think, Andy, my man? Could you handle a night out with the girls?'

Sal saw the look on Jen's face, and proceeded to kick her under the table.

'Yeah, sure, Sal, that sounds like a plan to me,' said Andy. 'I haven't had a good night out in ages. I think there's a band playing down there as well. Jen?'

Andy turned his full attention to her, and under his gaze she couldn't think of a good enough excuse to object.

'OK, I'm in,' she said, then added, 'I'll cook if you want. We can have dinner here first, and then take a stroll down.'

Sal could have kissed Jen when she heard that suggestion. There she was – playing ball! Jen was back. Just like the old days. She couldn't look at her for fear of bursting out laughing.

'Cool. I'll help you with the cooking, Jen.' Andy gave her a little shove as he got up to make tea. 'You might even learn a thing or two from me.'

'Well, Andy, you were the one who had an eight-year-old teaching you how to cut a sandwich this morning – so, although I appreciate the offer of your culinary skills, I think I'll pass.'

She stuck her tongue out and they all laughed.

'How is the planning going for the round-the-world trip, Andy? Are you still going?' Sal enquired innocently.

'Planning for it is going well, Sal. I have my ticket to Alaska booked. That's the first stop. Then head south – Canada, North and South America. I'll figure out the rest as I go along. Departure date is January the seventh. Just need to keep saving now.'

Sal wished she hadn't asked the question. She hadn't realised he had the damn ticket booked. There was no backing out of it now for him. Sal and Jen both knew that he had this trip planned. Aunty Pat had also talked about it with him, and that had led to some mirthful stories about her travel adventures back in the day.

'Are you going on your own, or are you going as part of a group?'

'Flying solo, and meeting a couple of friends from my college days somewhere in Vancouver. My friend Scott is thinking about joining me, but we'll see what happens.'

Jen listened with interest as Andy spoke about his planned

expedition. She couldn't get involved with someone who was leaving in a few months. It wouldn't be fair on any of them, especially not her little Danny. Sal was a romantic and what she was angling at was right: Jen did need to get out and start living a bit. But Jen was a realist and went out of her way to avoid any kind of drama. There would be no wild romance or seductions under this roof.

'That all sounds amazing, Andy, but when do you think you'll be back?' It was out of Jen's mouth before she could stop it. To try and correct the impatience in her voice, she added, 'I mean, are you going for good or are you just going on an extended holiday?'

Sal tried to suppress a laugh – she was well used to Jen's filter between brain and mouth going into shutdown.

'The answer is, I don't really know, Jen,' he said. He seemed oblivious to what had just happened. 'I guess with everything that's gone on over the past couple of years, I'll just go and see what happens. I want to get out of this place for a while and see what the world has to offer. The bigger picture, see what all the fuss is about.'

Sal changed the subject rapidly. 'So, Jen, what's your plan for the rest of the day?'

'I have to collect the boy from school and we are going to do something for the afternoon. I've had no time to just hang out with him lately.'

'Ah, he's a great little guy, Jen,' Andy said. 'And he comes out with some corkers all right. You should have heard him this morning giving out about how people were parking outside of the school. It was priceless – he had me in fits of laughter.'

'You know where he gets it from, Andy,' said Sal. 'Jen has no patience at all. She wants everything done yesterday.'

Andy laughed, and stood up to clear the table.

'What do you think, Andy?' Sal enquired as she stared at Jen. 'Would you be really patient if you wanted something in particular or would you just go and get it?'

The comment was loaded, and Jen felt like killing her friend. 'Look at the time!' She jumped up from the table. 'I'd better go get a parking space before the madness starts up there. Come on, Sal, I'll give you a lift.'

'Ah, you're fine, Jen – I'll stroll back down to Mam's in a bit.'

'Sal, I insist.' Her tone of voice ruled out any further protest. She grabbed her coat and bag and waited for Sal to do the same. He must think we're a pair of loons, she thought.

'OK,' said Sal. 'Don't forget Friday night now, Andy – it'll be great fun.'

'No bother, Sal, I'll be there. See you later, girls.'

Andy chuckled to himself as they left the kitchen. He remembered the two of them knocking around together in the harbour as teenagers. He was a bit older, but they hadn't changed a bit.

'Get into that car, Sal, before I kill you.' Jen fired up the engine of her beloved Saab, and they took off up the road giggling.

'Look, Jen. You need to just go with the flow for a bit. There is chemistry there, I'm telling you. I saw the way he looked at you, and he really likes Danny. Get it out of your head for now that he's leaving and let's just organise Friday night.'

'OK, OK, Sal.'

They sat in an easy silence for the rest of the short trip down the lane to Sal's parents' house.

When Jen pulled up, Sal gathered up her skirt and the rest of her belongings, and opened the car door.

'Jen, you won't cancel, will you?'

'I won't. Now get out of the car – I'll be late. Give your mam and dad hugs from me.'

Sal gave her friend a big squeeze and got out. If she makes up an excuse for Friday night, I'll brain her, she thought.

Sal was excited. She blew a kiss in the direction of the sea and thought: Aunty Pat, I've got it. I'll get them two together, but I need your help!

Chapter 7

He was more than comfortable with his own nakedness, and why wouldn't he be? He was flawless. He liked to lie there and watch their faces as they emerged from the bathroom in the cold light of day, to face him in all his glory. He liked to look at the discomfort that registered in their eyes as they came out through the door and saw him just watching. It was his house, his rules, and he would do as he pleased. Some of them would come back for second helpings before he kicked them out, some of them would be gone before he woke (that was unusual), and the small few would be dressed and fully made-up before he saw them. Generally it was the same old dance, the small talk, alluding to seeing them again as they scrawled their number on the notebook on the locker. Little did they know it was there for that exact purpose, and the page would go in the bin before they reached the ground floor.

Sometimes he thought about getting up and looking through

their bags before they woke, just to check what their name was. But that was all it was – a thought he never followed through with action. He rarely remembered their names, and he didn't care.

This particular gazelle emerged from the bathroom wrapped in a towel. Typical – and possibly coached from reading too many self-help books, or glossy magazines, she tried to look demure and alluring. She didn't. The bruise had faded, thank goodness, and for a second he felt sorry for her. She looked younger now than he had originally thought. Early twenties. Young and impressionable. Young and easily led. Young and compliant.

She was beautiful though: all legs and breasts. She looked awkward standing there, looking around in panic for her clothes. She would follow with the line 'I'm sorry for waking you' – they never meant it really – they always wanted him to wake, and cook them breakfast, and hold their hands and tell them he would love to see them again. Doesn't work like that, girls. You would need to be something really special to keep up with me.

He lay there as she sat on the end of the bed.

She felt so uncomfortable. Dammit, she thought, what was I thinking? He is a creep, lying there like a demi-god. I can't wait to get the hell out of here. If he hadn't got me so high last night I would never have stayed here. She looked around his room. Really spacious, typical modern man room – wealthy man room. Golf clubs in the corner, *Forbes* magazine on the floor, a wardrobe stuffed with expensive suits with a large selection of ties hanging on a rail. She needed to get home and get ready for the evening shift. Never again would she go home with a strange man. She wasn't sure if it was the come-down from the drink and the coke or his presence that was making her feel ratty. She knew who he was, and she also knew that he was the most eligible bachelor in Dublin. She had heard the stories, a real-life Lothario. Funny, she had never heard any stories of how he liked to play rough. It was all a bit hazy, and she couldn't really remember a lot from the night before.

She needed to get dressed and get out of there. She checked her phone – lunchtime.

This one is different, he thought. He could tell by her body language she was feeling prickly. Better sweeten her up, or she might go home to Daddy and tell him she was roughed up by a big boy but, then again, his friend owned the hotel she worked in, and she knew it. No, there would be no gossip out of her, thanks very much.

'Can I offer you a coffee or some breakfast, Anna?'

He had risen from the bed and was getting dressed.

He remembered her name, which was a start, she thought.

'A coffee would be lovely, thanks.'

Boom. He had her reeled in again.

She watched him as he rounded the bed, and planted a kiss on her cheek. Maybe he's not so bad, she thought, and began to feel a bit better about herself. It was a late night, she'd had way too much to drink and, as well as her own stash of coke, they had taken more when they got back.

They made small talk at the counter in his kitchen over a coffee. He was always the charmer and she had just opened up like a spring flower. He knew she had merely been a means of satisfying a sexual urge last night. She was beginning to think he was actually interested in her.

They sat exchanging pleasantries for a few more minutes, before he began looking impatiently at his watch. He informed her that he really must get organised for his three o'clock meeting, and unfortunately – after enquiring where she was going – he was going in the opposite direction.

She asked if he wanted to go out for a drink sometime this week, and he responded by telling her to write down her number on the notepad on the locker. He had a really busy schedule for the remainder or the week but would be in touch early next week to arrange dinner somewhere in town, perhaps The Dandelion: did she know of the restaurant and would she like to go there?

This little charade of course made her eyes light up. Everyone knew The Dandelion. It was the most expensive and exclusive restaurant in Dublin. It would cost more for dinner in there than she earned in a week.

And for the finale, he leaned over and kissed her on the lips.

'Now, Anna,' he said, 'I must go. I need a shower to wake myself up – you wore me out last night. I'll give you a call. Just let yourself out. The DART station is around the corner, keep left. See you soon. *Ciao ciao.*'

They fell for the same bullshit every time. He was growing tired of it. He had started to notice lately that he was feeling slightly guilty as they left. But easy come, easy go. They were all the same, gave in to the chase too easily. The women who stank of desperation. They wanted a man, and no amount of mascara could hide that look in their eyes. They all wanted a man, more specifically him.

The hot jet of the power shower washed away any feeling of guilt.

Suited and booted, ready to go event-manage for Mother, he stepped out into the daylight to meet the first client of the day. Weybridge Estate was an incredibly exclusive property and all his clients had deep pockets.

As he drove, he passed her on the road walking. Keep walking, girl, he thought, keep walking.

He was looking forward to the dinner party in Jen's with Andy and her friends. It all sounded very cosy. He might make a weekend out of it. He would book the usual place and just play it by ear on Friday night – surely he could get a taxi out of Hicksville at some stage?

He was looking forward to getting out of Dublin and seeing Andy. He was the only person whose company even registered as being anything worthwhile. It was up to him as his friend to always make sure he got what he needed. He was his protector. He was his friend.

Jen intrigued him. She was completely immune to his charm, which always made it interesting, and although she was pretty hot there was something a bit too frumpy and bland about her to even bother with the games.

He had to hand it to her though, she knew her own mind and, from what he had heard through Andy, was a great mother to that little rug rat. Andy seemed taken with both of them. That was something he would have to remedy – he had the trip planned and no woman was going to get in the way of that. He would make sure of it.

Chapter 8

Doc stood on the front doorstep of his home, wondering whether or not he should ring the doorbell. His bag sat beside him on the concrete.

This is all your fault, you know, Doc, said a voice in his head. *You need to clean up your act and save your marriage.*

This had been the general train of thought since he left his home the previous evening, albeit not a strong enough thought to keep him away from his fancy woman. He loved his wife more, and he had come home. He made a promise to himself – that was the last time – he would tell her soon it was over.

He turned the key in the door and walked in. He could hear Hugh up in his bedroom, playing on his drum kit – Tess had been less than impressed when he arrived home with that for Christmas. Hugh loved it, and all was forgiven in the end. He wanted to shout out to him, but he needed to face his wife first.

The sound of the television wafted from the sitting room. This in itself was unusual: she hardly ever watched TV and never during the day.

He opened the sitting-room door, to find her lying on the couch in front of a roaring fire. Crumbs were all that remained of the plate of biscuits and her cup was empty.

'You look cosy.' He was trying to be nice.

'I am.' Her eyes didn't leave the television.

He knew that this was a good sign: she hadn't launched into a tirade of shouting. He offered to make tea, she accepted.

When Doc returned from the kitchen, she had come out from under her blanket. He sat down in the chair beside the fireplace.

'Where did you stay last night, Doc?'

'In a B&B.' He cringed as the lie was said. But he couldn't tell her the truth, could he? 'Tess, can we talk now? We need to sort this mess out.'

'Doc, I don't know where to even start. Everything has gone to shit and I'm tired of it all.'

Her tone was gentle. She seemed to be beyond fighting. The drama of the day before had depleted her energy – she looked as though she didn't have the strength to argue. She was drained – and pliable.

'I did a lot of thinking last night, Tess. Most of what you said is true. Things are crap between us and we don't make time for each other any more. I love you and Hugh more than anything in the world, you have to believe me when I say that. I want us to get back to where we were, and you to see me as you did before – instead of the musician stereotype you now see me as.'

She shook her head and looked at him in amazement. 'Musician stereotype? So it's all my fault, is it? The problem is that I see you as a stereotype? *What about the affair, Doc?*'

'As God is my judge, Tess, you are the only woman for me.'

'That's not answering the question though, is it?'

She stared at him and his stomach turned to lead.

'Tess, I'm not having an affair. I swear on my life. You have to believe me.'

'How can I believe you? You did it before! You've been acting so weirdly lately, you can't blame me for jumping to that conclusion.'

He then knew by the tone of her voice that she didn't know for sure. She was guessing. He needed to convince her that she was being paranoid.

'Tess, I swear you've got it wrong. I nearly lost you the last time. It was a long time ago and I learned my lesson – you know that. I swore to you I wouldn't do it again and I meant it, and I promise you now there will only ever be you.' He meant that last statement with all his heart. He loved his wife, and they had been together for so long. No one knew him better than her, and she deserved to be treated right. He wouldn't tell her about his affair, but he would, from today, be the perfect husband and father.

'I don't know, Doc. I want to believe you, I really do, but I feel like we are housemates, living totally separate lives. You make me feel like I bore you to tears, and you can't wait to get out of this house and go where the wind blows you.'

'I'll give up the music.'

'What?'

'I mean it, Tess. You and Hugh are my number-one priority. I'll give up the gigs and get a job somewhere else – a "real job" if you want to call it that. I heard the fish factory is looking for staff.'

He looked at her, and he saw how his suggestion had affected her. She looked shocked, to say the least.

'It would kill you to give up music, Doc. It's part of your DNA.'

'Well, I'll only do local gigs then. I will do whatever it takes to fix this, Tess. I swear to God. If I have to get a job and hang up my guitar to prove that to you, that's what I'll do.'

'Doc, I just want us to be happy. You, me and Hugh. I want us to be a family again. And now ...'

'And now what?'

'It doesn't matter … The pub is struggling, Doc, and I'm under huge strain. I need to know we can support each other and take care of each other.'

'I promise, Tess. Things are going to be great from here on in. I'll be fecking Superman and you will be my Lois.'

He smiled at her and it was reciprocated.

'Teamwork, Tess. That's what it's all about from now on. I love you, you know that, don't you?'

He looked at her. She nodded her head and began to cry.

'I love you too, Doc, and I just want us to be happy,' she said between sobs. 'I can't expect you to give up music, it's your livelihood. We just need to figure everything out and make sure we put our family first.'

He joined her on the couch and hugged her. 'We will make this work, Tess, OK?'

She hugged him back. 'OK.' She hesitated. 'Doc, I've something to tell you.'

'What is it, love?'

Before she could continue, the sitting-room door flew open and in marched Hugh kitted out in his football gear.

'Dad! We need to go training. I'm going to be late, and I'm goalie tonight and I'm going to save all the goals and be the hero. Come on, Dad, quick, quick!'

'All right, mister, let's go. What were you going to say there, Tess?'

'It can wait, Doc. Don't worry.'

'Mam, do you want to come too?' Hugh was hopping from one foot to another, and nearly fell over his laces.

'I'll stay here and make something nice for dinner. I'll have a big bubble bath ready for you when you get home, OK? Now come here until I tie those laces for you.'

'OK, Mam.' He stood still just long enough for her to tie the laces on his football boots.

Doc looked at them, and in that moment he knew that things would be OK. He would put things right and wouldn't fuck up again.

'See you later, Mam!' Hugh gave her a hug and a kiss then scarpered in the direction of the car.

'I'll see you later, love, OK?'

'OK, love. I'll make dinner and we can just take it easy tonight. I'm exhausted.'

He went to kiss her goodbye but she turned her face and offered him her cheek.

Doc walked out the front door and felt lighter. He had dodged a bullet. He felt his guilt abating slightly and he knew he was out of the woods, so to speak. It would take time and effort. He would make it up to her if it killed him. His Tess, his one and only.

Chapter 9

He ended the call with his mother as he pulled into the wide drive of Cherry House Nursing Home. The modern building looked warm and inviting, as the windows took on the same colour as the evening sun.

The nurse on reception nodded to him as he walked down the corridor to room 17B, his shoes squeaking on the polished non-slip floors. The same faces greeted him on the corridor. It was a pleasant place, Cherry House: new, private and very expensive. The art work on the walls, the communal courtyard and the dozens of potted plants disguised the institution well.

He knocked gently on the door before opening it. It was just after five, and a rattle of crockery and a tea trolley could be heard in the distance over the din of the television immediately opposite him. This was the usual carry-on, until a nurse or an orderly came in and turned it down. As soon as they left, someone would turn it up again. Others would be sitting facing the window overlooking the courtyard, seeing nothing, oblivious to the chat-show theme tunes.

He pushed open the door and went in.

'Hello, Arthur, how are you this evening? I brought your favourites – Liquorice Allsorts.'

He sat in the chair at the side of the bed, and laid the sweets down on the locker.

'Evening, Scott laddie – how are you?'

He was really lucid and in good form this evening. That was a good sign: it hadn't progressed.

'Is that mother of yours looking after my garden properly up there?'

'She is indeed, Arthur. She has a young fella up there at the weekends, and she has left strict instructions for him to maintain everything exactly as you left it.'

This pleased him. Arthur Jenkins had been the gardener on Weybridge estate for decades. He had grown up with Scott's father and had watched Scott grow up. He knew that Scott was a cold fish and fond of the highlife but he understood how he had turned out the way he did. His mother was an awful wreck, and she had put his father in a grave too early. Young Scott had always been a pleasant chap in his company, and he looked on him like family. The Carluccio Randalls were the only family he had known. He had never married. Scott continued to visit him after he retired, and when he started to get a bit absentminded, and not quite able to look after himself, he would have been left alone only for him. Scott had found this lovely place for him, and he was only paying a few euros out of his pension every week for it.

'You're a good chap, Scott – you never forget my sweets.'

'I know how much you'd give out if I did!' Scott said, smiling at him.

He was pleased to see how well Arthur looked. He had persuaded him to come here four months ago after a nasty fall.

He had seen that he was struggling on his own and had recognised how his mind had started to fail him – the absentmindedness and the bouts of aggression. His hypertension was becoming too difficult to control, and increased amounts of medication were difficult to manage. He worried about him being in that little house on his own. Eventually Arthur saw sense and agreed to come. He didn't know that his stay was being subsidised out of Scott's money, and that was something he would never know. Nobody knew. He had been very clear in his instructions to the management and staff when Arthur arrived.

He was a good old man, and had been a good man to Scott all his life. He had taught him so many things over the years and filled the space that his parents should have occupied time after time. In truth, he loved the old man and visited once a week if he could.

They spoke about the weather and the usual things. Arthur had always loved sports, especially the horses, and he liked to have the odd flutter. He would study the form and place a bet online. Scott had got him an iPad, and given him grinds on how to use it. It had taken quite some time for him to get his head around the idea of WiFi but, once he did, there was no stopping him. Not bad for a 76-year-old. He also had mastered the art of texting, and Scott was able to keep in contact with him. Cherry House had a great reputation, but you could never be sure.

On a good day, Arthur was quite the storyteller. Today he regaled Scott with the tale of the latest romance between the residents of 5A and 9D, hilarious stuff. The last visit hadn't been so good, and it was distressing for Scott to see him that way. His suspicions about the onset of dementia had been confirmed. Days like this were a bonus.

It was time for Arthur's tea, the nurse informed them. Arthur got up from his bed, put his iPad back in the locker and then hugged Scott.

'See you next week, son.'

Scott watched him as he walked in the same direction as many of the other residents, and sighed. He always felt sad leaving him here in this institution. It was the safest place for him, and he knew he was happy but he also knew that his home was the gardens of Weybridge, a place he might never see again.

Chapter 10

'Now you be a good boy for Daddy and don't stay up too late,' she said.

Danny was excited and nearly fell over Butch as they made their way out to Will. A movie night was on the cards, and the dog was going as well.

'Have a lovely night, Jen. I'll give you a call tomorrow evening.' Will started the engine and they both waved from the car.

It was half past six and everyone was arriving for half seven. Jen was excited, and nervous. It had been a long time since she had entertained a group of friends, and if Sal had anything to do with the evening's proceedings, it was going to be interesting.

The kitchen looked lovely. She and Andy had been cooking all day. He wasn't joking when he said he could cook. He was in charge of the starter and dessert, and Jen had chosen the main course. The table was laid, the flowers were in the vase and the candles were ready for lighting.

Everything was in order. She glanced at Andy as he washed the last few dishes in the sink. He was a lovely person. They had discussed the menu last night, and had got all the supplies in first thing this morning.

'I'm running upstairs to get ready, Andy. Have we got everything under control?'

'Yes, we have, Chef. All we need now is the guests to arrive on time.'

'Well, Sal will be late, she always is. But Tess and Doc will be here early.'

'Scott will be early as well. He's really annoying like that. Now go get ready, woman!'

Jen took her time. There was no rush, and no Danny coming up the stairs every five minutes shouting at her through the bathroom door. She put essential oils in the bath and slipped under the water. She was looking forward to taking her time applying her make-up and blow-drying her hair.

At ten past seven Andy heard the doorbell ring.

It was Sal.

'Hi, Sal, come on in. It's not like you to be formal and use the front door!' He kissed her on the cheek. 'You're early. We thought you'd be the last to arrive. Jen is upstairs getting ready – she should be down in a bit.'

'Oh, the place looks lovely, and something smells great. I've been starving myself all day for this.' She plonked herself down at the counter, and handed him a bottle of wine.

'Would you like a glass now?' he asked.

'I'd actually love a coffee now, Andy – that Chablis could do with a few more minutes in the fridge.'

Jen walked through the kitchen door while applying her lipstick. She had heard Sal come in and there was no way she was leaving her on her own with Andy – goodness knows what she would say.

Sal stood up and hugged her friend. 'You look terrific, Jen. It's great to see you dressed up as a girl once in a while.'

The doorbell went again and next to arrive was Scott, a huge bunch of flowers in his hand, followed five minutes later by Tess and Doc. Drinks were served, and everyone relaxed into the evening.

Scott was chatting to Doc about music when Jen slipped over to Tess.

'How are you, Tess? Have you told him yet?'

She looked drawn and stressed, but from texts back and forth during the week Jen knew they were working some stuff out.

'*Shhh*, Jen, for goodness' sake!'

'I'll take that as a no then? You have to tell him. He's going to cotton on to it soon enough.'

Andy came and joined them. 'We should get some food out to this lot before they start eating those flowers, Jen.'

'You're right. OK, everyone, grub's up! Take a seat at the table and we will start serving up. Scott, would you open a couple of bottles of wine for the table – the corkscrew is there.'

Jen had decided to make an effort with Scott. He couldn't be that bad if he was such good pals with Andy. He seemed to be happy and relaxed around everyone and was fitting in well. Maybe she was wrong about him after all.

There was a wonderful selection of wines to choose from. Everyone had brought a couple of bottles.

'Something smells amazing, Jen. I hope you haven't been cooking all day?' Doc slathered butter over a slice of brown bread.

'Well, I knew you were coming, Doc – the bar had to be raised. We all know you fancy yourself as a Jamie Oliver. I can't take the credit on the starter though – it was all Andy, and even the brown soda bread to go with the seafood chowder is homemade. I'm impressed.'

'I'm no Jamie Oliver, Jen – I'm better!' Doc replied with a laugh.

The seafood chowder went down a treat. Andy had made the base the night before, and collected all the fresh fish – cod, salmon, prawns and mussels – that morning. It was beautiful, and fresh as fresh could be. Tess only toyed with her chowder, and the wine in her glass lay untouched. Jen noticed, but she seemed to be the only one to do so.

Scott turned his attention to Sal. He was really interested in her news about the Oscar Gallery.

'It's quite the prestigious place to be exhibited, Sal. Your work must be of an extremely high standard. Where did you study?'

'I went to NCAD, the National College of Art and Design. I loved it there, and it was a combination of talent and pure luck to have got the exhibition in Oscar. They have taken me on for representation, which is really exciting.'

Sal was so excited and proud of the latest developments in her career, but she really had no idea how gifted she was.

'That's a wonderful opportunity for you. Congratulations. I have a couple of friends on the Arts Council, and in the NMAG. I would be glad to pass your portfolio on to them – on the quiet of course.'

Sal nearly fell off the chair with delight. The National Modern Art Gallery! She couldn't thank Scott enough for offering to do that for her. She knew better than anyone how hard it was to get an audience with any of those high up the ladder in the art world.

As the soup bowls were cleared from the table, light began to fade outside and the candles threw shapes up onto the walls. Conversation was flowing and Doc seemed to be hanging on Tess's every word. Jen knew he loved her and hoped that things would get back on track for the two of them.

'Are you having a nice time, Jen?'

'Andy, I really am. It's been so long since I have spent the evening in adult company, I have almost forgotten how to behave. I'll be trying to get you up to bed for nine o'clock!'

They laughed together. Andy liked her. He tried to deny it

but, as the wine went down as quick as the evening light, he was beginning to see more and more things about her that appealed to him. It was a shame in one way he was leaving – she wouldn't be the type to get into something just for a fling, and he wasn't either. There hadn't been anyone really since Sharon, and no one that made him laugh like Jen did.

Sal saw the looks pass between them. It was just good luck they were sitting on the end of the table together, close to the kitchen. Aunty Pat, she thought, we are on track here.

The main course of pulled pork, Asian salad and sweet potato wedges was as good as the chowder. The pork was delicious. Slow-roasted all day, Jen informed them, as she put the platter and serving spoons in the centre of the table. She loved the idea of everyone sharing from the same big plate. They could take as much or as little as they wanted, and it always looked better presented in that way.

There wasn't a scrap left twenty minutes later, and Jen and Andy were delighted at how well the food had been received.

'Jen, my duck, if you ever want to come work for me, I'll fire that bitch of a cook,' Tess said. 'Andy, you can come too. Compliments to you both, you make a good team.' She couldn't resist the last remark, and she could have sworn it made both of them blush. 'I forgot to tell you, guys – the damn band cancelled on me last minute this evening so there's no music tonight. Doc was going to fill in, but we wanted the night together.'

'I'm sure you two aren't too keen about going down there on your night off,' Sal said, 'so I'm happy to chill out here if no one else has a burning desire to go and sit in the Gale?'

And so it was decided. Everyone was happy to relax in Jen's kitchen. There was plenty of wine, and dessert was yet to be served. Maybe Doc might even give them a song or two later, someone suggested.

Soon Doc and Scott had the table cleared of main-course dishes and Tess was doing the rounds topping up the wineglasses.

Sal was out the back smoking a cigarette, and Andy was bent over the vinyl collection trying to choose.

'No pressure now, Andy,' Jen said, 'but choose wisely, the party depends on it. Maybe you should supervise, Scott? Anyone for an Irish Coffee?'

Everyone was in great form at this stage. Everyone except for Tess was merry. Jen was no exception – she was also feeling the effects of the wine, but she didn't care.

'So five Irish coffees after I bring out the dessert.'

'I'll help you, Jen.' Sal materialised at her side. It wasn't hard to chat privately in the open-plan kitchen at this stage – the music had gone up a decibel or two. Jen knew there was no point in suggesting they should move next door into the front room. The group was more than comfortable where they were.

'*Wohoo*, the sparks are flying between you and the lodger tonight, hon,' Sal murmured. 'He wants to kiss you, for sure. I have been observing his body language all evening.'

'Sal, will you stop with the matchmaking! We are housemates and friends – nothing else. He's leaving in a few months. Even if I did fancy him it would be a pointless exercise.'

'Stop bullshitting, Jen. You can't hide the truth from Sally Pally Pee. Bullshitter! Bullshitter!'

'Who's a bullshitter?' Andy asked as the girls roared laughing. He had come over to check on the progress of the dessert.

'Jen is a bullshitter, Andy, and I suppose you have come over here now to supervise us plating up your dessert. Did you really make that from scratch?'

She pointed at the masterpiece, and Andy was in his element with the praise.

'Yes, ladies, I have come to supervise. I saw the little wobbles as you two walked across the floor, and I would have to give Jen a good whipping if she dropped my chocolate torte.'

'*Oh, behave!*' Sal added, trying to do her best Austin Powers impression. It was brutal.

Doc piped up with his version and it was brilliant. This of course started a whole new round of laughing and prompts from the girls. Doc's impressions, down to the ones of the dinner-party guests, had them all in fits laughing.

Jen was still thinking about the whipping comment as she ate her chocolate torte, daydreaming about Andy and cream. Jeepers tonight, she thought, get a hold of yourself, Jen.

Scott had taken up residence beside the record player and he was doing a stellar job. The conversation turned inevitably to music, a love they all shared.

Scott then said that he was going to choose a collection of songs that he felt perfectly represented each of the guests. This was greeted with enthusiastic applause. After some thought, he rapped loudly on the table and made his announcement.

'OK, here goes, ladies and gents. If you think I'm going to include any of the current crap in the charts that makes my ears bleed, you are mistaken. First up is the lovely Sal – for you, it has to be "Tiny Dancer" by Elton John.'

'Scott, I love that song. Good choice.' Sal was delighted.

'For you, Andy – "With a Little Help from My Friends" – the Joe Cocker version.'

Andy grinned as the others clapped.

'Tess, for you I choose "To Ramona" – the Sinéad Lohan version – much better than Bob's.'

Doc nearly had a conniption because he chose Sinéad over his hero, Bob, but let it go after a brief protest.

'I shall continue now that Doc has got back in his box. For you, Doc, and how apt – "The Devil's in the Jukebox" by Ray Lamontagne.'

That got a laugh out of everyone.

'And finally for you, Jen. Well, it has to be a Donovan number, doesn't it? So for you it's "Sunshine Superman".'

'And for yourself, Scott?' Jen asked.

'It could only be "You're So Vain" by Carly Simon.'

That ensured more laughter from everyone, including Jen.

'Now, Doc, here's a challenge,' Scott said. 'How about you sing each of these songs for us?'

Everyone applauded, whistled and drummed their heels.

'Yes, Doc!' Sal called. 'Time to warm up those vocal cords and see how many of them you know – or, more to the point, can sing!'

'Ah, come on, lads – Scott is doing a right job here, and it's my night off,' he protested in vain.

Scott quit the record player, and left Doc with little choice.

'Ah, he doesn't know any of them at all!' Andy said, laughing.

'As a matter of fact, smart arse, I know all bar one, that Ray Lamontagne one. Never heard of it, Scott.'

'No excuses, Doc, my lovely,' Tess said as she gathered up the dessert plates. 'The guitar is in the car. Why don't you go get it?'

'Oh, please do, Doc,' Jen said. 'I'd love a sing-song now.'

He got up and went out to the car.

'Oh feck,' Jen said, 'with all this music talk, I completely forgot about the Irish Coffees!' She made her way over to the kitchen.

The footed mugs were laid out and ready, cream was whipped and sugar and coffee were there too. But where was the Jameson? She rooted around in the kitchen cupboards until she remembered that it was, in fact, in the locked drinks cabinet in the front room – hard liquor needed to be locked away from curious children.

She darted into the front room and over to the cabinet under the bay window. Noticing that one of the windows was open a bit, she reached out to pull it shut and saw that Doc was outside with his back to her. He was on the phone, telling the person on the other end not to cry and that he would see them tomorrow. It must be Hugh, she thought, poor kid!

'You know I miss you too,' Doc went on, 'and if I could be there with you tonight I would be – but we need to talk. Things have changed now.'

Jen felt the hair rise on the back of her neck.

'Yeah – Dublin tomorrow. Just book the hotel, and I'll see you there. I'm looking forward to it. We can sort it all out then.'

Jen left the window open, grabbed the Jameson, and hurried back to her station in the kitchen.

She waited for the kettle to boil, going over and over what she had just heard. It wasn't his son on the phone, obviously. It was his mistress.

'Jen?'

'What? Oh, sorry, Andy, I was miles away.'

'What's wrong, Jen? You look like you've seen a ghost.'

'I'll tell you later.'

Tess followed Doc outside. She was uneasy. It doesn't take that long to get a guitar, she thought. What is he up to? When she got outside he was fishing around in the boot for a capo.

'There you are, pet – I thought you had got lost.' She was relieved he had a valid reason for the delay.

The capo found, they went back into the kitchen and he started to tune up the guitar.

Tess couldn't believe it when she saw Jen out the back with a cigarette in her mouth.

'Jen! What are you doing? Why in blue blazes are you smoking, you daft cow? And you, Andy! What has got into you all with the fags tonight?'

They just laughed and blamed the wine. They were soon lured back inside as they heard Doc begin to sing.

His voice was beyond compare. He was singing 'With a Little Help from My Friends', and he sang it beautifully. That was Andy's song.

Next he played the opening bars of 'To Ramona' for his wife.

Jen couldn't help but feel so sad for him and Tess. After witnessing that last conversation, it was clear that he was doing the dirty. She had no idea how she was going to tell her friend. And he didn't have a clue he was going to be a father again. It was all such a big sad mess. One she couldn't think about tonight, but the mess had taken the good out of the evening for her. She and Tess had spoken during the week and she now believed that Doc was faithful to her. He had convinced her.

Scott saw her change in demeanour and thought it was tiredness. He was impressed by her easy charm and skill at throwing a dinner party and, moreover, making everyone comfortable around each other. She looked tiny standing there beside Andy. It pained him to admit they would make a handsome couple. The wine from the evening had mellowed him, and he was enjoying everyone's company. And he knew nothing would come of Andy and Jen – tonight at least – because they both had too much baggage to go down the casual-sex route.

Scott turned his attention back to Sal. She was a wonderful girl and a very talented one at that. He really hoped he could help her out through his contacts.

The cheers and a round of applause brought his thoughts back to the room.

Next song on the list was 'Tiny Dancer'. Scott had chosen this for Sal – it suited her, and he had hit the nail on the head as she was a huge fan. Sal really liked Scott. He was a total ladies' man, she could see that, but their interest in each other was genuine and platonic. They had a lot in common as regards art and, for Sal, it was rare to meet someone with whom she could chat about her work. It was nice and she was enjoying herself. Jen seemed quite cold towards him, which wasn't like her. Sal could see that she was just trying to be nice for Andy's sake.

Sal joined in with the singing at this stage, and Jen couldn't help herself either. Neither of them were particularly good singers, but they weren't all that bad. Before long, everyone had joined in, even Scott, who had a great voice.

'Scott!' Jen said. 'You never mentioned that you could sing. What a beautiful voice you have!'

'There was nothing to mention, Jen. I can sing with a few glasses of wine in me, but I think we can leave it to the professional to take centre stage.'

Scott was taken aback by the praise for his voice. Sing-songs and sessions were rare things in the circles he moved in, and it was so long since he had sung in public he had forgotten he could.

Doc was in his element, and was getting pretty drunk, downing glasses of wine faster than anyone else.

'Scott, please tell me you know this one,' he slurred as he started to play the opening bars to 'The Sound of Silence'.

Scott started to sing, tentatively at first, then Doc joined him in the harmonies and they really did a wonderful job. More cheers and claps. It always amazed Jen – no matter how drunk Doc got, he never missed a note.

She slipped out to the deck for another of Sal's cigarettes and watched the scene inside. The candles cast a soft glow on everyone's face and her kitchen was full of friends, all happy and enjoying themselves … for tonight at least.

She sat down at the wooden table. From the distance she could hear the sound of the ocean. She was lost in her own thoughts and didn't hear the door open. She felt a hand on her shoulder and she jumped.

It was Scott.

'Sorry, Jen. Did I startle you?'

She stubbed out the cigarette as he sat beside her on the bench.

'Thank you for the invitation tonight, Jen. It's been a wonderful evening, and so far removed from my usual social gatherings. Refreshing.'

She couldn't decide whether he was being genuine or condescending. 'You're very welcome, Scott. I know you and Andy are great friends so it's nice to get to know you.'

'We are very good friends, Jennifer. I know him better than

anyone and I've always had his back. Andy is a nomad, and that will not change, dear. He has a fixed plan in his head, and no one will get in the way of that. It's who he is. He will never settle in this little one-horse town.'

Something in the tone of his voice made her sure that he was giving her a warning. She didn't like it.

'I'm sure Andy is a big enough boy to speak for himself about his plans and his wishes, Scott.' She stood up abruptly. 'It's cold out here. I'm going back inside.'

Scott placed a hand on her arm.

'Jennifer, he deserves the best. Speaking of which, I'm going to make some calls for your really good friend Sal. I have friends in high places on the Arts Council and in the NMAG. Wouldn't it be wonderful for her as a fledgling artist to get a solo exhibition there? Her career would be made. It would be a shame for anything to stand in the way of that.'

She shook his hand off her arm and folded her arms across her chest.

'Scott, if you have something to say to me, spit it out. I don't like your tone and I might remind you that you are in my house.'

Sal appeared with a cigarette before he could respond.

'Sal, I was just telling Jen here about our plans to make you famous!'

'Oh, Jen, isn't he just great?'

'It's great news, Sal, but it's chilly out here, I'm going inside.'

She forced a smile at both of them and went in. She was furious, but for now she was going to keep quiet about it all. She couldn't understand Scott's problem with her.

Inside, Tess and Doc were having words. She was wrecked and wanted to go home; he was having a great night and wanted to stay. Tess won the argument and made her way over to Jen for a hug.

'Jen, tonight has been lovely, thanks a million. I'm wrecked, so we're heading off. I'll give you a call in the morning.'

Doc was man-hugging and handshaking with the boys.

Sal and Scott had come in, protesting over the party coming to an end.

'Scott, do you need a lift to the guesthouse?' Tess asked. 'Sal, can we run you home?'

'Yes, please,' was the reply from each of them.

And then, they were all gone.

Jen and Andy sat down at the table, both with mugs of tea in front of them.

She told him about the phone call she had overheard. He shook his head and played with the candle.

'What are you going to do, Jen? Are you going to tell her?'

'I can't even think about that now, Andy, I'm wrecked. I don't know what to do. Doc is my friend as well and I am sick about this. Poor Tess. Maybe I picked it up all wrong, but I think that's wishful thinking.'

They sat in silence at the table, each wondering what was going through the other's head. He looked at her as she gazed into her cup, and he was struck, not for the first time, with how pretty she was. She could feel his eyes on her and it made her heart start to thump. She held on to her cup for dear life, and couldn't bring herself to look at him. There were no words in her head, or no silly jokes to make, and the energy had shifted to something almost tangible.

He forgot sometimes how physically small she was, as she had such a big personality. He knew he was headed into dangerous territory with her. He wanted to reach over and touch her hand, or her face, or that beautiful mop of hair, but he couldn't bring himself to do it. He needed to stick to the plan. He had got home from hell after Sharon, and he was never going to leave himself that open again. He thought about little Danny, and his little head of curls inherited from his mam. A sweet loveable little boy, fiercely protective of her. They were loveable, both of them. It was dangerous.

He stood up from the table so quickly he nearly knocked over the chair.

'I'm off to bed. Goodnight, Jen.'

'Goodnight, Andy.'

She breathed out a sigh, and picked up the cups. What a night, she thought. My friend's husband is doing the dirty on her, my other friend is about to get her foot in the door of the most prestigious gallery in Ireland, I have a thing for my housemate and his best friend is practically blackmailing me to stay away. Great, just bloody great.

The remnants of the party remained on the table and the counters: it could wait until morning. She began the nightly ritual of unplugging and checking everything before making her way up the stairs.

Andy's light was off and his door was firmly shut. Story of my life, she thought.

She got into bed and then it struck her. Scott is gay. He has to be. That's why he's warning me off. He's in love with Andy. Then she thought: No, he's not gay, I know he's not. They're just close friends and he wants to protect him after what happened with Sharon. Around and around the argument went in her head, around and around, until she finally drifted off to sleep.

Chapter 11

Scott had finished his breakfast and it was enough to cure the effects of the previous night. He had enjoyed himself. The group was an interesting mix, and he was quite taken with Sal's sheer talent. He would make a few calls on her behalf. Tess and Doc were easy to read – even though Tess had tried to keep her business to herself in their chats last night, he knew she was in real trouble in many ways. Doc was a lost cause and he was a heavy drinker. Jen's presence had been tolerable but it was very clear to him that there was something between Jen and Andy, and this could mess everything up for him. She was a problem, but he was good at solving them. Now was the time to act.

The view from the breakfast room in the Bed and Breakfast was stunning. The weather had changed dramatically overnight. The waves were pounding, grinding and roaring onto the beach, crashing down and sending white spray up into the grey sky. It was hard to tell where the sea stopped and the sky started. The rain beat on the window relentlessly, the wind driving it forward.

He picked up his phone and punched in her number.

'Good morning, The Gale, Tess speaking.'

'Hi, Tess, how are you this morning? It's Scott here.'

'Oh, hello, Scott. I'm fine thanks. How are you today?'

He knew by the tone of her voice that she was surprised to hear from him.

'Tess, I'm staying around for a couple of days. Would today be convenient for us to have a chat?'

'Em, yes, ah – OK. What is this in relation to, Scott?'

'I have a suggestion I would like to run by you about your pub that I feel may be of benefit to us both. How would three o'clock suit?'

'I'm intrigued, Scott. OK. I can meet you at three. Do you want to come here to the pub?'

'No – let's meet somewhere else, where we can talk. I need to go to town. Say, the County Hotel?'

'OK, cool, I'll see you there at three.'

Scott put the phone back on the table and returned to his coffee. He knew that Tess was a savvy businesswoman – she had a good head on her shoulders. The pitch would have to be right, and it would have to be above board. Doc had very little to do with the running of the business – he wouldn't be able to organise his way out of a paper bag. Scott did know how Doc could be of benefit to him, and would make it his business to get to one of his gigs soon, but this weekend was out. He wanted to stay around and spend a bit of time with Andy.

A short time later, he received a text message from Andy. They arranged to catch up over a few pints in the Gale later. He hoped that Jen wouldn't tag along – he was sick of looking at her. He wanted his friend all to himself. He finished the dregs of his coffee and went upstairs to get organised.

The bar in the County Hotel was small and full of character – of days of old. The oak panelling and the dark walls coupled with the weather made it feel like a cosy afternoon in December. Tess sipped on tea and watched as the locals at the bar counter scanned the daily papers for the next bet. They were deep in thought, and didn't seem to notice her sitting in the corner. It was quarter past the hour, and there was still no sign of Scott. He didn't strike her as one who would make a habit of being late for anything, but she felt irritated anyway. Sitting there, she recapped on the previous night's conversation. She hadn't said anything outright to him about how much trouble the business was in, but she hadn't lied to him either. He had made some suggestions to her, some of which she hadn't thought of. She had no idea what he was going to propose at this meeting, and felt under pressure as the time ticked on. Doc had a gig in Dublin and she needed to get back. I'll give him until half past, she thought. Of course she hadn't asked him for his number, and he had called the landline in the pub.

He arrived two minutes later, with no umbrella and soaking wet. Throwing off his light jacket, he apologised about his tardiness and ordered a coffee from the waiter who had materialised at his side.

'So, Tess. Have you been wondering about why we are here today?' He locked his fingers into a position of prayer, focused on her and looked like a man who was about to reveal the secrets of the Universe.

She took a moment to answer, taken aback by the lack of small talk. 'I have been wondering, Scott, but I'm sure you're going to cut to the chase. So tell me, why are we here?'

She had sprung into work mode, her demeanour very different from when they sat together in Jen's the previous evening.

'I want to invest in your business, Tess. That's the short answer.' He sat back in the chair and studied her reaction.

'You want to invest in my business? Why?' She didn't know where this was going.

He knew she was now on the defensive. 'Let's not beat about the bush here, Tess. Your business is in trouble and I have the means to help you out.'

'I appreciate you taking the time to meet me, Scott, but I have kept the business afloat up until now, without anyone handing me money in the guise of investment. I don't understand where you are coming from by making this offer, when you don't know a thing about the business. Not very business savvy.'

He had expected this kind of reaction. Pride tends to get in the way.

'Tess. This is not a trick.'

'I didn't say it was, but my father always taught me –'

'OK. Tess, your business is about to go belly-up. You are not in a position to turn down investment opportunities – that's not, as you put it, business savvy. I am offering you an investment, and I will of course get a return on that.'

She was getting annoyed now; it just didn't make sense to her. 'What kind of return are you looking for, Scott, just so we are clear?'

'When you pick up and you start making a profit, I will seek a percentage of it. I will get the paperwork drawn up, and your lawyer can do the rest.'

Tess was speechless. It was the last thing she expected to hear from him. An injection of money was exactly what she needed, but why did he want to do this?

As though he were reading her thoughts, he leaned forward and said, 'Tess, you need this. I have been in your pub enough times to see you are the brains behind the operation, and you run a tight ship. You have a prime property, in a perfect location that has pots of potential. I don't need to see historical accounts to know that.' He touched her hand before he continued. 'This is not a handout, Tess. It's a real opportunity for you to get back on your feet and get your business out of the gutter. It's not charity, it's a business deal. I have the means to invest, and I am always on the lookout for opportunities.'

He was right in what he was saying. She needed this, and she knew with the right backing that place could be a goldmine. But she was wary. It all sounded too good to be true.

'I apologise if I sound sceptical or indeed ungrateful, Scott, but what's the catch? It all sounds a bit fairytale-like at the moment.'

'No need to apologise. I haven't put much thought into the finer details, as it was late last night when the idea first came to me. Suffice it to say, I have a substantial fund for investment and I will be looking for a percentage share in the business.'

They sat in silence as he gestured to the waiter for a refill. He wanted to give her a few moments to process what he had just offered.

'Tess, let me get something down on paper and you can have a think about it. Would you be open to that much?'

'OK, Scott. This is a lot for me to think about, but I am interested in your offer. Get the paperwork to me and then we can talk further.' Her head was spinning with ideas and figures, but she didn't want to let him see her excitement – excitement that wasn't sullied by the notion of someone else now owning part of her empire.

He nodded and smiled, before putting out his hand. She shook it, nodded and smiled in return.

Scott's drink arrived and Tess refused one.

'So, Scott, when you are not throwing money at business owners, what do you do for a living?' She had visibly relaxed and sat back in the chair with her legs crossed.

'I manage Weybridge Estate for my mother and I am involved in the Opera Society nationally. Weybridge has been in the family for generations, and about ten years ago it was redeveloped into a high-end guest house.'

'Wow, that's amazing – I was there once. It's a stunning property.' She had been there at a business event about six months previously. 'Actually, I think I met your mother – Livia?'

'That's her, the Lady of the Manor!'

She was surprised by the sarcasm in his voice, but didn't comment.

'And how did you end up getting involved in the Opera scene?' She was really curious and couldn't help herself when it came to getting the lowdown on someone.

'My father was a board member years ago – that's how he met my mother. She was an opera singer, travelling with a troupe from Teatro di San Carlo. They were based in Ireland for the season, before travelling to Europe. She was young, beautiful and very gifted. My father fell in love on the spot, and I guess the rest is history. When he died, I was given his position on the board.'

'What a lovely story! The romance of it all, eh?' Tess was visualising all the glamour and romance, both of which were lacking in her life at that moment. She knew his father was dead, but couldn't comment.

'Hmm, well, I don't know about the romance part, but they had a great life travelling and partying. I was in boarding school and didn't see much of them. Anyway, that's a story for another day.' He stood up, and went to pay the bill at the bar.

They walked outside. The weather had improved slightly, a mere drizzle rather than the earlier monsoon.

'Tess, I will probably see you tonight. In the meantime, I would ask you to keep our discussion completely private. Until everything is finalised, I would prefer it that way.'

'OK, that's understandable. We can discuss it further soon enough.'

'Great. See you tonight.' He turned and walked down the street.

Tess was excited. She would consider the offer but, in her heart, the decision was already made.

The Gale was occupied by the usual suspects when Tess returned from her afternoon jaunt.

'Do you want me to get the order from the wholesalers out of the car, Tess?' Doc asked as she threw her bag in the cupboard under the till.

She had told the bar staff she was going to pick up supplies – no one would question that excuse, but now she was caught on the back foot.

'No, it's grand, thanks. I got side-tracked and never made it there.' Changing the subject, she planted a kiss on his cheek. 'I was thinking, Doc. Maybe if you got back from the gig tonight, I could take tomorrow off and we could do something nice? You, me and Hugh. Have a family day? What do you think?'

He was totally sideswiped by the suggestion, and the kiss. It made him smile. Things will be OK, he thought. I'm going to make this right for her. I love her.

'That sounds like a plan to me, but I had arranged to meet a couple of music promoters after the gig tonight.' He was bent over the glass-washer, filling the tray with Guinness-stained glasses.

'So does that mean you're not coming home then?' Her tone was short – she was instantly pissed off.

He didn't look at her as he continued on with the cleaning. 'Look, I'll text them and try to blow them off. I'll be up there again in a couple of weeks, I can rearrange. I'll come back after the gig and we can have a nice day together, as a family. I meant it when I told you I was going to put you and Hugh first, Tess.'

Tess was delighted. She would find someone to cover in the bar for lunch, they would have a lovely day together, and she would tell him about the baby when Hugh went to bed.

'Yay! Happy days, Doc. Will I book somewhere for lunch tomorrow? How about that place we like in town?' She was scanning the bar for her bag.

He opened the cupboard where she had thrown it five minutes before. 'Scatterbrain.'

She smiled at him and dialled the number.

He was surprised about her taking the day off. She always

worked Sunday, and if she wasn't working she was here with her parents having lunch. Always on duty. He heard her in the background, confirming the booking for half one. He would come home tonight but he had to come up with an excuse for the other one. They had booked a hotel for the night. It was time to knock it on the head with her. Tonight was the night to do just that. Enough was enough.

Tess hung up, having booked for lunch. 'Did you text the promoters? Are they OK with rearranging?'

'I will do. I'm going to shoot off home for a shower and then I'd better hit the road. I'll see you tonight, babe.'

She watched him as he walked out the door. For the first time in ages she started to feel positive about things. Scott had thrown her a lifeline – he had the means to do so after all – and maybe, with financial pressures gone, she could concentrate more on her now growing family.

'Tess, will you get me a bleedin' pint before I die of the drought!' her best, and grumpiest, customer roared at her.

'Oh, hold your whisht, Paddy! No fear of you dying on me anyway. I'm not that lucky.'

'And, if I did, shur I'd be back to feckin' haunt ya anyway!'

'I've no doubt, Paddy, me old darlin'. I've no doubt. Now give me your feckin' money so I can get this dump ready for another mad night.'

She handed over the pint, and got a smile out of him, as always.

'What has you in such good form, eh, Tess? Do ya have a fancy man or somethin'?'

'Not a bit of it, Paddy – sure you know I'm saving myself for you.'

'All ould talk out of ya! Whisht now, woman, and leave me be to drink me pint in peace.'

She laughed out loud at this response. He loved the banter really, the grumpy old git.

'Well, whatever has ya in the good mood, Tess, I'm happy for ya. Shur you've been a right bitch over the last few weeks.'

The way Paddy looked at her, and the way he called her a bitch was too much for her. She couldn't stop laughing. Rounding the bar, she hugged him and planted a kiss on the top of his little wrinkled head.

'Paddy, me old darlin', today has been a good day. A fortunate one. But if you call me a bitch again, I'll bar you.'

He chuckled to himself as she went to clear the empty plates from in front of the tourists. He had known her grandmother when she was young. He had also watched her mother grow up in the village, and drank at the bar every night since her father had bought the place. He watched her grow up, from a little girl in pigtails to the now beautiful woman she was. Never in all his born days could he understand how she ended up marrying that layabout. She could have had her pick of any fine suitable man, and she married that eejit.

He will break her little heart one of these days, he thought. There's no bit of good in him. Then I'll break his bleedin' neck.

He shook his head, took a swig of his pint, and roared at her for a Jameson.

Chapter 12

The feeling of the throttle easing back woke Andy from his slumber. The perks of being the skipper allowed him the first sleep on board as they steamed to the Smalls. They had arrived. The slowing of the *Mary Rose* indicated it was time to shoot the net.

He made his way up to the wheelhouse. The weather forecast hadn't lied. It was a cracking day with a slight sea and a warm breeze dancing over the deck. He loved the freedom of being out here, and never tired of the feeing he got in his legs with the roll of the boat.

'We reckon this is the spot, Skip.' His shipmate pointed to the sonar screen, as the other three did the final visual checks on the gear before they fired it into the depths.

All was well, and they were ready to go. Try as he might to get out of it, this was in his blood. No time for small talk, no messing about, then the few moments of trepidation as the 27 metres of net snaked its way out to sea, no glitches, no snags.

'Prep to trawl and shoot away!' The command came from his lips, and was repeated by his mate.

The other two on deck acknowledged the instruction by feeding the net off the back of the *Mary Rose*, and watching as the swell swallowed it. One misplaced foot or moment of daydreaming could cost a man his life. In the wheelhouse, Andy pushed down on the lever, as the beams woke up and got to work.

'Here, Liam, stop that fucking whistling and watch those winch brakes!' yelled Fran, one of the men on deck, at the new guy. 'The ropes need to be clear!'

Two big strong fisherman – one of the pair, the new guy, oblivious to the superstition of whistling on deck. Well, technically speaking, it only applied to the wheelhouse, but Fran wasn't taking any chances. Andy tried to deny that he too believed in the old tales, but he was relieved when his whistling shipmate shut up.

So far so good – the propeller was clear and the clump and trawler doors were doing what they were supposed to. No alarms in the wheelhouse, and it wouldn't be long before the net started trapping the haul. Although she could take a crew of eight, there were four on board for the trip. They were used to working with each other and, bar the new crew member, they knew each other inside out.

Fran gave him the thumbs-up, before the monitors indicated the net was in place.

Time to breathe. Andy would stay in the wheelhouse, Liam the new guy would go to the galley and the other two would take it in turn to get some shuteye before hauling in the net. This process would be repeated every four hours or so.

'All right, mate?' Fran entered the wheelhouse with a brew for his skipper. 'Cup o' cha for you there.'

'Ah cheers, man.' Andy was sitting with his back to Fran, watching the screens and keeping an eye on the rig. 'Did you check the pounds?'

'Yep. Everything is the way it should be and all temps are reading right. Thank Jesus for that. How have you been doing, man? Not like you to sleep on the way out?'

Andy laughed. 'Ah sure, Fran, I'm a wrecked man. I had a bit of a late one over the last few nights. Party in the house Friday and I was out with my mate Scott for a few in the Gale last night. Half five wasn't long coming around, I tell ya!'

'You durty dog, Andy! What about your new landlady, what's her name, Jen? Is it all right living with her and the little fella?'

'Yeah, she's nice. Weird living with a woman again though – well, you know what I mean, having a woman in the same house. Little Danny is grand – funny little guy – full of mischief.'

Fran was one of the few people that Andy felt comfortable talking to. He had worked alongside him since coming back to the harbour, and as a shipmate, and a friend, he trusted him with his life.

'I like her, man.'

'Well, it's about fucking time, Andy. For fear of sounding too blunt, you need to get over Sharon. She was beautiful and yes, you loved her, but she's gone, man. And her death wasn't your fault. It was a horrible accident.'

Andy looked out the window of the wheelhouse and focused on nothing in particular. Trust Fran to be so straight about it, he thought. No one ever mentioned Sharon to him. It was nice for a change to hear her name coming from someone else.

'Sorry, skip, I didn't mean to speak out of turn like that.'

'Nah, man, you're grand. It's been two years. It's about time I let her go. It's just hard, ya know? Jen is a nice girl, and she's pretty hot. I just don't want to get involved what with leaving at the end of the year.'

'Andy, she's a big girl – nothing wrong with a bit of fun over the few months while you're here. Anyway, I'd better get back to it. I need to check the rig.'

Typical Fran – drop a bombshell into the equation, and then

leave him be with his thoughts. He did like Jen, there was no denying it, but every time he thought about her the thought of the first night he and Sharon met haunted him.

Scott had called over to his apartment. Andy had just finished a big project for college, and he was in the mood for some live music and a few pints. Scott was always up for a laugh, and he always managed to get into the best clubs.

They hit the town and the first stop was the Twisted Lemon to hear a new band. The place was packed but they managed to pull a couple of seats at the bar. The place was hopping, the music was loud and the beer was flowing.

Andy was deep in conversation with a couple of girls he knew from the course when she arrived on the scene. She was the tallest and the most beautiful girl he had ever laid eyes on. He'd had his fair share of girlfriends over the years, but this one was way out of his league.

Scott was on the stool beside him, and she made a beeline for him. Andy was so conscious of her presence he couldn't follow the conversation with his classmates.

What felt like an eternity later, Scott tapped him on the shoulder and Andy turned to face him.

When Scott introduced Sharon to him, all he could manage was a 'Hey'.

'Hay is for horses,' she replied. 'Now scooch over, Scott, and let me in at the counter. I'm dying for a pint. Would you like one, Andy?'

And that was it. With the good grace of a gentleman, he paid for her drink, and from that moment they were inseparable. They didn't waste any time that night. After the gig, they went back to her apartment, and had drunken sex all night. They bunked off college the following day, went out that night again, and repeated the process. Before he knew what was happening, they had been together for a year.

As corny as he thought the whole idea of love at first sight was, he knew this was exactly what had happened. They both did. Made for each other. He loved her with all his heart, and he knew he wanted to marry her. It was all crazy – here he was, the quiet sensible college kind, thinking about marriage a year into their relationship. They decided to wait until they finished college, and three months after graduation they got hitched.

And now she was dead. He couldn't get away from the guilt. If he had followed her that night, the accident would never have happened, but his stubborn streak had got in the way, and he let her go.

'Andy, looks like we're good to go, man – we're ready on deck.'

'Thanks, man. I'll turn her now and we can haul.'

'*All hands on deck!*' Fran roared. He didn't have to say that of course, the turn of the trawler was indication enough, but it always made the lads laugh, as he did it in his best pirate voice.

Andy eased back on the throttle and brought her port-side into the wind. The net came up, steady and slow. All crew were present for the task, dressed in oilskins and heavy gloves. Fran and Liam guided the cod end over the pound, and the process of unloading and sorting would begin as soon as the net was emptied, checked and relaunched.

The conversation would start as soon as the fish hit the belt. The usual talk, about quotas and the ridiculous strain on the industry.

Andy liked the focus that came with sorting and gutting. Small fish back out to sea, guts out to sea, fish in the basket. It was a good catch, and they worked well together as a crew. No big surprises in there today.

Fran started on the story about the day he nearly lost his hand to a small shark still alive and hidden in the haul. He exaggerated as usual, and Andy wondered how long it would take for his tale to turn into one about the day they caught a great white. It didn't matter that they were in the wrong part of the world for Jaws –

if anyone could spin that story, it would be Fran.

They all seemed to be impressed with the work of the newest crew member. He didn't talk much, but he had a fast hand and knew how to use a knife. When the banter and the humour started at his expense, it was clear he had been accepted.

The afternoon passed like this, and a few hours later the first catch was gutted, cleaned, packed on ice, and stored away. The last of the water from the deck scrub was running out the scuppers, and *Mary Rose* was ready for the next drag.

Time for someone else to grab some shuteye, and for the other three to take up their posts as cook, coxswain and skipper. It took some getting used to, sleeping in a bed that was roughly the same size as a coffin, but after a long haul and an early start, the newbie deserved a rest. Fran went in the direction of the kettle and Andy and his mate went back to the wheelhouse to check equipment.

Fran came back into the wheelhouse with more tea.

'I'll take over here, Andy. You go below and get some grub. Won't be long before we're hauling that bitch up again.'

'Sound, thanks, Fran. I'm starving now.'

'Don't get too excited, man – the new fella can't cook for shit. I think it's supposed to be curry. No idea, but there could be a queue for the jacks later.'

Andy laughed and made his way down to the galley. He would eat it regardless, he was so hungry. He fired on the heat under the pot of curry. Pot of sludge more like, he thought. It's smell only vaguely resembled curry but on the plate it looked palatable enough. He sat down at the table.

The galley was the one place he made a point of bringing the landlubbers to if they wanted a look at the trawler. They were always surprised it was equipped with all the mod cons, down to a washing machine. It confused them: a home away from home.

Home, he thought, and he began to think about Jen. He had been so tempted to grab her in the kitchen on Friday night. He wasn't stupid – there was chemistry between them for sure, and if Sal had her way they would have been making out on the table between courses. Subtlety was not Sal's strong suit, and the impression he got from her with her one-liners and winks was that Jen might have a thing for him as well. He just couldn't do it, and he didn't want things to get messy. He would stick to the plan and be gone for Christmas.

Scott had also passed a few comments the night before. He seemed not to like Jen much, but Scott had always been so protective of him – to the point where it smothered him sometimes. He figured he was just looking out for him. Sharon and Scott had been great friends initially, but she had cooled in her affections towards him over the years because of his controlling ways when it came to Andy. Maybe that's why Scott didn't like Jen. Once he got to know her a bit better, he would see how lovely she was.

Like an old black-and-white movie, the scene always played out in his head in the same way, waking or sleeping. Most days he could push it to the back of his mind, and make himself busy. Other days it just played over and over.

It was the summer of 2011. Andy and Sharon were headed to Achill Island for a weekend college reunion. Adele was in the charts, and 'Someone Like You' was Sharon's song of choice to sing over and over on the way down in the car. They had taken the following week off work for a mini-holiday. The weather was fantastic and it was magical standing on the pier with old friends waiting for the ferry to begin the trip. The cottages couldn't have been more amazing, the half-moon-shaped beach looking as if it was smiling between cheeks of sheer rock.

Everyone in high spirits and, as the darkness swept in on the bay, the plan was to have a few drinks in the local pub, and then go back to one of the cottages for a party. Just like the old days, and oh had they partied hard in their college days!

He and Sharon had spent most of the evening sitting on the

beach, chatting. It was always like that between them, rarely a cross word. They were lucky in every respect really – a great relationship and they both had really good jobs in Galway and had bought property before the whole country went crazy.

The trouble started at around three in the morning. She had warned Andy before the weekend not to let Scott lead him astray as usual. She believed Scott was too fond of his cocaine, and she didn't want any part in his madness. 'Domineering' was the word she usually used to describe him, and 'fucking obsessive about you' was the language of choice when things got heated. 'The Puppeteer' she had named him.

If only he had listened, she would still be alive. She walked in on him and Scott doing drugs in the bathroom. She could see that they had been caning it. A row ensued. Scott went back to the others at the party, and she and Andy remained in the bathroom arguing. It all came out: she was furious with him, he had been like Scott's sheepdog all night, vying for his attention, and her being the butt of the joke. Enough was enough – first thing in the morning she was getting the ferry and going home. People leave college and grow up but Scott hadn't and he was not taking her husband back down that road with him.

He argued the toss of course, accused her of being uptight, being a square. He was partying with his friends, some of whom he hadn't seen since their wedding day six years before. He hadn't even taken that much, just a couple of lines. He didn't know what she was on about with the accusation of his ignoring her all night – she had been with the girls.

And round and round they went – all the talk of love, adventure, babies and retirement from a few short hours ago forgotten.

She stormed out eventually. He let her go and went back to the party.

He woke in his bed to the sound of the front door being banged and Scott screaming his name. The first thing he noticed was the empty bed, the second was the time – half seven. He opened the door. Scott was standing there, crying. Beside him was a Garda, asking him if he was the husband of Sharon McClean. An incident had been reported, and he needed Andy to come with him.

She looked like she was asleep on the beach where she lay. Her beautiful black hair was pasted to her face and barely hid the bruise on her temple. She wasn't moving. Scott was saying something to him, but he couldn't hear him. He just kept calling out her name and telling her to wake up. She looked small lying there with her head on his lap as usual. He was holding on to her cold hand and couldn't let go. A crowd had gathered, but he didn't recognise them. He couldn't breathe, and all he could hear was her, singing that Adele song in his head. The rest was a blur.

A memory of the coastguard helicopter, the drone of the chopper, landing at the same hospital where she was born. The Guards, her parents clutching each other as they stared in through the glass, afraid to walk through that door. Afraid of the reality of what lay before them. The hatred in her father's voice as he told him he had failed to take care of his little girl.

There was an investigation of course, questions to be answered. Scott had sat with him for all those hours. There wasn't much to say to the Guards. She had left the party that night. Why had she left? Well, they'd had a row. He couldn't mention the drugs so he had to say it was because he was drinking too much. Scott had seen her before she left. She had been so upset, he said, and a bit drunk herself. After that, he had gone back in to Andy.

The cause of death was eventually deemed to be accidental. She had gone up the cliffs. She had fallen in the semi-dark, into the sea, washing up on the beach.

But had she fallen … or was it suicide? The thought haunted Andy – as it haunted Sharon's parents.

He watched her go into the ground on that day, in her beloved Galway, and he never went back.

The curry lay untouched in front of him, and by now it was cold. He ate it anyway and washed it down with the last of the cold tea. Back to work he went, determined to put all thoughts of Sharon and his landlady out of his head.

Chapter 13

As Andy returned to his afternoon shift, back in Dublin Scott was getting up. He had left the harbour the previous evening, in time to get to the Twisted Lemon before closing. Tess had confirmed this as the venue for Doc's gig, and he had known it was an opportune time to get Doc involved in his little business venture.

He padded downstairs to the kitchen, in desperate need of a coffee.

Doc joined him just as the kettle had boiled.

'Morning, Doc,' he said without turning around. 'Coffee?'

'Tea if you have it handy.' Doc was hoarse from singing and from the late night. He fired up his phone, knowing what was to come. Message after message came in. He was sick with guilt and knew he had really fucked up again. How could he have been so stupid? He had planned to leave after the gig the previous night and go straight home to his family. But then Clara, and eventually Scott, showed up. The whiskey, narcotics and his mistress had scuppered the idea of hitting the road.

Doc couldn't believe he had given in to her charm again. She had been so upset when he told her he wanted to call it a day. What the hell am I playing at, he thought. It was all too much for him, and now Scott knew about his little indiscretions. I'm a lousy husband. I have to make this right.

'Scott, can we talk about last night?'

Scott put the tea in front of him and smiled. Now was the time to get Doc on board.

'Doc, what you do with your life is none of my business. I don't care how many women you are banging, so your secret is safe with me. We are all allowed to have fun, and if that's your fun, so be it.'

Doc didn't reply. He was playing with his phone on the table, the screen telling him he had seven unread messages. He pulled his cigarettes out of his pocket, and Scott gestured for him to smoke where he sat.

'Tess mentioned you were playing in the Twisted Lemon. I got back in time for the last couple of pints. When I saw you and her at the bar, I knew she was more than a groupie. I watched you for a few minutes before I joined you. You are careless. You need to cover your tracks a bit better.'

'It's a fucking mess. I mean, I love my wife and my son, but I really like Clara. Tess is hard work and I need a bit of fun in my life – it's all too much.' His guilt had turned to anger and he needed to apportion blame. He coughed out the lungful of smoke he had just inhaled. 'Tess treats me like shit and I've had enough. She's a fucking control freak and a workaholic. You can't blame me for being flattered when a hot young one throws herself at me. She had been chasing me for ages and I didn't go near her. I gave in eventually, quite a while back and now I can't keep away from her. She didn't want anything from me other than sex and a good time.'

So he was pretending his wife had pushed him to it – the fool, thought Scott. Tess impressed him – she was very strong and driven. He could see how someone as apathetic as Doc would drive her insane. Chalk and cheese.

'As I said, Doc, I won't say a word. You're a big boy, and if that's what you want to do, go for it. Just be a bit more discreet. And kudos to you for having two hot birds on the go at the one time. That Clara is a cracker. Total whore but a great rack on her.'

Doc laughed with relief.

'Doc, I have a bit of a business on the side that you may be able to help me with. I keep my mouth shut about your bit on the side, and you do the same about mine.'

'Go on, Scott, tell me more – is it legal, like?'

'No, it's certainly not legal, but the pay is good and all you have to do is collect the odd delivery in the harbour for me, and then deliver it where it needs to go. Do you think you can manage that for me?'

'Hmmm, I dunno, Scott. What am I delivering, and to whom?'

'Small deliveries of some top-grade cocaine, to some of my employees dotted around the country. You won't have to worry about money again, and you also get a percentage of the stuff to do with as you please. Money, women and drugs, man – what's not to like? They loved you last night at the party here – you need some fun in your life.'

Doc didn't respond. The party the previous night had just happened. Scott knew the barman in the pub and they had stayed there for a few late drinks. Another couple of his friends arrived, and were let in the back door. It was obvious to all and sundry that Clara was with him, so they didn't even bother hiding it. The party migrated to Scott's apartment, and carried on until the sun came up. The reservation in the hotel had been forgotten about, and they crashed out together in Scott's spare room. He could barely remember the names of who had been there, but it had been such good fun. He had felt so free.

By now, another two messages had come through on his phone, and he was afraid to read them. She was always moaning at him to come home – for fuck sake, he felt like a caged animal. Tired of being told what to do and when to do it. What was her problem? It wasn't like she knew about the affair – he had dodged that bullet and in the end she had almost apologised. He didn't think Scott would grass him up, but then again, why take the chance?

She's your wife, Doc, and you're having an affair. It's no surprise she's giving you a hard time, the voice whispered in his head. *She's your wife, you lying prick.*

'Fuck it, man, I'll do it.'

What are you doing, Doc? Have you got a fucking death wish?

'That's the spirit, Doc. We're in for one hell of a summer. Wine, women and song! And plenty of cash.' *Boom.* The deal was done. Doc was in the bag.

Doc needed to get home. Better late than never, he guessed. He picked up his phone and sent a text to Tess.

Baby, really sorry. Got drunk with promoters, they showed at gig. Crashed in their place, phone died. Just awake and hitting road now. I will make it up to you – promise. See you at home XXX

'Thanks for a great night, man. I'm back up next weekend in The Workhorse – give me a shout if you're free.'

'Brilliant, that sounds good to me. The code for the carpark is 3425.'

'Fuck, I forgot I drove last night. Saves me the walk to the pub though.' He found his jacket buried behind the cushions of the couch and gathered up his phone and cigarettes.

'I'll be in touch about our arrangement, Doc.'

Doc thought it sounded like a threat. He nodded and let himself out.

What are you getting yourself into here, Doc?

Scott and Clara had been quite friendly to each other the night before. If he didn't know better, he would have thought they were already acquainted.

The bright sun hurt his eyes, and he had to search for the car in the carpark. Time to go home, and face the music.

Chapter 14

'Something smells amazing, Jen.' Sal threw her coat on the back of a chair and flopped down at the table. She could hear Danny and Butch upstairs having what sounded like great fun.

'Don't get too excited, Sal – it's a whatever-was-left-in-the-fridge-thrown-into-pasta dinner this evening! How are ya anyway?'

Jen was at the stove stirring the sauce, and the smell of garlic bread was wafting from the oven.

'All is good with me, painting away and feeling motivated. I'm getting lots of shit done, Jen. I think it's the lovely weather that has put a bit of jizz in me. But, I have a bit of news. Scott rang me this morning – he has an interview lined up for me with one of his arty friends!'

'Oh Sal, that's great news!' Jen rummaged around and found the corkscrew. 'Is this the gallery person he was talking about?' She put the corkscrew and wine bottle on the table.

Sal grinned at her. '*Yes! Yes! Yes!*' She hopped up from the table and started dancing around the kitchen like a woman possessed. 'I'm so fucking excited, Jen!'

'*Language, Sal.*' The stern tone of Danny's voice made both of them laugh.

'Sorry, Dan, you're right – I shouldn't use bad language.' Gone were the days where she could sweep him up into a big hug, or spin him around the room, so she settled for giving him a kiss instead.

'*Eww*, Sal, *what* is *wrong* with you?' Danny pushed her away and started laughing. 'Mam, I think Sal's gone bonkers.'

'You're only seeing that now, Dan?' Jen quipped. 'Now, sit down there. Dinner is ready.'

'Can I eat mine by the telly, Mam? I have all my homework done! I want to watch some cartoons!'

'No, love, sit down here and you can watch them later.'

'But, Mam!'

'No buts, Danny, and don't argue. I've told you that before. Now come on, sit down and eat.'

He sulked, and wolfed down his dinner. Five minutes later he was in front of the telly.

When he was out of earshot, the girls got on to the subject of men.

'Well, Jen, what happened Friday night after we left? There was some serious chemistry between you two. How come you didn't kiss the face off him?'

Of course Sal had texted her the day after the party, looking for all the juicy details, but there was nothing to tell. It was all too messy. She had thought about him a lot during the week and was feeling a bit unsteady about it. Sure, he was lovely, and really handsome, but he was leaving.

'You were mistaken about the chemistry, Sal,' she lied. 'He was nice to everyone. It's not going to happen, and I don't want it to. Too complicated and I have Danny to think about. Let's just leave it.'

Sal was going to respond and tell her she was just being stubborn as usual, but decided against it. She needed to broach another subject with her.

'Scott seemed to fit in really well with everyone Jen, didn't he? He was great fun, and there's no denying he is fecking hot.'

'Sal, you can't be serious? He is a snob, and completely condescending. He is like a jealous child having to share his toys when it comes to Andy. I'm not a fan.'

'You made that pretty obvious on the night! Honestly, I thought you were quite rude to him at times. It didn't go unnoticed. He's all right, Jen – you just take things way too personally sometimes.'

'Jesus, Sal, I wasn't rude to him. He's just domineering and wants to be the centre of attention the whole time.'

'That's horseshit and you know it. He chatted to everyone and let Doc take centre-stage singing all those songs! Anyway, just give him a chance is all I'm saying. He's Andy's best friend at the end of the day, so he's going to be around. Make life easy on yourself and try and get on with him!'

Jen pushed the pasta around her plate. 'Sal, I just have a feeling about him, that's all. There is something about him that makes me really uncomfortable.'

'Jen, he's all right. He had nothing to gain by making calls for me, but he still did it. You said yourself what a great guy Andy is, so Scott has to be decent to be his friend. Naturally enough he's going to look out for his friend – and don't forget Sharon was a friend of his as well. You would do the same for me if the shoe was on the other foot.'

'OK, fair enough, Sal. I didn't think about it that way. I'm delighted of course that he's helping you – it's great. For you, I'll be nicer the next time.'

She tried to sound genuine but Sal wasn't convinced. Changing the subject, she asked about Tess and Doc. Something had been afoot with those two that night as well. Tess seemed really on edge, and Doc got wasted pretty quickly.

'Ah Sal, Doc is being a real pig to her. He messed up again on Sunday and they haven't really been speaking all week. He is just out of control at the moment. Tomorrow is Friday, and he'll be gone all weekend again. It's crap for her at the moment.'

She didn't mention anything about the affair, or the pregnancy for that matter. Tess had rung her in tears on Sunday, so she and Danny had gone for lunch with her. Tess had taken the day off to spend some family time together before telling him about the new arrival, and he had come home late, hungover and wrecked. She didn't tell him.

Sal topped up the wineglasses. 'Poor Tess! He was always so chilled out and quiet. What the hell has got into him?'

The sound of boots at the back door made both of them turn around in fright. The French door opened and Andy walked in.

Jens face lit up. 'Oh, hey there! I wasn't expecting you back until Sunday.'

'I wasn't expecting to be back either – trouble with the cold storage meant we had to come back in early to unload. Hi, Sal.'

'There's some leftover dinner there if you're hungry – I can reheat it for you. Help yourself to a glass of wine.' Jen stood up and cleared the empty plates to make herself busy, doing anything to avoid that gaze of his.

'Brilliant, I'm starving. Will just have a quick shower if that's OK.'

'Em, yeah, fine. Enjoy.'

Both he and Sal looked at her a little oddly and he disappeared through the door.

'Jen Harper, you are full of shit!' Sal couldn't stop laughing. 'You went bright red the minute he mentioned going to the shower!'

'Feck off, Sal.' She was mortified, as he had copped on to it as well. She was a blusher, an affliction which had always haunted her.

'On that note, my dear, I'm going home. Behave yourself now!' Sal kissed her on the cheek and was gone in a flash.

'Come on, Dan!' Jen called to the door of the sitting room, 'Time for bed!'

He didn't argue, even when she made him brush his teeth and wash his face. By the time she had read one page of his favourite story, he was fast asleep. She pulled the blankets up around him and quietly closed his bedroom door behind her.

She stood at the bottom of the stairs for a moment and just listened to the sounds coming from the kitchen. She smiled to herself before casually sauntering in.

'How's the pasta?'

He was sitting at the table with a steaming bowl of food in front of him. She was really bad at portion control and had made way too much as usual.

'Just as well I'm here,' he said. 'You cooked for ten instead of three again.'

She sat down at the table with him. She just couldn't help herself. He was barefoot and in shorts, his hair still damp, and he smelled clean. He was so handsome.

Her glass was still on the table. She shared out the last of the red between them. He was enjoying the meal too much to speak, and she sat there very aware of the silence. All conversational skills had left her, and she suddenly felt very awkward compared to him with his relaxed body language.

'So,' he said at last.

'So,' she replied, feeling like a complete fool.

'How are things, Jen? You must have had an early night on Saturday night?'

'Andy, I was in bed by nine. Shameful really – one night out and I'm broken for days. Why do you ask? Did you come back here that night? I thought you were out?'

'I was out all right, just for a couple with Scott. When he left I came back here – around eleven, I think. Gone again then, at five.'

'Jesus, I never heard a thing.' She heard Sal's voice ringing in her ears, and she decided to act on her advice. 'Did Scott enjoy himself here on Friday? He seemed to anyway. Sal thinks he's great.'

'He did indeed, Jen. He's looking forward to the next one. Yeah, he was really impressed with Sal's sheer talent. He's going to make a couple of calls for her – he knows everyone like.'

'He has an interview lined up already!'

'Brilliant – I'm delighted for her, Tess. Scott knows everyone.' He put his glass on the table and looked at her. 'Jen, I know you're a bit wary of him. He is a snob, but he's a good guy underneath it.'

'I'm sorry, Andy, if I appeared rude to him on Friday, but I have a real thing about snobbery. Anyway, once he had fun and got on well with everyone, that's the main thing.'

The conversation was ridiculously polite and stilted between them, and well she knew it. The big elephant from the other night was in the room, and she knew for sure he felt it too.

'Will I put on some music, Jen? It won't wake Danny, will it?'

'Not at all – he would sleep through a hurricane. Stick on whatever you like.'

She stood up to clear the dishes, but he insisted on doing it. Sit down and chill out, he told her, he would wash up. She sat sideways on the couch, and sipped on her wine as he washed.

'Did you talk to Tess after, Jen? What are you going to do?'

'Andy, I have no idea how I'm going to tell her. Maybe I should speak to him instead? It's a real mess.'

He shook his head. He was pretty disgusted by Doc's behaviour, but didn't know what she should do. He eventually spoke.

'I don't know, Jen, it's a tricky one. Should you just keep out of it altogether, pretend you know nothing?'

'I couldn't do that, even though I want to. I'll think about it for a day or two and see what happens. What a complete asshole though – why is he doing this to her? Hey, leave the drying-up, Andy – I'll do it later.'

She curled her legs up under her as he took a seat on the couch beside her. They chatted for a while about music and books. Nice easy conversation. When he suggested they open the last bottle of wine, she nodded her agreement. She shouldn't be drinking on a school night, but tomorrow was Friday. She rooted around in her bag until she found the pack of cigarettes. She had cursed herself going into the shop on Sunday to buy them, but the old addiction was back, as strong as ever. Danny didn't know and she would keep it that way. Wrapping herself in a blanket, she went and sat down on a pile of cushions outside, and Andy joined her with the bottle and their glasses.

'I love the peace out here,' she said as she lit her cigarette. 'The sound of the sea relaxes me.'

In the distance, they could hear the lapping waves on the shore. The lighthouse, the sea's constant companion, lit up the horizon. Nothing else could be heard, it was clear and still. The waning moon competed with the lighthouse, kissing the surface of the water, giving the landscape a silvery glow.

'We are so lucky to live here, Jen,' he said, looking off into the distance. 'Can you imagine being stuck in the middle of a city right now?'

'I think I would lose the plot, Andy. I would be out on the rooftops howling at the moon before they carted me off in a straitjacket.'

They both laughed at that image. She excused herself, and went to check on Danny. Fast asleep. By now she was feeling the effects of the heavy red wine – tipsy. But she was enjoying herself and didn't care. When she came back out to the decking, he had brought out a few cushions and a blanket for himself. She turned back and grabbed a couple of candles from the kitchen and put them down beside the ashtray. Andy was smoking when she sat down.

'What are you doing, Andy? I thought the other night was a one-off?'

'Ah I just fancied one, that's all – sure why not?'

Her first thought was that now if he kissed her he wouldn't notice she tasted like an ashtray, then she immediately reddened at the idea. She would have to stop this.

He leaned over and kissed her. Just like that. She was startled, but that didn't stop her kissing him back. She sure as hell didn't want him to stop but she was shaking. Chemistry indeed. His hands were around her waist and he pulled her over beside him.

'I have wanted to do that all week,' he whispered to her. 'I haven't been able to get you out of my head since Friday.'

She didn't know what to say back to that, so she kissed him instead. The chemistry between them was insane. She had never felt this kind of intensity towards another human being – ever. His hands were all over her, and hers were locked behind his head. He smelled of citrus fruits, and shower gel.

She stopped, and looked at him. She didn't know what to say, so she just smiled. She felt exposed under his gaze, and when he picked her up and lay her down on the cushions, she shook. His weight was on top of her and she didn't want him to stop. The glass got kicked over, and neither of them took any notice – they were too busy, kissing, biting and exploring each other. Before she could stop herself, she had his shirt off, and his gorgeous body felt so perfect to her touch. He was totally ripped, the body of a man who works hard for a living. He was stunning. He gasped when she ran her nails up along his back. They were impatient and hungry with each other. He kissed her again, and his hand tugged at her top.

She froze, and he could feel her tense up under him. As quickly as the passion had flamed, it turned cold. She wriggled out from underneath him, and wrapped the blanket around her.

'Jen, what's wrong?' He sat back and looked at her.

She felt like shit, but she couldn't let him see or feel the scars.

She wasn't ready to tell him that story yet.

'I'm sorry, Andy. I just think what we're doing is inappropriate with Danny in the house.'

He couldn't argue with that.

'Fair enough, Jen. I obviously just read the signals wrong.' He put on his shirt in a hurry, and bent over to pick up the broken glass.

Jen took this as a cue to escape, and went through the French doors. While she searched under the stove for the dustpan, she absolutely cursed herself. It was always the same, and she needed to get over it, but she was repulsed by her scars, and they belonged to her. If he saw them, he would run a mile. His hand on her shoulder made her jump – she hadn't heard him come in. He turned her around to face him. She didn't know what to do – she couldn't take a step back as the stove was in her way.

'Jen, I'm really sorry if I was too forward, and it was stupid of me to forget about Danny being in the house. I just don't want things to be awkward.' He spoke to the top of her head.

'It's fine, Andy, don't worry about it.' She was taken aback by his candid approach, and felt all the worse for making him feel as though he had done something out of line. She was such an idiot. The purple nail polish on her toes was chipped. She couldn't look at him, so she concentrated on that instead. He was waiting for her to say something to ease his torment, but her mind was blank. She was so uncomfortable she felt the urge to giggle. If I laugh now, she thought, he is going to think I'm totally crazy, but the more she tried to stop herself, the harder it became. He saw her shoulders shaking and took a step back, really alarmed.

'Oh Jen, I'm sorry. Please don't cry. I didn't mean to upset you.' He was in a complete spin.

When she tried to speak, a snort escaped from the back of her nose. 'Andy –' She tried to compose herself, but the look of astonishment on his face made it all the more hilarious.

Then he started. A chuckle at first, which quickly turned to an absolute booming belly laugh. They gasped for air and tried to talk but the words wouldn't come.

How strange a person can go through the whole spectrum of emotions in such a short space of time, she thought.

The wave of giggles finally eased, and he was the first to speak.

'You are a strange little woman, Jen Harper. I think that's why I like you.'

They were so close she could smell the shower gel from his skin. She wanted to reach out and touch him, but she stopped herself. 'I just have a lot going on at the moment, Andy. I don't want things to get messy between us. I do like you, I'm not going to lie, but it's not fair on any of us, especially Danny, and you are leaving in a while anyway.' There was no point in beating about the bush here. He had set the bar for straight talking, and she owed him that much. Dammit, she liked him, but it was true – there was no point.

'Jen, we all have scars and baggage. You know about mine, and I know about yours. I'm not one to enter into something on a whim. It was never in my nature, especially after what happened to me. If you think I'm the type of guy who just wants to get laid, you are wrong. The end of the year is a long time away.'

So, he knew about her scars. But of course he did – everyone knew. It had been the talk of the village all those years ago, and everyone had been so good to her and her mother. She hated it, and she sure as hell didn't want to get into a conversation about it here and now.

'I never said you were that type of guy, Andy – you misunderstood me. I know what you have been through. Scars and baggage eh, what a pair we are.'

The last statement hung in the air like fog.

His body language had changed, and the moment was gone.

'That's fair enough. Let's just leave it as is. It's fine.' He took the dustpan from her hand and disappeared out to the decking.

They cleaned up the mess in silence, each lost in their own

thoughts of shit and baggage and hurt. But there was no denying the chemistry, it was electric.

'I'll be heading back out in the morning, Jen, and if the weather holds I'll be out for a few days. Maybe we can go for a beer when I get back in? We can have a talk then?'

He was leaning on the kitchen door just looking at her, as she frantically tried to do anything to keep herself busy. She didn't want to look at him, afraid she might throw caution to the wind, and the boundaries just established would fly out the window. But then, they would be back to square one, her mental block about her body issues rearing its ugly head again. Ugly, that's exactly how she felt, and one look at her and he would think the same. It wasn't worth the hassle. He didn't wait too long for a response.

'Night, Jen.'

'Night, sleep well, Andy.'

Eventually, she climbed the stairs. She stood on the landing and looked at the door in front of her. The light was still on, and she heard the rustle of a newspaper. Her heart was pounding in her chest as she lifted her hand to knock. She dropped her hand back to her side, and headed into her own room instead. Sleep would not come tonight, of that she was sure.

Chapter 15

Sal knew from the feedback that the deal with the NMAG was in the bag. The best trip she had ever made to Dublin. She knew that Scott was delighted as well – he had been really excited earlier about the meeting in the gallery. He remained impassive when shaking hands with the panel before they left, and advised them he would be in touch to discuss further details. Sal thought she was going to pass out with excitement. She had a good head for business, but Scott was a master negotiator. He had been right when he'd told her to keep quiet, and let him do the talking.

They came out on the pavement and he grabbed her arm. 'Come on, quick – we're going for a drink.'

As soon as they were out of view of the floor-to-ceiling windows he jumped in the air and clicked his heels together à la Gene Kelly in *Singing in the Rain*. He was genuinely delighted. He hadn't told Sal that these things rarely got past the panel meeting, choosing instead to remain positive. But he had been confident enough when it came to her portfolio as she had an astounding talent. He took her by the hand and led her into the lobby of the Westbury Hotel.

'Very swanky, Scott. I could get used to this life of luxury.'

She didn't really mind how she stood out amidst a sea of power suits with her bright clothes and her portfolio under her arm. Scott nodded in recognition at a number of the suits. The beautiful high ceilings, polished marble and stunning paintings dotted around the lobby appealed to Sal's love of grandeur.

Scott had already reserved a table for afternoon tea, in the aptly named Gallery. She took a seat in the antique chair, upholstered in the most vivid blue fabric she had ever seen. They resisted the urge to have champagne with the selection of sandwiches and pastries, and opted for strong Assam tea instead. She turned her chair to face the window and the hustle and bustle of Grafton Street. From here, there was no sound from the sea of humans outside.

The silverware arrived, as did the china. The finger sandwiches and selection of pastries were presented to them like little works of art all in their own right. She had never tasted anything as delicious as the home-made jam, which accompanied scones and clotted cream. Pure indulgence.

'Scott, I can't thank you enough for setting this up for me. It really is a dream come true.' The reality had begun to sink in with her, and she was feeling excited and terrified in equal measure. Her eyes began to well with tears. 'I know my work is really good, and it's the only thing in my life I get really excited about, so to have had the chance for them to consider my work for that gallery is amazing.'

Scott was smiling as he listened to her. He was genuinely delighted to have helped. He had grown up with a love of art, passed on to him from his father. In Weybridge, they had a serious collection of acquisitions from over the years. She deserved a chance.

'Have no doubt, Sal, my little artistic protégé, it's a certainty that your work will be exhibited, hopefully for longer than the norm, and because my father was always a patron of the arts they will look upon you favourably for funding etc. I will also get in touch with the Oscar Gallery – just as a courtesy to square things off with them.'

He picked up another sandwich, and looked out the window as he chewed. This was the beginning of something big, but if she didn't get the funding it would be difficult for her. He would offer her a loan, if that was to happen, as he had no doubt he would make good returns on the investment. He had told her he didn't want her to worry about the finer details – he knew how these things worked, and would sort it out for her. All she needed to do was concentrate on her painting and getting herself ready for a launch. He would also try and get her a residency with them if she was available for the opportunity.

'Don't sweat the small stuff, my lady.'

'You are brilliant – thanks, Scott.'

'So, did you tell Jen about our meeting? I don't think she likes me very much, which is a shame.' Now was the perfect time to have a chat about it – she trusted him after all – he had said he would do something, and he had delivered.

'Don't mind her, Scott – she's the best in the world, but she has a hard time letting her guard down with people. She's quick to form an opinion of someone if she feels they are in any way threatening to her. If she can't figure someone out, it makes her nervous.'

'That's very strange . . . why would she find me threatening?'

'Sorry, I didn't explain that very clearly. She had a really nasty accident as a child – do you know about that?'

'No – go on, Sal.'

Ah, so here we are now getting to the intimate details of Jen's life, he thought. Her weak point.

'OK, but don't bring it up with her, she hates talking about it.

To cut a long story short, she was only a child when she pulled a big pot of boiling soup down on herself. Her mam had left her on her own in the kitchen. Her whole chest is badly scarred. She nearly died, and the burns did irreparable damage to her body. Her mam turned completely obsessive-compulsive over safety, something Jen inherited. She is obsessed with safety in the house with her and Dan.'

Scott was shocked by this. So that's why in all her pictures on Facebook, even in the summer, she always wore dresses and shirts with really high necks and long sleeves – it had struck him as odd at the time he saw them.

'The poor girl. That's frightening. Her poor mother too, living with the guilt of that.'

'Yeah, Jen was only four when it happened, and her mother never really forgave herself. I think that's probably why she didn't have any other kids. Jen went on to college, and the only boyfriend she has had was Will – Danny's dad.'

'What a burden for the poor girl to carry!' He filled Sal's cup and gestured to her to continue.

'That's why I'm so excited about her and Andy getting on so well. There's certainly chemistry between them, don't you think?'

'I think there may well be but, considering Andy's story, I can't see him pursuing her.'

Sal was enjoying herself now – it felt like they were conspiring to get Jen and Andy together. She was sure he would want the best for his friend, and Jen deserved a good man in her life.

'Well, I don't think we should push anything between them. I could see what you were doing the night of the dinner party. If it's supposed to happen, let them sort it out themselves. To be honest, after my chat with Andy the other night, I'm not really sure if he's interested.'

'We are both protective of our friends here, but I think a gentle nudge in the right direction is no harm,' Sal said. 'I also beg to differ about whatever Andy may have told you. Chemistry doesn't lie, my dear Scott.' Her tone was playful, but her eyes were serious.

'Jen is also incredibly protective of you, my dear. She practically told me that if I hurt you in any way she would break my legs. I tried to explain that our relationship moving forward would be a professional one, but she was having none of it. I gave up and came back inside.'

Sal's face had started to burn, and he wasn't sure whether it was from embarrassment on the foot of some kind of crush, or if she was angry.

'I will speak to Jen, Scott. I am very much aware our relationship is nothing other than professional.' She didn't sound convincing.

She was the first woman in a long time he had met whose company he simply enjoyed. He didn't want to bed her, he respected her. She was different to all the women he spent time with in the city. As gifted as she was, she was void of ego, and was comfortable in her own skin. She was also great fun. That said, he couldn't help but notice how pretty she was.

'Scott, you're staring at me. Have I got something on my face?' She scrubbed at her face with the linen napkin.

He laughed. 'Sorry for staring, Sal. I was just thinking about how gifted you are. I'm excited for you. It should only take a few weeks to get everything in order.'

'Enough about me and the other two, Scott. It's your turn. I know very little about you. Spill the beans – I want to know everything!'

'The direct approach. I like it. Some would call you nosey, but not me.' His voice dripped with sarcasm, but his eyes were smiling. 'What would you like to know?'

'Oooh, now there's a question. Hmm, let me see.' She pondered for a minute, with a real glint of mischief in her eye. 'Ready? This will be like a rapid-fire round.'

'Shoot so.'

'Do you have any brothers or sisters?'

'Nope.'

'What's your favourite colour?'

'Royal blue.'

'What's the last book you read?'

'Aristotle's *Poetics*.'

'Interesting. Have you ever been in love?'

'Yes. Twice.'

'What happened?'

'One wasn't good enough for Mother, the other fell in love with someone else.'

'Would you like to have children one day?'

'Nope.'

'Who is your favourite artist?'

'Apart from you? Jackson Pollock. Last question, Sal. Make it count.' He was loving the attention, and really enjoying being this honest with someone. It had been a while since a woman had been interested in his life, rather than just his reputation and wallet.

'Do you believe in Karma?'

'Absolutely not.'

Sal laughed and excused herself to go to the rest room. It was getting close to the time where she would have to get the bus back to Wexford. What a lovely day it had been!

When she returned, the table had been cleared and the bill settled.

'Come on, Sal, I'll walk you over to the bus terminal. I'll leave the car where it is – the walk will be quicker than driving and it's not far.'

They strolled down the length of Grafton Street in the May sun. Scott, being a gentleman, carried her cumbersome portfolio, and she was free to people-watch. She was always amazed at the volume of people on the street, and the amount of tourists. A group had gathered beside the statue of the iconic Molly

Malone. She overheard the tour guide telling the tourists that Molly and her wheelbarrow would be leaving the spot where she had stood since 1988, to make way for improvements in the rail service. She would be kept in storage until 2017. The street was alive with activity and the smell of diesel and flowers filled her nostrils. A couple of paces up the street, the smell was replaced with fresh coffee and the daily specials on the restaurant menus. How she wanted to move here! The harbour was lovely, but it was lacking in the bustle that inspired her.

The terminal was crazy busy as usual, and she held tight to her little handbag. Pickpocketing was rife here – it was a universal rule in transport terminals all over the world. The victim oblivious of a crime until the driver demanded payment.

Scott handed her back her work, and gave her a big hug. 'I would have dropped you down to Wexford, you know – I meant it when I offered earlier.'

'You have done more than enough for one day. Thank you so much, Scott. I like the bus anyway – gives me plenty of time to daydream.'

He stood and waited for her to board, and she waved at him from the window as the bus snaked into the evening traffic.

She settled back in the chair and closed her eyes. She would convince Jen how lovely he was, get her and Andy together, and they would all have a great summer together. She rummaged around her bag for a pen and a notebook, and jotted down a few ideas.

It really had been a wonderful day, but what Jen had said to Scott about their 'relationship' really tormented her. She would speak to her about that when she saw her.

Chapter 16

Scott had just turned the key in his front door when the phone rang. His bladder screamed at him to ignore it which he did and went straight into the bathroom. He was tired from the excitement of the day, and was looking forward to a takeaway and crap Friday night TV. He discarded his shoes and sat on the couch with a bundle of takeaway menus. The phone rang again. Grabbing his suit jacket from the back of the couch, he fished in the pocket and pulled out the source of his annoyance. The screen read '**Cherry House**'. The nursing home. His heart skipped a beat, and he hoped he was mistaken.

'Hello?'

'Hello, Scott. This is Dermot, from Cherry House.'

He could hear the solemn tone in the caller's voice, and it made him uneasy. 'Hi, Dermot. How can I help you?'

'Scott, I'm afraid the news isn't good. Can you come here this evening?'

'I can be there within the hour. Is Arthur sick? Has he had another fall?'

'Scott, I'm so sorry. Mr Jenkins died an hour ago.'

The news knocked the wind straight out of Scott.

'Is there someone there with you, Scott, or can I call someone for you?'

'What do you mean, he died? He was fine when we spoke yesterday.'

'We believe he had a heart attack, Scott. We can talk face to face when you get here. I'm so sorry.'

'I'll be there in twenty minutes.' Scott hung up without saying goodbye.

He hadn't got as far as turning the television on, and the quiet in the room made him dizzy. It had to be a mistake – he had only been with him yesterday. During his last visit, the nurse had mentioned something about him not feeling well, but he had been in good spirits, lucid for most of it. On autopilot now, he put on his shoes, got his coat, and made his way to the car.

Dermot was waiting for him when he got to reception. The chaplain was present, as was Arthur's favourite nurse. She looked as though she had been crying, and this struck him as odd. The chaplain shook his hand, and they began the pilgrimage to room 17B. Scott was sweating, and his hands had begun to shake. He didn't want to go inside, but he would have to. Dermot was speaking in hushed tones to him, and he could barely hear him over the sounds of life on the corridor, the sounds he had become so familiar with.

The chaplain opened the door softly, as though he were afraid of waking someone. The blinds were drawn against the evening sun, and the room was bathed in a soft peachy glow. Scott stood inside the door, his back pressed to the wall, and his eyes eventually made their way from the foot of the bed to Arthur.

There he was. Just like he was asleep. *The Racing Post* and his

Liquorice Allsorts from yesterday were nowhere in sight. A lifetime of memories flashed through Scott's head at that moment, and the first of his tears began to fall. He didn't remember getting to the side of the bed – everything was so surreal.

The blanket was tucked up under Arthur's chin, and his fingers were interlocked over the blanket, grasping a rosary beads.

Dermot assured him he had gone quickly and peacefully. His history of high blood pressure and a previous small heart attack, combined with his age, meant that this could have happened at any time. They had taken care of him in his final moments, and the priest had been present when he died. This soothed Scott – he couldn't give a shit about God and religion, but Arthur had been a man of faith. 'God is good,' he would say. 'God is good.'

They told him to take as long as he needed. All the arrangements were in place with the funeral director, and they would be here in a while to take Arthur to the funeral home. Scott asked why he wouldn't have to have a post mortem, and they talked about Arthur's General Practitioner signing off on the cause of death, based on the medical history. The words, aimed at him, bounced off the walls. All he was thinking about was that this was the first time he had ever seen Arthur's hands so spotless.

The door shut behind him, and they were alone. He found the courage to place his hand on top of Arthur's head. The cool skin and the tinge of blue in his face made him feel ill. Everything was happening too fast. He couldn't wrap his head around it all. Yes, he was old, and had a good 'innings' as they would say about an old man, but he was the closest thing to a grandfather Scott had. He loved him.

Arthur had always been there, as advisor, disciplinarian and friend. Filling the void of his absent parents most weekends. This all flooded into his mind as he stood beside him. He spoke out loud to him, and willed him to respond.

A gentle knock came to the door, and two solemn men

entered with Dermot. He introduced them as the funeral directors, who had come to take him. Before he invited him to his office, Dermot, on behalf of a number of residents, asked if they could come and say their goodbyes. Scott nodded his assent, afraid to speak.

He was met by several people outside the door of 17B, Arthur's friends and fellow residents. They shook his hand, telling him how sorry they were for his loss, and how Arthur would be missed.

In his office, Dermot advised him of procedures. Scott had been surprised at how savvy Arthur had been. Long before the dementia had set in, he had insisted Scott would have enduring power of attorney. 'God is good, but I'm an old man,' he said. 'I have made my will, with my solicitor, and now I want this to be done.' And it was done. Everything had been in order and legally Scott, the son he never had, would look after things for him.

Scott realised he would have to get in touch with the solicitor, and let her know Arthur was gone.

Arthur's belongings sat on the passenger seat of the car. He would have to get his affairs in order, and sort out his cottage. He couldn't think straight, his head was swimming. He needed to hear a friendly voice, someone to comfort him and tell him things would be OK. He needed to break the news to someone.

Andy, he would ring Andy.

Chapter 17

'Mam! Where's my rucksack?'

Jen stood in the hall and shook her head. She would have been quicker going upstairs and doing it herself.

'It's in your bedroom on the bottom shelf! Make sure you pack your toothbrush this time! Hurry up, the picnic is packed, we're leaving soon.'

'Where's my socks? I can't feckin' find any.'

'Danny Harper, you watch your language, mister, or I'll ring your dad and cancel your sleepover.'

'He gets that word from you, you know.'

As usual, she hadn't heard him come in. For a big guy, he moved around like a ballerino.

'Hey, Andy. How are you? How is Scott?'

'Ah, he's pretty gutted to be honest. We went for a meal and a few pints after the funeral. Sal was there as well.'

Andy looked tired. He had left the harbour to head out

131

fishing, and then got the call from Scott. He turned the *Mary Rose* around, and got dropped off. The boys would cope without him for one trip. He left Fran in charge, and knew everything would be in safe hands.

'Was she? I'm surprised she didn't mention anything about heading up. It was all last minute, I guess.' A thought crossed through her mind, and she let it go. Another thought came to her then and hesitantly she spoke. 'Andy, Danny and I are heading up to Raven's Wood for a picnic. You know what I'm like when it comes to portion control. Packed way too much for just the two of us! Do you want to come?' She knew she was blushing.

'You know what, Jen? That sounds lovely. Do I have time to change?'

'Of course, rock on. I was about to make a quick cuppa anyway.'

He took the stairs in twos, and Jen skipped into the kitchen to pack extra crockery. This could be fun, she thought, and it will make a nice change having a strong man carry the picnic basket. She thought about those big strong arms of his, and how good they had felt wrapped around her the other night.

'Let's just see what happens.' She spoke out loud, and Butch answered her with a bark.

Less than an hour later, they had arrived at the woods, and what a glorious day it was for a picnic! A number of families had had the same idea, and were pulling picnic baskets and camping stoves from their cars.

Danny and Butch were ahead. Butch didn't mind the leash too much, but clearly wanted to be running free, chasing the dandelion clocks that floated in the air.

'Jen! How long do you expect we'll be out here? You've packed more food than I would for a week on the trawler. It weighs a ton.'

'Nearly there. Come on, Andy, don't be such a wuss. I didn't moan like that when I've had to carry the basket halfway up a mountain. We're on the flat here, almost, for goodness' sake.'

'*Why I oughta!*'

They both laughed at the catchphrase, and followed Danny and Butch off the main walk, down a dirt track through the woods. They rounded a corner into a clearing. Jen knew this place like the back of her hand. She and Danny loved to come here for 'pick-a-nics' as he used to call them. They always came to the same spot, and they always found it to be unoccupied.

'We're here.'

It was beautiful. A slope down the wooded hill opened out onto a valley about the size of a football pitch. The other side sloped back up and, through the top of the trees, a distant mountain could be seen. Jen always felt like Julie Andrews when she stood in the middle of the clearing. Resisting the urge to do the iconic twirl, she set about getting the picnic organised.

Danny had taken Butch off his lead. He wouldn't go far, he never did.

Andy was standing to one side, swinging his arms, not sure what to do.

'Come on then, Andy,' Jen said. 'Can you get the flask out? We can have tea before those two come over ravenous. The mugs are on top of the basket.'

'Jen, that flask is ridiculous. I don't think I've ever seen one so big in my life.'

'Steady on, dear. What will the neighbours think? Size doesn't matter, you know – it's the quality that counts.'

He was amused by her humour – he hadn't seen this side to her before.

'Here you go.' She handed him the steaming mug, and sat cross-legged facing him. 'Tea always tastes nicer outdoors. I love coming here – it's so peaceful.'

They sat sipping their tea, luxuriating in the wonderful sunshine.

'Jen, are you not bloody roasting in your long sleeves there?' It was out of his mouth before he could stop it. He flushed in embarrassment, remembering why she always covered up.

'I can't wear short sleeves, Andy. The scar comes down along my left arm, just short of my elbow. It's really obvious, and I don't like people staring at it.'

'Sorry, Jen. Me and my big mouth.'

'Danny gets agitated when people comment, that's all. Bless him, he's really protective.'

'He's a good kid, Jen. You should be proud of him.'

'Ah, I am. He's my little angel.' She looked over to where her little boy was trying unsuccessfully to climb one of the biggest trees in the woods. She kept her eyes on her boy as she went on. 'It's not easy with these scars, Andy. They're really bad, and that's not just me self-deprecating. Some days I don't feel so bad about them, but I never feel good enough to let people see them and not give a shit.'

He let her speak, afraid of interrupting her. He felt that it was important she knew he was really listening.

'I've lived with it all my life, but I can never get used to the look of it.' She laughed at herself, but it was an empty, almost bitter laugh.

'Ah Jen, what exactly happened to you?' He couldn't help himself. He had only a vague memory of the story. Everyone had known about it at the time, and Aunty Pat had made reference to it once or twice.

'Me trying to be Miss Independence as a child. Pulled a big pot of boiling soup off the stove. I was only four. I was never one to listen to Mam, but I paid the price for that one. Nearly killed myself into the bargain, and we have both lived with the consequences ever since. I think Dad always kind of blamed me for Mam not wanting to have any more children. She never trusted herself after that. '

'Oh, Jen!' Andy was horrified.

'It missed my face, I'm grateful for that much, but it totally destroyed my chest area and upper arm.' She reached for the flask and replenished their mugs. 'Mam and the local postman saved my life. Third-degree burns, and months in hospital. I'm over that now – it took me a long time, but I have managed to put it behind me for the most part. I still remember it though.'

He took her hand in his, and squeezed. He didn't know what else to do. He looked at her and felt protective towards her.

She pulled at her top and exposed her left shoulder. The scar looked like solidified candle wax, raised and white. She slipped her top back up to its rightful place, her secret safe again.

'So, Andy, if you are ever trying to woo me, don't buy me a lacy negligee.' She squeezed his hand, and stood up. Her legs were shaking, but she felt a little bit lighter. 'Come on, you two! Time for the picnic!'

Andy bowed his head, deeply shaken by Jen's revelations. He busied himself helping to unpack the rest of the contents of the basket. When everything was laid out on the blanket, it was a sight to behold. Beautiful crusty bread with dips and a round of cheese. The leftover roast chicken from the day before, with a mixed salad and coleslaw. Wedges of the juiciest watermelon, famous Wexford strawberries bought on the side of the road en route, and ruby-red grapes. Iced sparkling water was served from a flask, and three wedges of Jen's Chocolate Cola Cake lay in the basket for dessert. Butch had retired to the shade of a tree to gnaw on a bone.

They were having a great time, all of them. The afternoon slipped by nicely. Danny was quizzing Andy about the life of a fisherman and the Loch Ness monster, and Andy was teasing him about girlfriends and stunt scooters. Danny was soon full, and darted back to play with his best buddy. Butch was having none of it of course, preferring the gigantic bone and the shade to football.

Jen and Andy were now sitting beside each other, facing the

same direction. Their legs were touching, but neither of them moved away.

'What did you want to be when you were growing up, Andy?'

'Well, when I was five I wanted to be a fisherman like my dad.' He liked these games, and Jen was a great one for coming out with all sorts of random questions. He had listened with real interest the day she and Sal had argued over which African animal they would come back as in their next life. 'But then I began to think that I wasn't all that suitable for life on the high seas. I decided to be a doctor instead. I was lucky in school – my brain was wired for study and retaining lots of information quite easily but, like any teenager, I got distracted by girls and summer jobs. I also can't stand the sight of blood or needles, so that ruled me out!'

'Hang on a minute. You're a fisherman – what do you mean you can't handle the sight of blood? Sure, are you not up to your elbows in fish guts most days?'

He was laughing. 'That's different. I realised that I was afraid of needles and blood one afternoon in our kitchen. That's how I got that.' He pointed to the Harry Potteresque scar over his left eye.

'I have to hear this one. Go on!'

'Well, Ma was out for the day, and me, my sister and the lads thought it would be cool to pierce our ears. My sister wanted to be a beautician when she finished school, and convinced us all that it was part of the job she did on Saturdays. Sure we didn't have a clue, and the fact she actually worked in a hairdresser's made it all the funnier – and don't forget, young lady, I'm a few years older than you, so it wasn't like your fancy salons with the cappuccinos.'

'All right, Grandad.'

'Anyway, we were sitting at the counter in the kitchen, all lined up like ducks. She had the clothes-pegs on our ears, and the ice, and one by one, she got to work on us.'

'Please tell me she sterilised the needle between each ear?'

'Course she didn't, are you mad? Anyway, Ben was before me,

and the minute I saw that fecking needle pop out of his ear, and the blood drippin' onto his Def Leppard T-shirt, I fainted. Fell off the stool, cracked me head off the counter, and landed in a heap on the floor.'

'You are the biggest wuss I have ever met! That's hilarious.'

'What's worse was my ma chose that moment to come home. There we were, two of the lads topless with her sleepers in their ears, while I was bleeding all over the floor and her fancy tea towels. We were in the super shit that weekend, and I got five stitches into the bargain. If my dad had his way, he would have superglued it closed. Jesus.'

'But you can gut a fish no problem?'

'I can gut a fish like a pro – especially with my new hunting knife which works a treat.'

'So, what happened when you decided not to study medicine, you wuss?'

'I did my school exams, and then went to work for my dad for a few years. Eventually went to college, studied Theoretical Physics, fell in love, got married, had an amazing job and a beautiful house, was widowed, sold up, travelled for a bit, came home, back to work for Dad, and here I am.'

'I'm sorry about your wife, Andy. It's very sad.'

'Thank you, Jen. Now, enough of that. Let's get that cake out, right?' Then he called in the direction of the trees, with forced joviality. 'Danny, I'm just going to eat your cake! Hurry up!'

Danny sprinted out of nowhere, and practically dived on the basket. Butch came flying too, but had to settle for chicken instead.

Cake eaten, Jen was became conscious of the time – she had to drop Danny over to Will's. Reluctantly they started to pack up.

'Well, it's just as well we all have big appetites – the basket will be easier for you to carry on the way back, Andy. It's practically empty.' She was delighted – nothing pleased her more than people enjoying her food.

Andy seemed a little bit quieter on the trek back to the car. They were tired from the heat of the sun, and their bellies were full. She walked behind him, with Danny leading the procession. She wondered what he had looked like on his wedding day, and thought about how beautiful his wife must have been. She knew it was irrational, but she felt jealous of this poor dead girl. He seemed to have an air of melancholy about him most of the time. Could you fall out of love with someone after they died?

In the midst of all her ponderings, she failed to notice the big stick right across her path. Down she went, and the pain from her ankle blinded her. Danny came running back, and Andy went a bit pale looking at her bleeding knees.

'I am a total fool,' she gasped. She knew straight away that her ankle was swelling, but it wasn't broken. A sprain – she had weak tendons and it wasn't the first time it had happened.

'Can you walk, Jen? What can I do?'

'Don't pass out on me, for goodness' sake, anyway! Just don't look at my knees, and help me up. Don't make a fuss, cos Danny will panic.'

'Mam!' Danny was nearly in tears, and Butch was licking at her ankle.

'Lads, stop fussing. I'm fine. Let's get out of here before anyone sees what an eejit I am.'

The pain was lifting her out of it by the time she got back to the car, propped up by Andy. He would have to drive, she couldn't. It was decided. He shuffled her into the car, pulled the seat back, and Danny put a cushion in the foot-well for her. All was good. She had a first-aid kit, and would strap the ankle as soon as she got home. They could drop Danny to Will on the way.

By now, the codeine had kicked in. Her ankle was nicely swollen and bruised, but she had strapped it and it now rested on the arm of the couch. Andy was flapping around the kitchen and she was grateful to have him in the house. It wasn't the first time she had injured herself in this manner, and she knew, although it was only a sprain, she would be incapacitated for a while.

'Jen, are you sure you don't want me to take you to the emergency department?' He had materialised at her side with a cup of tea and a plate of chocolate biscuits. She took the tea, and balanced the plate on her good leg.

'Honestly, there is no need. But thanks, anyway. If you could dig my old crutches out of the garden shed, it would be a great help. I kept them from the last time I did this.' Her voice had a slight slur to it, and her eyes looked heavy.

He went outside in search of the crutches. Before long he was back with them, cleaned, and he placed them beside the couch.

He eventually roused her from her sleep and suggested that she go to bed. The effects of the strong codeine had started to wear off, and he could see she was uncomfortable. Again he suggested the hospital, but she assured him, having suffered the same injury on more than one occasion, that she knew what she was dealing with and there was no need.

'Come on, Jen. I'll help you up the stairs. I've left water and pain relief up there – you should try and get a proper sleep.'

She winced as she swung her foot down to the floor. He gently pulled her up and supported her as she arranged the crutches. She felt clumsy as she made her way, slowly, to the bottom of the stairs, the click of the crutches rhythmic on the floor.

'I can carry you if you want?' Andy stood like a sentry beside her.

'OK.' She didn't think she had the strength in her arms to get up the stairs.

He took the crutches from her and put them aside, then picked her up very gently. He was careful not to whack her sore foot against the wall in the narrow hall, taking his time to manoeuvre her sideways in his arms. This made her laugh. He had no trouble getting her to the top, and she enjoyed the feeling of being taken care of for a change.

'Where to, m'lady?' He rocked her gently in his arms.

'Bathroom, please.'

She supported her weight on the hand basin as he went back downstairs to get her sticks.

'Could you grab my PJs off the end of the bed for me!' she called after him. 'It would be easier to get changed standing in here.'

He came back with her PJs and stood the crutches against the sink. 'I'll wait for you outside,' he said. 'Don't lock the door, just in case you slip.'

He went out and closed the door softly.

She started to undress, cursing herself for having a faded washed-out pair of pyjamas with teddies on them.

Ready at last, she called him back in.

He opened the door to her room, and guided her in. The water had been left within reach on the locker, and he had turned down the bedclothes.

'You are incredibly thoughtful, Andy. Thank you so much.' Pushing the bedclothes back further, she sat down on the bed, and gently swung her legs up onto it. 'The pain is not so bad now really.'

He smiled and gently propped her leg up with a pillow. 'Can I get you anything else?'

'You could kiss me goodnight?' Her voice was a whisper.

He didn't have to be asked twice.

He sat on the side of the bed, and kissed her very gently. He was nervous – she could feel his arms shake on either side of her. They both knew this time there was no backing out from what was about to happen. He stopped, looked at her to make sure she was OK, before carefully swinging his legs up on the bed and lying beside her. The chemistry between them was now a palpable force.

His hands slid up her leg and traced circles on her thigh with his fingers. She propped herself up on the pillows and pulled his T-shirt up. He helped her pull it over his head. She tugged at his shorts and he removed them. Then he gently removed her pyjama bottoms. Her hand rooted around the top drawer of her locker until she felt the little foil package – kept there 'just in case'. They didn't speak at all, but kept eye contact with each other. He put the condom on, and she guided his hips where she needed them to go. He moaned as he entered her, and she moved her hips in time with his rocking, slowly at first, until their bodies took over and their impatience showed in how they pulled and bit at each other. She knew he was holding back, waiting for her. The intense waves of pleasure took her by force, and she let go, the pain in her foot forgotten. Her moans excited him, pushing him over the edge. He thrust harder and harder until he too cried out in pleasure. He buried his face in her neck, and inhaled the gentle smell of her perfume. They lay like that for a while, both lost in the pleasure and the realisation that there was no going back from this moment.

Eventually he got up and went to the bathroom. When he came back he lay down beside her.

'Jen, I'm mad about you.' He kissed her on the temple and put his arm across her waist.

'And I am about you, Andy.' She kissed him. 'Stay here with me tonight.' She wanted to fall asleep with him beside her, and wake up to his face in the morning.

He smiled and nodded, then pulled the bedclothes over them.

She wasn't sure where this was going. They would have to be so careful in the house when Danny got home – she needed to figure where this was headed before he knew anything. And there was the slight problem of Andy leaving at the end of the year – she would cross that bridge later. For now, she just wanted to lie here, in the arms of this kind, lovely man and feel excited about what tomorrow would bring. His breathing was soft and regular beside her, and she gave in to sleep as well.

He woke during the night, and thought it was Sharon's warm body beside him. He was dazed and confused as to where he was. Then he remembered. He was here with Jen, not his dead wife. He had not lain with a woman since her, and he felt as though it was some form of betrayal of her, and her memory. He still loved her, he knew that much, but now he was faced with new feelings for this woman, and her little boy. His analytical brain was his worst enemy at times, overthinking everything to the point of talking himself out of things. He went to the bathroom to clear his throat of the lump of emotion caught there.

He stood outside Jen's door, faced with a choice: to take a leap of faith or to stay put, living with a ghost.

He sneaked back into the bed beside her, wrapped his arm around her and went to sleep. Tomorrow would take care of itself.

Chapter 18

She awoke to the sound of gale-force winds and driving rain, the beautiful weather of the previous day long gone. Feeling the warmth beside her, she couldn't help but smile and toyed with the idea of getting up and making breakfast until she remembered her damaged ankle. And she didn't want to break the magic spell just yet, so she lay there waiting for him to wake.

'Morning,' he said as he turned over. 'How's the foot?'

He smiled at her, and she felt relieved. She had wondered if he would think he had made a mistake the night before but that smile reflected what she was feeling.

'It's sore, but not as bad as yesterday. It's quite stiff.'

He grinned at her and guided her hand under the covers. 'It's not the only thing that's stiff,' he said before he placed his mouth on hers.

They made love again, slow and lazy this time, taking time over each other, discovering the favourite spots. He made no attempt to remove her pyjama top, and for this she felt real warmth towards him. She wasn't ready to reveal herself fully to him, and she knew that he wasn't ready to see the scars.

'M'lady, I'm starving. You stay there for a bit and I'll get breakfast on.' He untangled himself from the sheets and headed in the direction of the shower.

Jen lay back on the pillows, and tried to process what had happened in the last twenty-four hours. He was gorgeous, he was charming, and he seemed to be pretty keen on her. As the smell of bacon wafted up the stairs, she thought to herself – what's the catch? If something seems too good to be true, it probably is.

He shouted up the stairs to tell her breakfast wouldn't be long and to get her sexy little ass out of bed.

She sat up in bed, and took the bandage from her foot. Her ankle was a lovely shade of purple and green, but the swelling hadn't got any worse. The compression bandage and elevation always did the trick.

Freshly showered and dressed, she hopped into the kitchen as breakfast was being laid on the table. Poached eggs, bacon, tea and toast were on the menu. He had even picked a flower from the soaked garden and put it in a little vase in the centre.

'You got down the stairs unaided then, fair play to you! Something must have given you pep in your step this morning?'

'Haha, very funny, Andy.' She blushed as she laughed.

'So, what's your plan for the day then, Jen?'

'Well, let me see.' She pondered the question for a moment. 'I'm going to have a jog on the beach, before I go rock climbing.'

'You are a cheeky little cow really, aren't you?' He leaned over in the chair and kissed her on the cheek.

'I have nothing on the cards. I called my boss to let her know I won't be in this weekend. What about you?' She hoped he had no plans, and he would just stay here with her for the day.

'No plans at all. The guys are still fishing so I'm at a loose end for a few days. When will Danny be back?'

'Tomorrow. It's another mini-midterm in school. He was delighted, bless him.'

'Would you like to go to the cinema, then down to the Gale for a bite to eat and a few drinks?'

Although the idea appealed to her, she didn't really think it was a good one going to the Gale for dinner. Like any local pub, questions would be asked if they were there for food and drinks. Beers, totally acceptable, but with a meal as well the locals would have them married off in weeks. It was too soon for the tongues to start wagging.

'Maybe we could go for food somewhere in town before the movie, then for a pint afterwards?'

'It's a date,' he replied with a smile.

As they came out of the cinema, Andy's phone began to beep in his pocket. They had caught the earlier show – the choices were limited, but they had enjoyed the movie – Will Smith and his son, saving the earth, the usual.

They were sitting in his car, laughing about some of the outlandish scenes in the movie, when his phone beeped again.

'No coverage inside – they are all coming through together here,' he said, as he looked at the screen. It was Scott. He sent a reply and immediately got a response. 'Brilliant,' he said. 'Scott is coming down for the night. He is going to be in the Gale around ten.'

'That's cool! Great.' Jen tried to sound as enthusiastic as he was, but she was pissed off. The one night that she and Andy could be alone, Scott had to appear. Then she felt guilty – the poor guy was in mourning for goodness' sake – he needed to be around his friends. She admonished herself for getting territorial about Andy already. Easy there, Jen. 'Listen, Andy. If you think Scott would prefer to have a pint with you alone, I don't mind going home. I'm just mindful of the fact he's bound to be feeling a bit shaken still.' She wanted to sound genuine, and hoped she did.

'Don't be daft, Jen. You can help me cheer him up – we'll have a nice time. He likes you, he told me so yesterday. Don't worry – he's not a bad guy.'

She couldn't get out of it, and didn't know whether to be worried or flattered by the notion she had been a conversation point between them.

'OK, so. I'm sure we'll have a laugh. I'd just worry that he wouldn't feel free to talk with me around.'

'Jen, it's settled. We're going together.' He noticed her reluctance, and was slightly miffed. Scott had really been his saviour after his wife died. He needed to be there for him.

It had turned out to be a better night than expected. Scott and Jen had a good time, chatting about music, and she could see their camaraderie pleased Andy no end. Sal had turned up, Scott and her in cahoots over all things art-related. They filled their friends in on the meeting with the panel at the NMAG, and the fun they had afterwards in the incredibly posh Westbury.

Jen, of course, was a centre of attention on the crutches, having to regale numerous acquaintances with the story of how it had happened. This led to a number of sympathetic neighbours buying her copious amounts of wine. 'Get that down ya, Jen love, 'tis right stuff to numb the pain.' She had visions of falling flat on her face after a few drinks, but she was in good hands, and they all took good care of her. Sal insisted on escorting her to the bathroom, where Jen filled her in about the romance.

Back at the table, Scott insisted they all attend his mother's next garden party in a couple of weeks. They should come for dinner the night before and spend the night. They enthusiastically agreed, except for Jen whose heart sank at the thought.

None of them had had the foresight to book a taxi home. There was no way Jen could walk it, and it was too far for piggybacks – as much as the idea appealed to her when Andy suggested it. But Tess had saved the day by offering to take her.

Jen's carriage home was sorted.

In her post-lovemaking cocoon with Andy in the wee hours of the morning, two things struck Jen as odd. Firstly, how familiar Scott and both her friends seemed to be and, secondly, why had Sal insisted on walking home in the rain with Scott? She would ask her tomorrow and Tess too. There was something going on with them, she knew it – she just needed to establish what exactly.

Chapter 19

'Doc, I'm pregnant.'

He stuck his head out of the ensuite with the toothbrush still in his hand.

'*Wha dod ou jus say?*' he muttered through a mouthful of minty foam.

Hurriedly spitting and rinsing, he rushed out to the bedroom.

'What did you just say? Tess, did you just tell me you are fucking pregnant?'

'Yep. About ten weeks. And, before you ask, yes, it *is* yours.'

'Fuck sake, Tess! I wasn't going to say that. Ten weeks. Ten weeks preggers! I'm going to be a dad again!'

His face cracked into the nicest smile she had seen in a long time. The old Doc's smile.

'Tess! That's fantastic news. Come here, my darlin' mama!'

He knelt on the floor in front of her, and wrapped her in a hug. When he looked up at her, tears formed and fell freely down his face.

'I love you, Mrs Martin, do you hear me? I love you, and I'm going to make it right.'

'I love you too, Doc.'

He started to sing to her navel, and she cried as she recognised the lyrics to their wedding song: 'A Rainy Night in Soho'.

I've been loving you a long time
Down all the years, down all the days
And I've cried for all your troubles,
Smiled at your funny little ways …
I took shelter from a shower
And I stepped into your arms
On a rainy night in Soho …
Still there's a light I hold before me
And you're the measure of my dreams,
The measure of my dreams …'

Things would be OK, she decided. The idea was firmly rooted in her brain. No more tension or sadness. He would come back to her, now that he was going to be a dad again. Hugh would be over the moon – he always wanted a little brother or sister.

'How long have you known, darling?'

'A few weeks. I wanted to tell you that Sunday I had lunch booked for us. But it's OK – you know now.'

'Ah, I should have bloody guessed! You've been off the booze! Told me you wanted to lose a bit of weight. You're a good liar, Tess!'

He said it with good humour, but she couldn't help thinking she wasn't as good as him at concealing things.

'When is the little button due?'

'My calculations say around the end of January. I went to the surgery, just to confirm it and get the ball rolling. We'll see what they say at the first scan.'

'It was the bar counter night? That was the end of March, wasn't it?'

'Yep. You gave me more than splinters that night, my love.'

'Tess, I'm sorry I've been such as asshole. Things have been shit, and I've been neglecting you and Hugh. I promise I'll cop on, and be a proper husband to you.' He looked genuinely stricken, all the arguments and the angry words silenced in his head.

'I'm sorry I accused you of cheating on me, Doc. Things were just getting so bad, and I felt so scared. I just jumped to conclusions. I should have known you would never do that to me or Hugh.' She knew that had been a low blow, but she had been so confused at the time. Even Jen had tried to talk her out of that one.

'It's OK, baby, all is forgiven. I can't blame you for being a bit irrational really. Let's just call it quits and start over, eh?'

Tess was irked by being labelled irrational, but she would have to let it go. Her imagination had run away with her. He was a good man, and he worked hard. Things would work out between them. She needed to draw a line in the sand, and get on with it.

He felt sick. Sick for lying to her, sick about the affair, and if she knew what was stowed away in the bag in the spare room, she would have him arrested. He hadn't wanted to bring it into the house, but he'd had no choice. He had collected the packages as per Scott's instructions, and would deliver them to him this weekend. But today was only Tuesday for Chrissake and the stuff had to stay hidden in the house all week. And there had been a lot more than he expected – several kilos of it. He just wanted rid of it.

He looked at his wife, and realised what an absolute bastard he had become. Drug-running and cheating, nice one, Doc. Real husband material. He would sort this mess out once and for all this weekend. This time he wouldn't back down and give in to her. He needed to stay off drink and that other shit – keep a clear head. He had made a promise to Tess, and he would keep it. He knew all the stress was taking its toll. She had lost weight – well, she could spare some as she had never managed to shift the baby weight from Hugh, but it worried him. She hadn't been sleeping. He needed to take care of her. He would get over the other one, and Scott would just have to find himself a new delivery boy. The money was great, but it made him nervous. Some of the characters he had encountered of late looked like they were out of a Mafia movie.

'When can we tell Hugh?'

'Let's just wait, Doc, until we get past the three-month mark at least – a couple of weeks.'

'Have you told anyone else?'

'Not a soul,' she lied.

'January, eh?'

'January.'

'It's going to be brilliant, Tess. Another little person in the house, wrecking the place and keeping us up all night. Hugh is going to be in his element.'

'I hope so anyway. He'll be a great big brother.'

'Girl or a boy?'

'Does it matter?' She was beginning to get excited now. She thought he would go off the deep end and be really angry about the news. Instead, he was ecstatic.

'Course not, but do you have any inkling?'

'Another boy. My feeling is that it's a little boy.'

'Another little chap.' He took her in his arms and told her again how much he loved her.

She was overwhelmed with relief and love for this man, the father of her children.

'I'm just scared we won't get back to where we were, Doc. Things have been so shit lately, and we have been so distant with each other. I'm scared that there's too much damage done.'

'As God is my judge, Tess, I will make this up to you. We are a family. I love you.'

She believed him.

'Are you hungry, Tess? Do you want something to eat?'

'Doc, it's midnight!'

'Last time you were pregnant, you ate all around you at all hours.'

'I did, but I'm not hungry at this minute.'

'Oh. OK.' He looked almost disappointed.

'While we are on the subject of good news, there's something else I need to tell you.'

'It's twins! Please tell me it's twins!'

'No, it's not twins – well, I don't know that yet, but this is to do with the pub.'

'Hit me.' He was like an excited puppy. He settled down cross-legged on the floor in front of her.

'I need you to trust me on this, Doc. I have a better head for business than you, right?'

'Right. Sounds a bit dubious, but go on.'

'I have been approached by an investor.'

'Who?'

'That's the bit I can't share with you at the moment. This person was very clear they wanted absolute confidentiality for now. They have money, and they are keen to sink some into the business.'

'Is it Scott?'

She was surprised at his guess. How did he cop that one?

'Yes – but Doc, you've got to swear to me you won't let on to him. He's really cagey about letting anyone know, and he asked me not to tell you.'

'Why the hell would he not want you to tell me?'

'I think he doesn't want to bruise your ego. Point is, we're in big trouble with the pub. I have hidden the worst of it from you and, if I don't accept, we will lose the pub. But how the hell did you guess it was Scott?' Doc wasn't usually the sharpest when it came to things like this.

'He's the only one who fits the description.'

'Doc, if we lose the pub, we will also lose the house. I couldn't say no. He's offering eighty grand in return for a stake in the business. He will share in the profits when we start making them.'

Doc had turned pale. If he pissed Scott off now, he would probably pull out of investing as well, and no doubt tell Tess exactly why. This was a complete nightmare. What was Scott playing at? Had he stitched both of them up, and why?

'Doc, you need to trust me on this. Everything will be done formally through solicitors. It's not a handout, and I will still be the boss. He doesn't want to run the place. He is just investing, and then we can eventually buy him out. That money will get us out of debt, and we will be able to refurb the place.'

She tried to convey confidence in her voice, but truth was she was also feeling nervous over the proposition. She didn't want to give away any of the pub, but what could she do?

Doc said nothing. He had a feeling of dread in his stomach, but couldn't tell her why. He eventually spoke.

'Do you trust him, Tess?'

'Yes, I do, Doc. I don't think he does anything without self-gain, but he is a good businessman.'

He trusted his wife. He knew she was as good at business as Scott was, the only difference being she didn't have access to wealth like him. Things had really got out of control in the harbour – few were working and they weren't spending their few quid on luxuries like drink and food. The pub was wholly reliant on the tourist market. The place needed a real overhaul.

'OK, Tess. I'm going to trust you on this – but if he hurts you or interferes with the business in any way, I will have words with him.' He wasn't smiling, and there was real venom in his tone.

'You need to just play dumb! He mustn't guess I told you! I'm a bit uncomfortable that he won't let me tell you – it is a wee bit odd – but he holds the purse-strings, and if he wants to be odd about it, so be it.' She paused, studying his face, trying to gauge his reaction. 'Oh, and, before I forget, we're invited to his stately home next month, to one of the famous garden-party shindigs. Jen and Sal too – and Andy of course. I'll let you know the date so you can make sure you don't book any gigs then, OK?'

'A fucking garden party? Well, OK.' He fell silent for a few moments. 'But, Tess, are you sure there are no other options? Could we remortgage the house?'

'No, Doc. This is the only way. I have a meeting with him and his solicitor on Thursday, so we will see what comes from that. Now, enough business talk, let's talk about babies again, or at least the bit about making them.'

He stood up in front of her and took her in his arms. He loved his wife, and he knew he had to make things right.

Chapter 20

She was surprised to see Scott at the front door and, even though Andy was back out at sea, she felt obliged to offer an invitation to come inside for a coffee, which he accepted.

'Good to see you're on the mend, Jen. Only one crutch?'

'Getting there now, Scott.'

Jen led the way into the kitchen and gestured for him to take a seat.

She switched on the kettle and put coffee in the cafetière. He made no attempt to help her as she hobbled back and forth between the counter and the table with cups and cutlery, but she didn't ask.

'I had fun the other night, Scott. It's been ages since I've been out for a few drinks.' She was trying to give him the benefit of the doubt and make the effort, but she still felt on edge in his company.

'Yes, indeed, it was fun. Andy and I had a really nice meal in there the following evening. The food is good.'

'The food has always been great in the pub – it's packed in the summer with tourists going mad for crab rolls and bowls of mussels. On a sunny day, it's glorious down there for lunch in the beer garden.' She carried the cafetière over to the table and went back to fetch him a slice of cake.

'Yes, I've been speaking with Tess and made a few suggestions to her about the place,' he said.

Hmm, that's interesting, she thought. Tess had mentioned in passing that things were looking up financially – she wondered if he had something to do with that.

As she placed the cake in front of him he looked up at her.

'So then, Jen, you and Andy? Should I be booking caterers for the impending wedding or is it just a fling?'

Jen's cheeks instantly flushed. 'Jeepers, Scott. Steady on with the wedding talk there.'

'I'm joking, Jen. Just having you on.'

He was guffawing at his own joke, but it didn't feel like a joke to her. She wanted to stay as far away from him as possible but for the sake of being polite she sat down opposite him, putting her crutch on the floor at her feet.

'Honestly, Jen. Lighten up, I'm messing.'

He patted her leg under the table, and it gave her the creeps.

They made small talk about her work and the Opera Festival. The minutes seemed to drag by for her. He was waffling on about the Opera Society but all she could think about was an excuse to get rid of him. He finished his monologue and turned his attention back to her love life.

'So, Andy said you're seeing each other now. He likes you.'

'He's a nice guy, and I like him too, Scott, but I'm just taking it as it comes.'

'That's wise, Jen.'

'Dammit, my tea tastes weird, there must be lime in the water again. Would you like a fresh coffee, Scott, or do you need to get going?' Jen didn't like the way this conversation was heading. He was too forward for her liking, and she didn't like the way he almost assumed ownership over her.

'Here, allow me. I'm in no rush at all – you sit there and I'll make it.'

'Fine. The water filter is in the fridge. But I'm a little pushed for time, Scott. I need to leave shortly.'

As he rose from the table, he picked up Jen's crutch and propped it against the kitchen counter. It was now out of her reach and the action unnerved her. Her mobile phone was in her bag on the hall floor. She could get around without the crutch, but very slowly. The fact she was thinking about having to move at speed alarmed her. Something in his demeanour felt all wrong to her.

'Andy is a very good friend of mine, Jen, and after everything he has been through I worry for him. He is still vulnerable, you know?'

'Scott, Andy is a grown man. I'm sure he's capable of making his own decisions. It's early days, and we are simply enjoying each other's company.' She was getting pissed off by his tone – it sounded more like he was warning her off than looking out for his mate.

'Aren't you curious about Sharon, Jen? Do you wonder about her? She was the love of his life after all.'

'Of course I wonder about her, Scott. She was his wife and, as you say, the love of his life. It's part of his history. I'm sure she was lovely, and I would imagine Andy will tell me about her when he feels ready to.'

She felt disloyal to Andy – it wasn't appropriate to be sitting here, engaging in a conversation about his dead wife.

'Lovely, Jen? She was absolutely flawless – that's why he fell for her. Every inch of her was perfect. Andy seeks perfection in everything – surely you can see that much?'

'Beauty is in the eye of the beholder, isn't that what they say?'

'They also say beauty is only skin deep, Jen.'

She was listening forensically now. He was taunting her, and she knew it. How could he know about the scars?

'She was the absolute belle of the ball, everywhere she went. Everyone wanted to be her friend. So interesting and graceful – not frumpy or bland.'

'Sounds like you had a crush on her too.'

'I did.'

He let that one hang in the air, and she was certain he was enjoying this.

'So, why didn't you two get together then? Didn't you know her before he did?'

'I met someone else.'

'So what happened to your girlfriend? What was she like?'

'She disappeared, just before the end of Uni. Never saw her again.'

She was glad the conversation was steering away from Andy and Sharon, but it wasn't for long.

'Sharon and I remained friends, of course, during college, and straight after that they married. But, she had changed by then.'

He was talking to himself now. He wasn't in the room with her – he was off somewhere in his past.

'Sharon had become so controlling. They were both working and they had a beautiful house. Living the dream some would say, but I could see Andy wasn't happy. He was trapped. All she wanted to do was work and spend romantic weekends with her husband. He was never allowed to go anywhere with his friends.'

'Isn't that what all couples want to do, Scott? And I'm sure Andy isn't a pushover.' She was intrigued now, and couldn't stop herself. She wanted to know about this woman, the ghost she was being judged against.

'She was always hassling him about starting a family. He didn't want to, never could stand kids really. He would have had one out of duty eventually, but she kept nagging and nagging. She was becoming a real problem.' He was clearly angry now, his words coming out in short bursts.

'Hang on a second, Scott. How can you say he can't stand children? I've seen him around Danny and that's not the impression I get. Did he actually tell you he didn't want kids? Surely that's something he would have discussed with his wife, not you?'

She got his attention with that.

'He tells me everything,' he said, looking agitated. 'Everything!'

'Scott, I feel uncomfortable discussing Andy's marriage with you. It's not appropriate. I need to use the bathroom and then I need to get going.' She had to get away from him. Her heart was hammering in her chest and she wasn't quite sure where this conversation was going to end up.

He didn't listen to her. 'Depression, she claimed she had. She wasn't depressed at all, you know – she used to just blackmail good old loyal Andy with that one.'

Jen stood up.

'What are you doing?' he barked.

'I need to use the bathroom and, as I have just said, I need to get going.'

'Oh, sorry, Jen. Listen to me, rambling on here.' He stood up too.

She leaned her weight against the table – she needed to get her crutch. If she had to, she could walk on her bad ankle, but it hurt like hell.

'Jen, I'm sorry. I shouldn't be painting such a bleak picture about Sharon. She wasn't the worst, and she had mellowed until that night on Achill Island. Poor Andy, I'll never forget his face when he saw her on the beach. I found her, you know.'

'No, I didn't know that, Scott. It must have been hard for you as well.'

He was standing between her and the door to the hallway. He was blocking her.

'I had to tell him his wife was dead. I think in the end, though, it was for the best and he was grateful.'

The comment frightened her. He's sick in the head, she thought.

He looked her straight in the eye. She was rooted to the spot, and he was smirking as his eyes travelled down her body and back up to her face.

Jen limped over to the counter, grabbed the crutch and made for the door. She forced herself to hobble straight at him and he stepped out of her way.

She awkwardly climbed the stairs and sighed with relief when the bathroom door was firmly shut behind her.

What was he trying to imply there? She was frightened of him, of that she was certain. Think, Jen, think. OK, pull yourself together – you're reading way too many crime novels.

She couldn't hide upstairs in the bathroom all day. She washed her face and went back down to the kitchen, picking up her bag on the way.

Scott was sauntering around as though he owned the place.

'Scott, I'm going to have to get going now. I have a couple of things to do before I pick Danny up.'

'How can you drive, with a bad foot?'

'Dad drives an automatic, so we swapped until I can manage the manual again.'

'You are a clever girl, Jen. A problem-solver like me, eh? It was suicide in the end, you know.'

'Sorry. What?' She was fussing around trying to find her phone and her keys. She pulled her phone out of the bag, only to realise the battery was dead.

'Sharon. According to the death report, it was an accident. But she didn't fall. She committed suicide that night. Jumped off the cliff. But the riddle always remains: she was afraid of heights. Why did she go up there? Maybe somebody forced her? Maybe someone pushed her?'

'Poor girl. It's sad.' She was no longer trying to make sense of what he was saying. She had to get out. 'Scott, I have to go. I'm sorry to rush you out like this.'

'That's OK, Jen. Maybe I can come back another evening and keep you company while Andy is away. You can tell me how you like him to turn you on.'

She couldn't believe her ears. I have to get out of here now, she thought. He's a dangerous man.

She scooped her bag up on to her shoulder and stood to her full height.

'Scott, that's not a good idea. You need to leave. Now.'

He smiled and licked his lips. 'I don't need to do anything, Jen. You are not fucking me, so you don't get to tell me what to do. Maybe I'll fuck you here, right on the table, and you can then control me. You women are all the same. You get the leg over, and you think you own us.'

The blood ran cold in her veins. She was screaming at herself to get him out. Her hands were clammy and she had a feeling of dread in her stomach.

'What is fucking wrong with you, Scott? Get out of my fucking house!'

'Let me see your scars, Jen. I have a bit of a fetish about women with scars.'

He lunged forwards, and pinned her up against the table. She tried to swing the crutch, but she couldn't move.

He's going to rape me, he's going to rape me, was on loop in her head. The air had drained from her lungs and she couldn't breathe. All she could hear was the blood in her ears and his breath coming in gasps.

Then he stopped.

'I'm joking, Jen.' He stood back and laughed at her, as though she had just told him a joke. 'You're very easy to wind up, my dear, but perhaps I took the joke a bit too far.'

'Scott, please leave.' She was shaking now, and her legs were like lead.

He straightened his jacket and grabbed his keys from the table. He started to whistle. Every fibre in her body screamed at her to run, sore ankle or not, but she was frozen to the spot. She couldn't move.

'Oh, and before I leave, Jen, I just want to tell you this. If you breathe a word of this to Andy or fail to show up at the garden party next week, not only will I make sure Sal's deal falls through, I will also cancel the funding for your other friend, Tess. Eighty grand is a lot of money to lose over the whim of a friend, don't you think? Andy won't believe you either. And let's not even get started about your little boy. You have him to consider too. Tread carefully, Jen, or I will come back and fuck you for real, in every sense of the word. *Ciao*, dear!'

He was gone.

The sound of the engine in the driveway was matched by the sound of her retching into the kitchen sink. She sank to the floor and sobbed, unsure of what he had just admitted, and what he was capable of doing.

She needed to pull herself together and figure this out. With difficulty, she managed to pull herself up off the floor, and back on to the crutch. If that monster ever threatened her again, she'd have him arrested. He had threatened her little boy – he would pay for that one – and no, she wasn't going to give him what he wanted. Trying to scare her off Andy, like a jealous teenage girl.

She hobbled upstairs and sat on her bed. She wished Andy was here – it would never have happened had he been at home – but, then again, if she hadn't been with Andy in the first place, it wouldn't have happened either. Scott would have no reason to threaten her if she wasn't involved with him.

Her eye fell on a small pile of underwear at the end of the bed. They belonged to Andy and had got mixed up with her laundry. She picked them up, hobbled to Andy's room and opened the door. She hadn't come in here since she moved in. Maybe I shouldn't be doing this, she thought as she put the clothes down on a chair – it's an invasion of his privacy. Am I just using the underwear as an excuse to nose around?

The room smelled of him, citrus fresh. His jumper was on the end of the bed. She picked it up and pressed it to her face, breathing in his smell.

The bedside locker was inviting her to have a look in the drawers, but she refrained. Get out, Jen, stop encroaching on his space. Don't open the drawers. She didn't, but she did spot a black box wedged between the locker and his bed. Picking it up, her hands shook as she opened the lid. It was his wedding album, lovingly preserved in a lightproof box.

The book itself was beautiful, a cover of embossed leather edged with cream lace – no doubt from her actual wedding dress. There it was, on the front cover: *Sharon & Andy – The Wedding.* She ran her finger over the names, tracing the outline. She wondered if they had picked the design together, or if Sharon had free rein about everything. It felt as beautiful as it looked, delicately padded.

She opened the book, almost afraid that Sharon would jump out of the pages and ask her what the hell she was up to.

'I just have to see you for real, Sharon,' she said to the book.

She was even more beautiful than she thought she would be, and Andy was just as stunning. He looked so happy staring at her from the page, his grey morning suit in perfect harmony with her vintage ivory-lace gown. So understated, so glamorous. The pictures were all the same, a sea of smiling happy faces, all full of love and wishes for a wonderful life for the happy couple.

Scott was there too. Younger of course, and it went without saying he was best man. It was a small and expensive-looking gathering, judging by the grounds and the backdrop. They looked very much in love, and perfect for each other. How could she compete with her? She was perfect and eternally worshipped by everyone.

Jen was feeling a whole host of emotions which she wasn't

sure how to deal with.

Flicking through the book, she noticed that Scott was in most of the photos. Always there, right beside Andy or never too far away.

How can I tell anyone I suspect Scott killed his best friend's wife, made it look like a suicide and spilled the beans to me just before he threatened to rape me on my own kitchen table? They would all think I'm stark raving mad. He's already got my two closest friends on side, and now I'm being blackmailed with that. Why is he doing this, what does he possibly stand to gain from it, and why is he so possessive of Andy?

She packed the wedding album back into the box, and put it back exactly as she found it.

She tried to think straight for a couple of moments. Would he come back, she kept asking herself, would he have the capacity to come here one night and follow through on his threat? She had a feeling he just might. She needed a plan, and fast. Andy was due back in a few days, and something would have to be said or done.

Slightly out of breath from trudging down the stairs and out the door, she sat into the car and closed her eyes. She tried to rid herself of the memory of Scott's face breathing down on top of her. His eyes were so full of hatred towards her that murderous was the only description.

She eased the car out of the drive, and pointed it in the direction of school. She would collect her boy, and do the usual, then figure out the madness after dinner that evening.

Chapter 21

The view of the house was breathtaking, and absolutely huge. Jen felt sick at the prospect of seeing Scott, but hadn't had any choice but to come. Andy was driving, and his excitement was in direct opposition to her feelings of dread. She hadn't said a word to anyone about the incident in the kitchen, but hadn't slept for nights thinking about it – unable to find a solution. The sweeping drive on the approach to the house was long and stately, but in her head it would never be long enough.

The large windows on the ground floor lit up the terrace. She could see Scott and Sal standing at the front door. They looked lost beside the huge supporting pillars, there in their finery ready for the events of the evening. The smell of roses on the warm evening air wafted in through the car window. Of course there was a valet service for the car and staff on standby to take luggage out of their sweaty hands and up to the guest rooms. Jen was uncomfortable at the whole notion of this place – it was a real cliché and she wouldn't be one bit surprised to see a lord in a top hat beating a servant, or a horse and carriage roll up to the front door.

'Andy, Jen, welcome! Welcome!' Scott said, approaching with outstretched arms. 'You're late!'

'That was my fault, Scott,' said Andy. 'I got stuck late with work.'

'I was beginning to wonder if your woman had talked you out of coming.'

'Why would she do that?'

Scott ignored him.

'Jen, darling. It's an honour to have you here in my home. If you would like to go upstairs and freshen up, your room is ready. I assume you will insist on sharing with your new lover?'

'I'm not letting her of my sight this weekend, Scott, so make sure you have us in the same room,' Andy laughed.

Sal came down the steps and gave her a hug. She was wearing a beautiful black Chanel dress, and patent shoes. Jen had never seen her so dressed up.

'Sal, you look great. Where did you get the dress?'

'Scott bought it for me, Jen.' She was beaming and couldn't take her eyes off him. 'Isn't it gorgeous?'

'You look wonderful.' Jen wasn't going to tell her what she really was thinking. Sal was dressed in an outfit she would never have chosen for herself, and was conducting herself like Scott's prize bull at a fair. The price of success, she thought dryly. She had seen very little of Sal in the last few weeks, and only the other day she had cancelled on her as she had to go to Dublin with Scott to plan the launch. When she did see her, he was always around. She couldn't tell for sure if they were sleeping together or not. She was reluctant to ask.

'Has Tess arrived yet?' she asked.

'Yes,' Scott said. 'You're the last to arrive, so perhaps you can hurry upstairs and get ready, in the hope we can get on with dinner. Mother is waiting and she is not known for her patience.'

Jen and Andy were escorted up to their room, where their bags lay waiting for them. Jen knew before the door was opened what the room would look like: four-poster bed and heavy on the mahoganies. Beautiful, but predictable. The view from the window, however, was stunning. The fading evening light kissed the array of wonderful flowers, in all shades.

'Jen, will you get a wriggle on there? Scott is waiting.' Andy was scrambling into his suit, and looked frazzled.

'All right, Andy. Chill out. Prince Charming will only have to wait for a few more minutes. I'm bloody getting ready now.' She was getting fed up of everyone hero-worshipping Scott, including Andy. She had to listen to him the whole way up in the car, saying how amazing he was, and how he threw the best parties. Little did he know! She snatched up her overnight bag and slammed the door of the ensuite behind her. She wished she was at home in her PJs with Danny curled up beside her, but she was trapped here for two days. On the upside, at least she would get some time with Andy, just the two of them. She struggled into her dress, and quickly re-applied her make-up. She had chosen a dark-green dress – the colour suited her skin tone and made her look fresh and healthy.

'Jen, you look beautiful.' Andy stood and admired her as she came out of the bathroom.

He was looking stunning in a suit, and she couldn't help but think of the wedding photos.

'Look, Jen. I know you're not Scott's biggest fan – he winds you up, I can see that much. But for my sake I'm asking you to make a bit of an effort. You two are really important to me, and I would love for you to be friends.'

She was furious with him, but hid it. 'OK, Andy. I'll be nice. Now come on, let's not keep him waiting any longer.'

'Wait, Jen. Come here.' He took her by the arms and kissed her.

She kissed him back, and fought the urge to drag him over to the bed and just stay there for the evening. She couldn't get enough of him, and anytime they were alone recently they ended up in bed. She was getting more comfortable with him, and even though he hadn't yet seen her fully naked she knew it wouldn't be long.

'Right, come on now or we won't get down there at all,' she said.

Just then, a knock came to the door.

'Come on, people, are you ready?' they heard.

It was Scott.

Jen looked at Andy and rolled her eyes. Scott was a pain in the arse.

'Nearly ready, Scott!' she called out. 'Just having a moment with Andy. We'll be down in a minute.' Her tone was incredibly dismissive, and she could see by Andy's reaction that he wasn't impressed.

Opening the door, he called after Scott. 'Coming, Scott, hang on there!'

Then he was gone down the corridor after him, without waiting for her, or giving her a second glance.

Jen was the last person to enter the drawing room, and all eyes were on her as she did.

'Jen, darling, you look simply ravishing,' Scott said, as he walked over to her.

She knew all eyes were on her, and she had to be careful. She had begun to figure out what he was trying to do.

'Scott, my apologies for holding everyone up. Your home is simply beautiful – I got distracted on the way down here. I'm excited to be here, and I must say you look wonderfully handsome in your suit. Dark colours suit you.'

She knew by the smirk on his face he had clocked her game straight away. It felt as though they were two lions on the plains, dancing around each other, sizing each other up, not knowing who was going to strike first. No one else seemed to notice the exchange. Andy was standing with his back to her, laughing at something a striking woman had just said to him.

'Where are your manners, Scott? I assume that is your mother Andy is speaking to. Can you introduce us?'

'Of course.' His response was clipped.

Interesting, she thought. His body language had changed straight away. He had lost a bit of that swagger, and Jen could see where he was coming from.

Livia oozed an air of authority and charisma. She had the demeanour of a person who always got what she wanted, and never took no for an answer. Scott was a dead ringer for her, but the darkness he exuded wasn't there in her. She was a snob, absolutely, but not as sinister as Jen found Scott to be.

'Mother, allow me to introduce Andy's girlfriend.' He practically shoved Jen in front of this woman.

'I assume this beautiful young lady has a name other than "Andy's girlfriend", Scottie. Perhaps you would be obliging enough to share it with me?'

She had cut him to the quick, and in front of everyone.

'Yes, Mother, she has a name. Jennifer.'

Jen noticed how he looked at her with the same contempt he had shown her in her kitchen and it disturbed her.

'Jennifer, it's lovely to meet you, and I'm delighted to hear Andy has met someone.'

'Thanks, Mrs Carluccio Randall, but you can call me Jen.'

'And I'm Livia, dear. Scott, can you see to drinks for our guests, please? Jen, you are very welcome here to my home. Andy has been telling me what a wonderful hostess you are. I hope my little party tonight won't disappoint.'

She was smiling, and Jen knew she wasn't being sarcastic.

'Ha! Certainly not, Livia. Your drawing room is bigger than my whole house, so you have won that battle already, I think. It's a beautiful room, so tasteful.'

'I do all the interior designing myself – little else to do at my age when I have a whole house full of staff. Now, go say hello to your friends and we will chat again soon.' She glided across the floor and disappeared towards the sounds coming from the adjoining room.

Tess and Doc were on the far side of the room. Everyone looked so great, all done up. It felt like a wedding reception rather than a meal. Tess was dressed in the most beautiful floral Lila Calypso dress, with a perfect swing skirt to hide her little bump.

'Tess, honey. You look amazing.' Jen kissed her friend on the cheek.

'I'm leaving you girls to it,' Doc said. 'Jen, you scrub up well!' He gently touched his wife's stomach before making his way over to Andy.

'So, you've told him then?'

'I did, Jen. We've worked an awful lot of stuff out, and things are looking up. I couldn't have coped if we had split up, but now things are really good. I've so much to tell you, Jen.'

'Ah, we'll have plenty of time this evening! Have you told anyone else?'

'No, not yet – we don't want Hugh to know too soon.'

Jen studied her for a moment. She hadn't seen Tess look this relaxed in a long time, but she couldn't get that phone call she had overheard out of her mind. She would have a word with Doc about it when she could get him on his own.

'Thanks for being there for me, Jen. Everything is back to normal now – crazy Tess is gone. How I thought he was having an affair is beyond me. I just got so paranoid. It's all good now and I have a bit of news about the pub – but you have to keep your mouth shut about it. Scott is investing, meaning I'm out of the shit financially.'

'Tess, I'm happy for you, but are you sure it's a good idea? I mean, it's your pub, and you barely know the guy.' I'm caught in the middle of a bad conspiracy, she thought, not for the first time. She was caught in the middle of it, and the only way out was to let go of Andy.

'Jen, my duck, I've known you a long time, and I know you well. What is going on in your head when it comes to Scott? We all know you don't trust people easily, but what has he done to you to make you dislike him so much? For goodness' sake, you are bordering on downright rude around him! That's not like you.'

'I think he has a real problem with me and Andy, Tess. He has passed a few comments about it, and he was up in the house the other day and was on about it again.'

She stopped herself before she told Tess the whole story. She couldn't. It would ruin everything, and he would fuck up her friendship with both Sal and Tess.

'So, what did he say to you that was so bad?'

'Ah Tess, it doesn't matter. I just don't particularly like him, that's all.'

'You like Andy, Jen. It makes him uncomfortable when you and Scott are not getting along. Make the effort for his sake.'

Andy approached them just then and they swiftly changed the subject.

Doc was standing at the sideboard, helping himself to a drink under the disapproving eye of a waiter, when Jen casually made her way over to him.

'So how're you doing, Doc?'

'Flying form! And you look great. Being in love suits you!'

Jen felt awkward, and steered the conversation to school and the boys.

They moved away from the sideboard and the attendant waiter. Everyone else was engaged in conversation – it was now or never.

'So, Doc, things seem to be good with you and Tess again?' she said quietly. 'I haven't seen her so at ease in a while.'

'Aye, things are great, pet – we are really back on track now. Turned a bit of a corner so to speak.'

'I'm glad. She's a wonderful person, Doc, and she loves you more than anything. You know that, right?'

'What are you saying, Jen? Spit it out,' he muttered. 'I know you well enough to know when you're angling at something. I know you know all about our rows, and I also have a feeling you knew about our news before we told everyone – she denied telling you, but you knew about it, didn't you?'

'Yes, I knew.'

'You know I love her, Jen. I love Hugh and I love this baby. I'm not going to do anything to mess that up. I've been an eejit in the past, but things are different now.'

'Are you denying the affair, Doc?'

He stared at her, shocked. 'What? What affair?'

'I overheard you on the phone that night in my place. You weren't talking to your mother!'

'Jen, leave it now. I'm happy and I have sorted things out with my wife. That's all you need to know – none of it is any of your business after that. Don't meddle in other people's business.'

The conversation was very stilted and subdued – neither of them could afford to draw attention to themselves.

Doc was panicking. Two people now knew, Jen and Scott. It was getting dangerous. He had tried to walk away from the affair, several times, but he couldn't. Then he told her the other day it was the end, and hadn't heard a thing from her after, so maybe it was over for real this time. He couldn't risk it any more. Clara, she had been a fling, albeit a fling that had lasted quite some time, but he was walking away. Tess would never know and Jen would have to keep her little mouth shut.

'I won't meddle, Doc, for Tess's sake, but if I think you're up to no good, ever again, I will blow the whistle on you. She deserves better than what you give her, so shape up or ship out.'

'What are you two talking about?'

Scott was suddenly at their side.

'You seem to be solving the problems of the world?'

'We're talking about the upcoming school sports day, Scott,' Doc answered, 'and the hilarious carry-on of some of the crazy parents. They are so competitive it's funny. There's one couple in particular that never fail to disappoint with their side-line antics.'

He's good, she thought. Quick recovery, off the cuff, just like that. She had to buy into it.

'Yes, we never fail to get a laugh out of them every year,' she said. 'The poor child is probably in training for months before the egg-and-spoon race, and goodness knows what kind of drills he has to go through for the sack race.'

They all laughed at that one, at the idea of the poor child doing laps of the garden in a potato sack for months, while his parents screamed and swung a giant stopwatch at him. There was always one in every school and their school was no exception.

She excused herself from the conversation and went over to Andy.

Livia returned and clapped her hands, drawing the guests' attention to her. She had a couple of announcements. Breakfast would be served in the dining room at nine sharp. And dinner was now about to be served.

They all made their way to the dining room next door.

The large oak table dominated the room. Livia took her place at the top of the table. Then Scott seated the others: Sal, Andy and Tess on one side – and Jen and Doc on the other, opposite their companions. He himself took the remaining seat to Livia's right, opposite Sal.

They were all intrigued to see that the place at the end of the table was also set, and they wondered who that might be for.

Livia only seemed to notice the empty place at that point and she enquired of Scott what time his friend would be arriving.

'Apologies, Mother, I expected her to be here by now. She should be here soon, but we will start without her.'

Jen glanced at Sal and she looked as though she was about to be sick. Tess clocked the glances between the girls – she too had an inkling Sal was interested in more than just a business relationship with Scott.

Of course there was a pre-dinner speech from the man of the moment. Jen tried to hide her contempt behind her glass of wine as he waxed lyrical about new friends and old, business deals and Weybridge estate playing host to the cream of society the next evening. More wine was poured and the candles cast shadows on the walls.

Scott, Livia and Sal were chatting about art, and kept up the same conversation throughout the starter course. It was obvious to Jen that Livia liked Sal, and it was glaringly obvious that Sal was trying hard to get on with her possible future mother-in-law. She laughed just a bit too long each time Livia said something, and she didn't swear once. A feat in itself for good old Sal. Meanwhile Scott was behaving as if he were enamoured of Sal, but the mystery date hadn't yet arrived.

Tess and Andy were talking about music and fishing, and the characters they both grew up with around the harbour. Andy was engrossed in conversation about one particular character and his funny ways when he suddenly turned and looked at Jen. He simply smiled at her, asked her if she was OK, and in that moment she knew she loved him. It frightened her, but the wine allowed her to sit with the notion for a bit.

The main course arrived, and the meal did not disappoint. Beef Wellington, cooked to absolute perfection, with all the sides. The wine was also glorious, not Jen's usual tenner-a-bottle choice from the local supermarket.

Doc and Jen were sitting next to each other and, after their exchange in the drawing room, conversation was strained between them. They played it safe and talked about the boys and school, weather and the opulence of the house they were in.

Crème brulées and coffee were served and Jen was beginning to enjoy herself. Livia was a lovely host, very attentive, and good at engaging everyone in conversation. She had regaled them with stories of being part of a travelling opera troupe, and the high life that came with it. She had also shown them the side of touring that wasn't so romantic or glamorous.

Scott excused himself from the table as everyone finished their desserts.

Then, as coffee was being poured, they heard him announcing: 'Everybody! I would like to introduce my mystery guest to you.'

They all turned in the direction of his voice.

'Everyone, say hi to Clara.'

They all chimed out a greeting, except for Doc.

'Oh Jesus! Sorry about that.' He had jumped up out of his seat and, red in the face, was mopping at his coffee which he had spilt on the carpet.

'Doc, leave it. No use in crying about it, the damage is done now, old chap.' Scott was smiling down at him, Clara on his arm. 'Clara, this is Doc. He is a musician.'

Clara smiled and Doc nodded.

Scott led Clara to her place and then, standing beside her chair, completed the introductions, beginning with his mother and going around the table from there.

Clara turned to Doc, who was seated on her left, when Scott was finished. Everyone else had settled back into their conversations.

'Nice to meet you, Doc, you look very familiar. I'm sure I may have come across you before somewhere?'

'Nice to meet you, Clara.' He didn't know whether to laugh or cry. There she was, in the same room as his pregnant wife, and she looked as though she was enjoying every minute of it.

Soon after he excused himself.

Scott followed him out to the hall.

'I know you're getting cold feet about our little business arrangement, Doc. Doesn't work like that, chum. I don't like people letting me down and Clara doesn't like to be let down either. She came to me, heartbroken, after you finally dumped her the other evening.'

'Scott, man, you don't understand. Tess is pregnant, and Jen knows I was having an affair. This shit has to stop. I have to be real about it.'

'No, you don't, Doc. You can have your cake, and eat it. Clara wants in on our deal as well, so now you have an assistant. I can't be dealing with heartbroken mistresses with big mouths. You will preserve the status quo, and you will leave that Jen to me. Here's a little present for you to take the edge off your nerves.'

For the first time, Doc felt intimidated by another man. He was a good deal taller than Scott, but he was afraid of him. He could ruin everything. He had no choice but to take the little package of cocaine.

'Now, Doc, go back inside, keep your mouth shut, and your wife happy. She isn't drinking tonight and is a sharp woman. Don't fuck this up.'

Doc did as he was told, and went back to join the party.

Livia suggested they retire to the drawing room where after-dinner drinks were to be served. The room had been prepared to receive them. The drapes were drawn and even though it was an early summer's evening, the fire was lit. The room had a lovely relaxed feel to it. The women gravitated towards each other and took their seats on various embroidered chairs and armchairs, while the men took a stand round the fireplace.

Doc went and took a large brandy from the waiter at the drinks cabinet. He wanted to get shitfaced and forget about it all, but unfortunately had to keep his wits about him.

Tess beckoned him over to the group of women.

'Are you all right, Doc? You look as though you've seen a ghost.' She took his hand.

'Love, I'm fine. I'm just embarrassed about spilling coffee all over myself and on the fancy carpet.'

'You big, clumsy lug! Give me a kiss.'

He bent down and kissed her.

'Ah, that's so sweet – how long have you guys been married, Tess?' Clara asked.

Doc wanted the ground to open up and swallow him. He would have to get her out of here somehow.

'Years, Clara. Bless him, sure he's the love of my life, isn't that right, Doc?'

'Whatever you say, love.'

He went back over to his brandy and the boys.

'He hates it when I wind him up like that – not a one for public displays of affection.' Tess was smiling as he scurried off like a scalded rat. 'What about you, Clara? Is there a Mr Clara on the scene?' She glanced sidelong at Sal as she waited for an answer.

'There is indeed, but he was otherwise occupied tonight. He's not one for commitment and social engagements, but he's a keeper and I won't be letting him go anytime soon.'

'So it's not Scott then? I assumed you were his date for the evening?'

'No, it's not Scott, ladies – he wouldn't be my type at all. Too polished, all white teeth and charm. Not for me! I prefer the more down-to-earth type.'

Sal looked so relieved.

Jen was listening to this exchange with real interest. Clara certainly had an air about her, but there was something else – a nervousness or shyness. She seemed really on edge, and Jen assumed it was because she was in the company of strangers.

'So, how did you and Scott meet, Clara? Have you known him long?' Jen asked

'He's friends with my boyfriend. I haven't known him terribly long, but I couldn't miss out on tonight, having heard so much about all of you.'

Scott called her over to join the men, and the three women were left alone.

'Hmmm, what do you think, girls? Is she sleeping with him?' Sal said.

'Does it bother you if she is, Sal?' Tess asked.

'Spill the beans, Sal,' said Jen. 'What's going on in that head of yours?'

'Oh girls, I don't know. We just get on so well and he's so nice to me, and he just makes me feel – I don't know – nice, I suppose.'

'For feck sake, Sal! You are not sixteen and he's completely not your type!' This came out of Jen's mouth like a dismissal and louder than she had anticipated.

'Jen, you need to back down on the Scot-bashing here,' Sal said. 'Just because you don't like him doesn't mean we have to follow suit. I'm getting a bit sick of it now to be honest. What *is* your problem?'

'I don't have a problem, Sal. I simply think he's an asshole. You're as bad as Andy – why don't you get over the hero-worshipping of Scott and remember who your friends are?'

'Well, Jen, if two people are calling you out on the same thing, maybe you need to look at your own behaviour rather than theirs?'

'All right, girls. Chill out.' Tess was speaking, but her eyes were on her husband. He was deep in conversation with Clara.

Sal vacated her chair and went over to join Scott and the others. She looked really pissed off and Jen knew their problem wouldn't be solved here tonight.

She turned to Tess and found her staring across the room. 'You OK, Tess?' She followed Tess's eye-line to see what she was staring at. 'Tess, he's just chatting. They have all had a fair few drinks now. It's all good.'

'I'm fine, Jen, I'm just tired. I should probably head off to bed. It's getting late and I was up at the crack of dawn. You're right, it's all good. Being sober with you lot is hard work. Don't stay up too late, and keep an eye on my husband for me. He doesn't look like he's ready to go anywhere just yet.'

She kissed her friend on the top of the head and made her way over to Livia. She thanked her for a wonderful evening, and made her apologies for leaving early. She then joined her husband's group to say goodnight to them.

'Stay for an hour, Tess, and then we can both go up together.' Doc was sitting tuning his guitar which had materialised out of nowhere. It looked alien in the stately room amongst the suits and posh dresses.

'Doc, I'm going up now. You stay for the hour. It's OK.' It wasn't OK with her really, but she didn't want to make a scene.

'Great. I'll walk you up so.'

Doc propped the guitar against his chair and left with Tess.

Andy joined Jen on the couch.

'Are you having a good night, Jen? Can I get you a drink?'

'Another glass of wine would be lovely, thanks.'

He went to the drinks cabinet and Livia came over to sit beside Jen.

'Livia, the meal was beautiful. Thanks for having us here.'

'You're very welcome, Jen. I've always enjoyed entertaining in the house. Tomorrow night will be a great event.'

'I'm looking forward to it.'

Andy returned with Jen's wine and, though he noticed the glass of brandy in Livia's hand, he offered to fetch her a drink. She declined and Andy went back to Scott, Clara and Sal.

Jen and Livia made small talk about opera and parties. Jen felt slightly out of her depth, but from living in Wexford with its rich history of opera festivals, she knew just about enough to maintain the conversation.

Livia drained her drink before standing up.

'Jen, darling. This is an evening for young people. I have a packed schedule tomorrow, so I'm going to retire. It was wonderful chatting to you.'

Jen stood up and they kissed each other on the cheek. Jen liked her.

'Now for a nightcap to take upstairs with me.' Livia winked over her shoulder as she made her way over to the brandy decanter.

By now it was getting quite late, and Jen was tired. She didn't want to be a lightweight, but didn't relish the thought of listening to Scott's bullshit any longer. Andy and the two other women were laughing at something Scott had said.

Jen planted a smile on her face and went over and stood beside her man.

Clara seemed to have got over her initial nerves, and was having a great time with Sal. They were drinking brandy like it was water. You can dress them up, Jen thought.

Sal hadn't forgotten their earlier altercation and made no effort to include her in the conversation.

Scott simply irked her. He was playing the part of lord of the manor very well – monopolising the conversation and enjoying the sound of his own voice. She knew she was going to be seen as being rude, but she didn't care. At the first opportunity, she was going to bed.

As soon as Scott stopped talking long enough to draw breath, Andy turned to speak to Jen.

'You're very quiet there, Jen. Are you tired?'

She could have kissed him. 'I am wrecked, Andy. The beautiful meal and the wine has done me in. I'm going to head upstairs. You stay here though, and have another drink.'

'No, I'll come up with you, babe.' He placed his glass on the table.

'Jesus, you two, you're going to bed now? It's still early.' Scott wasn't impressed.

'It's nearly one o'clock, Scott. I was up at seven this morning.' Jen tried to be light-hearted in her response but it didn't sound like that.

'Andy, stay for another brandy?'

Scott was getting quite loud now, and it wasn't lost on Jen that he hadn't invited her to stay.

'You stay, Andy. I'm tired. Scott, thanks for a lovely evening and I'll see you in the morning.'

'No, no, I'll come up with you,' Andy said.

'You're such a lightweight, Jen,' Sal said. 'Stay and have a couple of more drinks with us.'

'I'm sorry, guys. I was up really early this morning and I'm fecked. Tomorrow night I'll be the last woman standing.'

'If you insist, then so be it,' said Scott. 'Clara? Sal? I assume there is still life in you lovely ladies? You're not going anywhere?'

'Hell, no!' they answered.

Jen and Andy said goodnight and left.

'Get your arse up to that room, milady.' Andy grabbed her by the hand. 'I would like to take your clothes off and ravish you, if you're not too tired.'

'I thought you would never ask, Andy. Now come on, before Scott comes out and drags you back for more brandy.'

Doc could hear them giggling as they raced up the stairs. He had tucked his sweet wife into bed before ducking into the little bathroom on the ground floor and snorting a couple of fat lines from the earlier package up his nose. He knew he was in a dangerous position but, as the drug hit his system, he didn't really care. He just knew he had to speak with Clara tonight, while his wife lay sleeping. He needed to get her out of the house before the morning, but he wasn't sure if he wanted her to go. He was confused over the whole thing. Clara had bewitched him, and he couldn't help himself. Sal wouldn't be a problem – she was pissed and was only interested in Scott. She would be oblivious to everything.

Chapter 22

Jen's body clock always let her down. She was on a break but her body still believed she had to get up with her boy. Half past six in the morning and they had only been asleep a few hours.

She could feel Andy's heat beside her, a feeling she was growing used to. She loved him, she knew that, and she wasn't stopping herself. She could see it in him too and had decided to just let it go wherever it was supposed to. She curled into him and went back to sleep.

What seemed like only a few moments later, her alarm woke them. They pulled themselves out of bed and got ready quickly. Livia had been very clear that everyone needed to be in the dining room at nine sharp.

Jen and Andy entered, hand in hand, at the prescribed time, to find everyone else already there. Doc, Scott, Sal and Clara looked like they'd been up all night and, judging by the steely look in Tess's eye, this is exactly what had happened. There was way too much laughter and insider jokes going on between the four of them.

Jen joined Tess at the table, while Andy went to the buffet sideboard for toast and coffee.

'Morning, Tess. You all right?'

A miserable Tess turned to her. 'He came up to the room an hour ago, Jen. Up all night partying with the other three and, judging by the state of them all, it was hardcore. Funny thing is, I came down around half five, and there was no sign of life at all.' Tess was really wound up, and there were tears suddenly in her eyes.

'Maybe they went out to the gardens or something? Have you asked them where they were?'

'I don't have to, Jen. Look at the body language.'

She was right. If a stranger had walked into the room, they wouldn't be blamed for thinking Clara and not Tess was Doc's wife. It was the ease and grace two lovers had around each other. It wasn't the body language of strangers. Jen had a sick feeling in the pit of her stomach. They were too close for comfort and Clara couldn't take her eyes off Doc.

'Ah, Tess, what is he playing at?'

'I don't know, Jen, but I know for sure I'm going home today. I don't want you to breathe a word. I'll make up an excuse, but I'll make a real scene if I have to spend the day with her.'

Jen didn't argue. It was very clear Doc and Clara had either slept together, or were about to.

'I'm leaving him, Jen. I am not spending another minute with him. He had me convinced we would be OK, but we won't be.'

'I don't know what to say, Tess, but I wouldn't be running off and leaving him here to have whatever the fuck he wants for the weekend though.'

'Morning, girls, how are we?' Sal asked. She put toast and tea on the table in front of her and just about managed to sit on the chair without falling.

'Sal, are you still drunk? What time did you go to bed?' Jen asked.

'It was about half four I think – or was it later? Gawd, I can't really remember.'

'Did you all go up together?' Jen enquired, trying to sound innocent.

'Don't know. I had enough trouble getting myself up the stairs to worry about where the others were. But, to answer your first question, Jen, I'm not still drunk. I'll be fine once I eat. Are you both coming on the picnic today?'

'What picnic?' Jen and Tess looked at each other. It was the first they had heard of it.

'Apparently the kitchen is preparing picnic baskets for everyone and we're going down to the lake. Livia is busy getting ready for tonight, and I think she wants us all out from under her feet.'

'Oh, OK then.'

Tess shrugged her shoulders and then saw that Doc was making his way over to them, full of smiles and good cheer.

Jan stood up to go to the buffet and Sal excused herself to go to the bathroom – she was the same colour as the linen tablecloth – snow white.

Tess stared at her husband and took a deep breath. 'Where were you last night, Doc? Where were you until eight?'

'Tess, I fell asleep in the toilet! Wine kills me, you know that, and we had a few brandies as well. I just passed out in the jacks.' He looked embarrassed.

'And what's the story with you and Clara?'

'What do you mean "what's the story with me and Clara"? Jesus, Tess, not this shit again!'

'You two look very chummy, that's all.'

'We are chummy. We had great fun last night – what's wrong with that, for Chrissake?'

'All right, Doc, no need to get so agro. I'm only asking.'

Jen arrived back from the buffet and hovered in the background when she heard the last piece of the exchange. What the hell is going on with Tess, she thought. A few minutes ago it was so bloody obvious to her that Doc was up to no good last night, and now she has just let it slide.

Jen had wanted to tell her all about the affair, but how could she now?

After they all had breakfast – or just coffee in some cases – Scott gave them a tour of the house, and even Jen was impressed. It was massive, and still retained so many of the original features. The house was about three hundred years old, and history seeped out of every wall. Scott brought them into an annex, where all their historical prized possessions were kept. He was a real history buff, and filled them in on wars and rebellion. He spoke with real pride about the family history.

They moved from there out to the gardens, complete with picnic baskets. It was time to walk to the lake.

The recital was due to begin at eight, and dinner would be served in the marquee afterwards. They had enough time to see the lake, have their picnic, get back to the house, have a nap and then get ready for the black-tie event.

'Jen, wake up!'

'What time is it?'

'It's seven o'clock. You were out cold for the last hour. And you were snoring.'

'Feck off, Andy. I don't snore.' She laughed.

He was naked, and his hair was flattened on one side from his nap. He looked at her, and she felt a real rush of love towards him. The Beatles' 'All You Need is Love' was blaring in her head.

'Take a shower with me, Jen. Let me see you.'

Jen looked him straight in the eye, and felt the heat spread over her face. Her eyes moved to the floor and she nodded her assent. She climbed out of the bed, and he took her by the hand into the bathroom.

The water hitting the tray was the only sound they could hear. She stood in front of him as he bent down to kiss her. Lifting her arms, he removed her T-shirt, as though she were a child being taken care of by a parent. She saw the reaction in his eyes. It was a mix of shock, revulsion and sadness. She didn't blame him. The scars were horrendous. Where breasts should have been, only a splat of solidified skin. The angry red had faded over the years, and now her body looked and felt as though someone had thrown candle wax all over her. She held her breath, and waited for him to leave the room. He didn't. He regained his composure and kissed her again. He didn't speak – he just took her hand and led her into the glass block. The steam obscured their vision only slightly, and she was grateful for everything taking on a blurred look. He picked up his sponge and started to wash her. She started to cry. He washed her everywhere, and then washed her hair. She stood there, and allowed him to do it. She allowed herself to be taken care of for just a while.

He allowed her to touch him, but she knew he didn't want to turn this into wet steamy shower sex – it was a deep and emotional moment for both of them. But she wanted him. She let her hands travel all over him and, as she guided him into her, she knew that they had started to heal each other's scars. It was just a start, but they were together on this part of the adventure.

He wrapped her in a towel, and dried her. He knelt in front of her, and traced his finger along the ropey bumps on her chest.

His hand moved lower and he grinned up at her.

She swatted his hand away and laughed.

'Get off me, Andy. I have to get ready.'

'OK, OK. I will leave you alone, for now. I should get ready too. Scott will have a hissy fit if we're late.'

'We won't be, I won't be long. Shit, Andy, look at the fecking time – it's ten to eight.'

'Ah, crap!'

Jen stuck her hair up in a French pleat, after a quick blast with the hair-dryer. She didn't have time to style it properly, but it looked the part. Her make-up never took long, the advantage of inheriting her mother's beautiful skin, and she was ready quicker than Andy. He was still running around the room in a shirt and underpants, looking for his cufflinks.

'Will you hurry up, man?'

Jen tried in vain to help him with his dicky bow, but had no clue how to tie it.

'Come on, Andy. Just get Scott to do the damn thing downstairs.'

They heard him in the hallway before they saw him, greeting guests with compliments and thanks as he pointed them in the direction of the waiter with champagne. Jen got the feeling that most of them were regulars – they knew where to go anyway without Scott having to direct them.

Scott laughed at Andy's request, and had the tie knotted perfectly in seconds.

'I knew how to knot a bow-tie before I could walk,' he said to Andy, as his hands rested on his shoulders. 'You look great. Now go out to the garden – I'll see you at dinner.'

Jen thought he was about to kiss him, the way he stood there eyeing him up. She wondered had she left a big glob of lipstick Andy's face, and secretly hoped she had. They exchanged pleasantries, him complimenting her dress as he ushered them through the doors.

The large walled garden was full of tuxedos and evening gowns. They spotted Tess and Doc and took their seats in the audience. The performance was going to last for an hour, and then dinner would be served.

'Where is Sal?' Jen whispered to Tess.

'Off somewhere getting pissed with Clara, I'd imagine. They were knocking back the champagne when we came down. Sal is being weird this weekend.'

'Weird how?'

'If I didn't know any better, I'd swear the two of them were off their heads on something.'

The tinkle of spoon on glass and the *shhhh* of the opera enthusiasts put their conversation on hold.

The hour passed very quickly. Jen was surprised how much she enjoyed the excerpt, Livia's voice not giving away her age or her love of cigarettes to the untrained ear. Jen wondered if she had lost any of the range or the length she could hold a note over the years – if she had she must have been truly phenomenal at the height of her career.

Andy materialised at her side after the encore, and walked Tess and her into the marquee, which had been transformed into a beautiful dining room.

The rest of their little party arrived at the table, and everyone was in high spirits. Sal, Clara and Doc in particular seemed as though the champagne bubbles had gone to their heads. The three of them were chatting a little bit too loudly about life after death and were drawing the attention of guests at the next table. Jen and Andy exchanged glances, just before Tess asked them to quieten down.

'For fuck sake, woman! Lighten up and stop being such a square all your life!' said Doc.

This made the other two girls giggle, and Jen was mortified.

Andy spoke up. 'Doc, have a bit of respect for your wife there, and for our sake take it down a notch. Girls, I would suggest you two eat something before you drink any more. You're acting the eejits and it's beginning to grate on my nerves.'

Doc was stunned into silence.

Scott arrived at the table, and looked around at them. There was very obviously an atmosphere, but no one said a word.

'I hope you are all hungry – the caterers are fantastic,' he said as he took the only vacant seat, beside Jen.

The meal was served and he hadn't lied. The food was

fantastic, and the service impeccable. The group got over their awkwardness and the wine and the conversation flowed. Even Jen and Scott managed to make sociable conversation. No digs, no jibes, just small talk. She observed him as he interacted with the rest of the party, and wasn't surprised at how they could be so enamoured with him. He sure could talk the talk, and did so the whole way through dinner. The plates sat empty as he continued with yet another story of the highbrow social life in Dublin. Compliments came as easy to him as drawing breath, and he could speak with authority on any subject. He enjoyed holding court as usual, but he made Jen's skin crawl. She couldn't believe that everyone else couldn't see through him.

'Where are you off to, Doc?' Tess asked as her husband stood up.

'I'm going to chat to the band. I can see them setting up over there.' He walked over in the direction of the stage without a second glance at his wife.

She was left sitting with Sal and Clara, neither of whom involved her in the conversation.

'Sal, I need some fresh air – let's go out to the garden.' Clara wrapped her shawl around her shoulders and they were gone.

Before Jen had a chance to move over and sit with Tess, she mumbled something about the bathroom and left the table. Jen was worried about her, she looked so pale and sad.

'I hope my beloved son hasn't been monopolising the conversation here.'

Livia had appeared out of nowhere.

'Jesus, she never gives him a break,' Andy whispered to Jen as Scott stood up.

She didn't answer. She didn't feel in the slightest bit sorry for Scott, and she warmed to Livia every time she put him in his place.

'A skill I obviously inherited from you, Mother dear. Excuse me, Jen. I must do my duty and mingle. Come, Andy, I'd like to introduce you to some friends.'

Livia took Andy's seat, and placed her champagne glass on the table. It was instantly refilled by a hovering waiter.

'So, my darling! Are you having a wonderful time? Did you enjoy the performance and the meal?'

Jen complimented her, for both her performance and her hospitality. As Livia told her opera stories from around the world, the staff refilled water jugs and wineglasses, and made empty dishes and cups disappear into thin air.

'Scott tells me you have a little son, Jen – Danny?'

'That's right, Livia. Danny is eight. With his dad this weekend.' She didn't know why, but she felt compelled to let her know that there was a dad on the scene.

'I remember Scott at that age. Such a sweet little boy, and oh how he loved his mother! I don't know where I went wrong after that really.' She laughed, but it was hollow.

Jen wondered if all the champagne had gone to her head.

'We know our boys inside out, Jen, that's one thing that doesn't change as they get older. It never changes. A mother's intuition is a strong thing.'

'I agree, Livia. Mothers understand their sons – and will do anything to protect them. I would for sure anyway. It's hard to imagine Danny all grown up, but I will always be there for him. He is the love of my life.'

'Jennifer, dear, I like you. From the moment I met you, I liked you, but I have seen how you are with my own son.'

'Livia, if I have offended you, I apologise. Scott and I don't gel. I'm sure he's a nice person, but I can't pretend to like someone when I don't. I am trying to be gracious here, but I'm not a liar. That said, I am very grateful to you for having me here, and your hospitality has been wonderful.' Jen scanned the room for Andy. He was nowhere to be seen, and there was no sign of Tess either.

'You don't need to apologise, Jen. I know my son, and I have seen how he looks at you. I'm sure by now you have had words, or he has done something to offend you. If you repeat this conversation, I will deny it of course, but you need to listen to me very carefully.'

Jen felt dread in her stomach. Before it was even said, she knew where it was going.

'I have suffered from depression all my life, dear. The real McCoy, not your off-days, and it has taken its toll on Scott. I tried to hide it from him as he grew older, but in his head over the years he has turned me into a monster. I have made mistakes, as all of us do, but when my husband committed suicide, Scott blamed me for it.'

'I'm so sorry to hear that, Livia. But you don't need to tell me any of this.'

'You need to hear this conversation, Jen.' Livia took a slug of the champagne, as if to steady herself, and continued with her story. 'Andy reminds Scott very much of his father in ways, which is strange as there is only a few years between them. I can see where he is coming from. Andy is a gentle kind soul, but he is easily led. Scott is a persuasive man, and I know you can see a change in Andy's personality when they are together. Scott feels the need to protect him, namely from wanton women like his mother. He believes all women are out to get what they can. He has never been fond of Andy's love interests.'

Jen couldn't argue with that one. Her brain had now gone into overdrive. Scott blamed Livia for the father's death, he hated women and, remembering what he had said about Sharon, she was starting to feel real fear.

'The last time I saw Scott look at or speak to a woman in the way he does with you it was Sharon. She was a lovely girl, but she had Andy on a short leash, at least when it came to Scott. You know what happened to Sharon, Jen?'

'Yes – she fell from the cliff …' Jen said hesitantly.

'Did she?'

'Livia, what are you trying to say here? Are you trying to tell me that her death wasn't an accident?' She could hear the panic and the fear in her own voice.

'I am Scott's mother, Jen, and like you said mothers will do anything to protect their sons. I will never admit anything and I will deny this conversation ever happened. But you need to protect your son now, and get as far away from Scott as you can. Your gut is right about him, dear. You need to listen to it. Protect your boy, Jen, and keep yourself safe. I am trying to put things right. I saw it coming last time and I did nothing.' She stood up from the table and wobbled slightly.

Jen was frozen to the spot.

'Now, my daahlliing! You don't want to be stuck with an old crone for the night. Get out into the garden and enjoy yourself. The band is about to start.' She looked at Jen, and then she walked away, calling to one of her friends.

Jens legs were like lead. She could see Scott out of the corner of her eye, but he wasn't looking in her direction. He appeared oblivious to the conversation that had just taken place.

'Hey! Earth to Jen!' Andy had returned.

'Sorry! I was dreaming.'

'What were you and Livia whispering about there? Aha, you look a bit pale – did she tell you she was charging you for the night or something?' He slipped his arm around her waist and kissed her on the cheek.

'Just mother stuff, Andy. That's all.'

She wanted to get the hell out of there, but was too scared to do anything. If she left now, Scott would wonder why and maybe he would guess about his mother saying something. What would happen then? Would he come after them? Who the hell could she talk to about this? She couldn't exactly chat to Andy. Sal was following Scott around like a lapdog, and Tess had enough of her own shit going on. Speaking of Tess, she looked around to see where she was. Doc was over with Sal, Clara and Scott. No sign of Tess.

'Come on Andy, let's join the others.' She was teetering on the verge of paranoia and didn't want Scott to suspect anything.

They walked over to the laughing group.

'Doc, have you seen Tess?' she asked.

'No. Haven't seen her. She's around here somewhere,' he replied, and turned his attention back to Clara, clearly irritated by the interruption.

A minute later Jen slipped away and made her way through the candlelit garden and back to the main house. She was about to head up the stairs when Andy called out to her.

'Whoa there, Jen! What's going on?'

'I can't find Tess anywhere, Andy. I'm worried about her. I think she might be heading home. Doc is being a real asshole.'

'Maybe she's up in her room, having a rest? Will I come with you to find her?'

'No, I'll go up to her. Can you go back out to the garden and see what the hell is going on with Doc and that Clara? There's a real vibe between the two of them.'

'What are you implying, Jen?'

'I don't know what I'm implying, Andy, but something is not right. I can feel it.'

She walked up the sweeping staircase, which was an accomplishment in heels, with a dodgy ankle. She had a really bad feeling in her stomach. The night had taken a turn for the worse, and she couldn't help but feel Scott had a hand to play in it, inviting Clara in the first place.

She knocked on the bedroom door. 'Tess, are you in there?' she asked as she turned the brass knob. It was locked.

'Jen, is that you?'

Jen could hear the distress in her voice and when Tess opened the door she knew she was in trouble.

Tess was as pale as a ghost. She staggered across the room and bent double over the vanity unit. Traces of blood had started to seep through the back of her dress.

'Oh, Tess!' Jen rushed over to her friend and tried to hold her up.

'It's the baby, Jen. I'm losing the baby.' She didn't move from where she was. 'I'm scared, Jen.'

'Tess, we need to get you to a hospital. I'll drive you. You need to sit down – or better, lie down.'

She guided her down to the floor as she moaned in pain. She was sweating now, and crying.

Jen's heart was in her mouth. She tried to dial Doc on Tess's phone, then Andy. She tried to recall her first-aid training from work, and drew a blank. She remembered something about lying down, elevating legs and putting a blanket over the patient, and that's what she did.

'Tess, can I leave you for a minute? I have to get Doc. I can't get anyone on the damn phone.' She tried to keep her voice even.

'OK.' Tess was sobbing now and had curled herself into a ball – the bleeding was getting heavier.

Jen kicked off her shoes and ran to the garden as fast as her ankle would allow. She scanned the crowd for Doc's head – he usually stood a foot taller than most. She saw Clara and him in the same place she had left them. She was out of breath and feeling almost hysterical when she reached them.

'Jen, what's wrong?' Andy grabbed her by the arm. 'Are you OK?'

'I'm fine.' She grabbed Doc hard, to turn him away from Clara.

'What the fuck, Jen? *What is your problem?*' he shouted.

'Doc, you need to come with me now.' She could see he was really drunk, and high on something.

'I don't need to do anything with you – are you for real, like?'

'Doc, it's Tess. She needs you.'

'Oh for gawd sake! What's wrong with her now? I'm trying to enjoy myself here. If she wants to go to bed early let her!'

'You selfish prick! Your wife is upstairs, having a miscarriage. We need to get her to a hospital *now*.'

Jen heard a roar, but it wasn't from Doc.

'*You never told me the bitch was fucking pregnant!*' Clara screamed at him, as her hand connected with his face. She too, was high as a kite.

Scott had the good sense to grab her, and tell her to stop making a scene.

'Jen, will I call an ambulance?' he asked as he shunted Clara in the direction of the house.

'No, I'll drive,' Andy said.

'Come on, will ye? We need to get to her.' Jen was nearly in tears by now. Andy couldn't drive, as he had been drinking – obviously not as much as Doc but still over the limit, and Doc was in no state to take his wife to the hospital.

They were back up in the room within minutes.

'I'll wait outside, Jen,' Andy said.

'Tess, honey, we're back!' Jen called softly as she opened the door.

Tess was grey in the face and clearly needed to get to hospital fast. Jen threw a couple of things into her weekend bag, before wrapping her in the throw from the bed.

Doc stood like a hare in the headlights, not knowing what to do or say. He had sobered up slightly. 'Tess, baby, are you OK?'

Jen cringed at his choice of words, and at how loud he was.

'No, I'm *not* OK, and you're in bits! You're not coming anywhere with me. Go back down to your drink and your woman! I fucking hate you! I've seen how you've been around that whore!'

He didn't even protest. He just looked at her, and walked out of the room in silence, past Andy and back down the stairs.

Andy knocked on the door and came in.

'Go get the car keys, Jen, and bring the car round to the front door,' he said as he crouched down beside Tess.

Jen didn't question it, she just went.

'Tess, honey,' Andy said. 'I know this isn't ideal, and you are scared, but I need to get you down to the car and to a hospital. Jen and I will come with you and look after you, OK? It's not far from here, OK?'

Tess nodded as the tears ran down her face.

'Do you think you can walk?'

She tried to stand but her legs were like jelly. She was lightheaded and looked as though she was about to be sick. She slumped back down onto the floor.

'I'm going to carry you, Tess. Is that OK?'

Again, she nodded her consent.

He scooped her up, still wrapped in the throw, and headed out of the bedroom.

Livia met them at the bottom of the stairs.

'Can I do anything, Andy?' she said with real concern.

'Sober her husband up and get him to the hospital in the morning,' he replied over his shoulder. 'Ring the hospital and tell them we're on the way in.'

Outside, he laid Tess on the back seat of the car, and jumped in the front.

'Take it handy now, Jen.'

They were at the hospital in less than twenty minutes, and a team was waiting there. Livia had rung in and explained the situation.

They sat hand in hand in the relatives' room and waited for some news. As the sun began to rise, Jen nodded off on Andy's shoulder. She was really amazed at how calm and together he had been in the situation. Calmer than her, and so kind to Tess.

The door opened and a doctor in scrubs came in with a nurse.

'Are you the husband?' He was quite gruff and less than polite.

'No, I'm not. I'm her friend. We brought her in last night.'

'How is she?' Jen asked him.

'Are you a relative?'

Jen wanted to lie and tell him she was her sister, but she went red at the thought and just shook her head.

'I can't go into specifics but she is out of the woods. She was quite poorly, but is going to be fine. She's out of surgery.'

'What about the baby?' Jen asked.

The doctor ignored her question. 'You can pop in to her for a few minutes. One of you. She needs rest, so don't stay long. Is her husband on the way in?'

The look that passed between Jen and Andy made it obvious to the doctor the husband wouldn't be running in with flowers any time soon.

'Keep your visit short. Well done for getting her in here when you did. She was lucky you were there for her.' He nodded and smiled before leaving the room.

'Go on in to her, Jen. I'm sure she could do with a hug.'

Tess was dozing on the bed when Jen came in.

'Jen … hi,' she croaked.

'Ah, Tess!' Ignoring the machinery and bags, Jen gave her friend a hug.

'The baby is gone, Jen.'

'Tess, I'm so sorry. You poor darling.'

'I'm OK.'

'You need to try and get some rest, Tess. I'll come back in a few hours with a bag of things for you. I can take Hugh for the few days as well. Leave it to me and your parents. We will sort it out for you, and I will talk to the staff in the pub.'

'Thanks, Jen. You're a real pal. He's having an affair with Clara, isn't he? He's gone, Jen – I've lost him too, to women and drugs.'

'Come on, Tess, you can't think about all that stuff now. You need to get some rest. We are here for you, it's going to be OK.'

Jen's words sounded so empty. Tess began to doze off – the after-effects of the anaesthetic. Jen slipped out the door and let her sleep. She needed to get back to Scott's house to collect Tess's things and her own, and then she would go see Hugh and his grandparents. Tess's mam and dad needed to know what was going on.

She also needed to find Doc and see if he had sobered up. After his behaviour over the last while, she would be mighty surprised if he was still at the house.

Chapter 23

She felt strange rocking back up to the house in daylight, still in her dress from the night before. All she wanted was a shower and some breakfast, but the urge to get away from Scott and never come near his house again was overwhelming.

Livia met them at the front door. It was half seven in the morning, but she looked bright and fresh. She insisted they go upstairs, shower and change while the chef prepared a good breakfast for them. Scott was in bed, but would be up shortly. She also informed them that Clara had left and, sometime after, Doc had gone too. That was hours ago.

'He didn't come to the hospital,' Jen said.

'Then we can assume he went after Clara,' said Livia.

Jen and Andy went up to the room. There was a real closeness between them now, the drama of the previous night having brought them together even more.

'Poor Tess,' he said. Freshly showered, he looked less shook.

'What kind of person would you be, to leave your wife and chase a bit of skirt like that, and under those circumstances? I could actually punch him.'

'I don't know, Andy. Doc was always fairly decent. It's mental – he has gone totally off the rails lately. It's no coincidence that this has all happened since he and Scott have become so pally.'

'Jen, you can't blame Scott for Doc having an affair. Come on, that's nuts.'

'Look – Scott invited Clara here, knowing that Tess was coming – a nightmare scenario for Doc. I don't know why Scott did that but I do know he's plying Doc with coke or something – and you know that as well as I do. So no, I don't blame him for the affair – I just blame him for everything else.'

'Why do you have it in for him so much, Jen? Is it a jealousy thing? Scott is a very good friend of mine. Do you feel threatened by that? He's never done you any harm.'

The memory of the day in her kitchen and the conversation with Livia from the previous evening were at the forefront of her head. If only you knew, she thought.

'Open your eyes, Andy. He's not all that he is cracked up to be. Just ask yourself why he brought Clara here. What was he trying to achieve with that?'

'Jen, I don't know, do I? Maybe he didn't know what was going on. Maybe he's sweet on her.'

He was getting really short with her now, and it hurt.

'He has no interest in her that way, Andy. Just trust me on that. Let's just go get breakfast and get out of here. I need to collect Tess's things and get down to her parents. They probably have no idea. I don't want to argue with you, pet.'

They arrived into the dining room to Sal and Livia at the table, waiting for them. Sal looked very hungover, as if she hadn't slept all night.

'How is she, Jen?'

'Not good at all, Sal. She lost the baby, and had to have surgery.

I'm not too sure of the details really. Are you OK?'

'Not really.' Sal started to cry.

Jesus, what now, Jen thought. Her heart went out to her friend.

'It all kicked off after you left last night. I was in the loo, and when I came back out Clara, Scott and Doc were having a big row. Oh Jen, I should have listened to you about him. He's a real asshole! Em, sorry, Livia.'

Livia swatted her hand in the air, and told her to carry on.

'Well, Clara was having a go at Doc about Tess being pregnant. It turns out they've been seeing each other for the last couple of years. Scott knew all about it too. Then Doc rang her one day out of the blue and told her that it was off, that he was trying to do the right thing by Tess. So Clara started sleeping with Scott, just to spite Doc I guess. Scott invited her here just to score off Doc. Then she and Doc saw each other, and they got it on again.'

'Two years? What an absolute prick!' Jen couldn't believe her ears. She knew that he was playing around, but it was incredible that it was for so long. 'Go on, Sal – what are you not telling me?'

'I kinda thought Scott and I had something. He was so upset the night of Arthur's funeral, I stayed with him, and one thing led to another. We've been seeing each other ever since. I thought he liked me, ya know?'

'Ah, Sal!' Jen let her cry on her shoulder.

Poor Andy looked on, slack-jawed. All this high emotion and drama in the last few hours was hard to get a handle on.

'Sal, my poor girl, I am so sorry,' Livia said, 'and I can only apologise to you all for the behaviour of my son. I'm embarrassed to admit it, but you are one of many, Sal. Scott doesn't have it in him to be faithful to a girl, or his friends.' She gave Jen a loaded look, as if to say: keep your mouth shut about last night's conversation.

'It's not your fault, Livia – he's a grown man,' Jen said. 'Anyway, we'd best be off. Sal, do you want to come with us?'

'Please eat before you leave,' Livia said. 'Breakfast is just about ready. I insist.'

A breakfast of Eggs Benedict was served, along with brioches, fresh fruit and steaming coffee. What's wrong with a fecking rasher sandwich and a mug of tea, Jen thought, but kept it to herself. She'd had a bellyful of all this pretentiousness and couldn't wait to get home to normality. After all this bullshit, surely now Andy would see through Scott? Jen would broach the other subject when she had done a bit more digging.

'So, when it all came out in the wash, Sal, what happened then?'

'Clara went up to her room, packed, and left. She was pissed – I don't know how she drove the car. They tried to reason with her, but she just ignored them. She just kept shouting at Doc about all the lies he told her about leaving Tess and moving in with her. Then Scott and Doc asked me to go get some drinks, which stupidly I did.'

Jen could feel the embarrassment and humiliation from her, and she felt so bad for her friend.

Sal stirred more sugar into her coffee and continued. 'When I came back into the drawing room with the drinks, the boys had decided to take the party to the next level, and they were snorting a load of coke. They were kinda oblivious to me being there and were resolving something – a dispute they were having. Doc told him he would keep working for him. His life was fucked now, he said, so in for a penny, in for a pound. When they clocked me there, they changed the subject. Shortly after that, Doc said he was going to see Tess. I told him the hospital wouldn't let him in at that hour. He just shook his head. He said he knew I was right, but he was leaving anyway. I tried to talk him out of driving as he was wasted. He just wouldn't listen. I thought he had gone to the hospital, and you would be able to deal with him.'

Andy stood up and walked out, without saying a word. He

looked completely disgusted by the whole story.

Livia said nothing – she just sat there with her head down, picking imaginary lint from her skirt.

'When Doc left, I challenged Scott about Clara. He laughed at me and told me not to take it all so personally. For Scott, it was all about getting the leg over, but it's so weird, we had some really nice times together over the last few weeks. I really thought he liked me.'

'I'm sure he does, Sal,' Livia said, 'but all this is a game to him. He will put himself first, always. He is charming, charismatic, and spontaneous. Whip you up into a whirlwind, and then let you down. My advice to you is not have any more contact with him, and move on. Don't worry about your exhibition – it was through my contacts he got you in there anyway. Now I think it's for the best if you all left.'

'Thank you *so* much, Livia – I'm very grateful,' Sal said. 'I'll just go get my bags then.' She got up and left the room.

'Livia, I am truly sorry your night was ruined,' Jen said. 'Thank you for your kindness, and your advice.' She looked at Livia, and felt so sorry for her. She knew in that moment she had been cleaning up Scott's messes all her life.

'Jen, I hope Andy is worth the trouble you have brought to the door of your friends. Arthur Jenkins' death was the turning point for Scott. He's out of control now. You need to be very careful from here on in. Scott hates you, like he did Andy's wife. He won't stop until you are out of the picture. He is beyond obsessive and possessive.'

'I will go to the Guards.'

'There is no point, dear. I will deny everything I ever said to you, and it will look as though you are as obsessive over Andy as he is. Which, in a way, is the truth. You are just coming from a good place, unlike him. Goodbye, Jennifer. We both know you are no longer welcome here.'

And with that, she was gone.

Jen went up to the room Tess had been staying in and gathered up her belongings. There wasn't a trace of her husband in the room. He had taken everything with him, including the last of Tess's money – Jen spotted the purse, open and empty on the vanity unit – it hadn't been there the night before. She went to her own room to get her things, but Andy had already packed it all up and taken it to the car. She was in love with him, and she knew he was worth it.

Andy and Sal were at the front of the house when she came downstairs.

'He's not here,' Andy said.

'Are you surprised?' she asked as she opened the boot. 'Sal, are you sure you're OK to drive?'

'Sal, I can take your car if you want to travel with Jen – it's no problem.'

Sal gave Andy a massive hug.

'You are one in a million, Andy. I hope you realise that. Thanks for the offer, but to be honest I just need some time to myself. I'll come round tonight for a cuppa and a chat.' She released him out of the hug, and turned to Jen. 'I'm sorry I was such a shit to you over the last while, Jen. We'll talk about that soon. He really did a sales number on me and I'm ashamed how I let him influence me.'

'It hurt, Sal. We do have some talking to do, but it's OK. We will sort it out, Sally Pally Pee.'

Sal knew that Jen didn't hold grudges, and they would do just that. Fight and argue, debate and solve. The habit of a lifetime.

'Don't text him, Sal. He's not worth it.' Jen looked at her before getting into the car. 'I mean it. Let it go, Sal. See you tonight.'

Jen watched her in the rear-view mirror as they drove away.

'You do that a lot when you're thinking about something, you know.'

'Do what, Andy?'

They had been sitting in silence for about twenty minutes. It was an OK silence.

'You pull at your earlobe.'

She smiled at him. He always noticed the little things about her, and it was a welcome distraction from the shit-storm raging around them.

'What are you thinking about?' he asked.

'I was just wondering if Doc had gone home to Hugh, or if he's up in Dublin with that trollop.'

'He's most likely in Dublin, Jen. He's not going to be ready to face the music yet.'

Jen was heartbroken for Tess and Hugh. She also felt so guilty about not telling Tess about the phone call she had overheard that night in her house. It probably wouldn't have made a difference, but she felt as though she had been deceiving her friend. When she's feeling better, I'll tell her everything, she thought.

It was only half nine in the morning, and it was Sunday. She knew that Tess's parents would be up and heading to ten o'clock Mass. They were creatures of habit. She would go over to the house for two o'clock – no point in spoiling the Sunday roast on them. Tess had texted her, and asked her to tell them. She wasn't up to speaking to anyone just yet. Jen told her she would be in as soon as everything was looked after. Hugh was going to have a sleepover with Danny – that way her parents would be free to go in and chat. Against Andy's advice, Jen tried to ring Doc. His phone was turned off. She left a message anyway.

It was going to be a long day. Jen closed her eyes and just let it all wash over her. She couldn't think straight about anything. Each of them was in a private hell, but none more than her. How could she tell the man she loved that she believed his best friend to be a killer? It was all surreal and frankly crazy. She had texted Will early in the morning to see how Danny was – he was fine, and he was safe with Will.

209

'I think the best thing for you, Jen, is a couple of hours' sleep and then we can face everything together. How does that sound to you?'

They had just pulled up to the house.

'I could do with a nap. I'll make some tea and bring it up for us – you warm up the bed.'

Andy was in his own room when she got upstairs with the tea. He was sitting on the bed, staring at a photograph.

'Jen, have you been looking through my things? Specifically my wedding album?' He held the picture up for her to see. It was a wedding photo.

Her face absolutely burned with shame. He was calling her out on invading his privacy. She couldn't deny it. The damn picture had obviously fallen out of the album.

There was no getting out of it now. She laid the cups down on the locker and sat beside him on the bed.

'I'm sorry, Andy.'

'Why did you nose around in my stuff, Jen?'

'Your laundry was mixed up with mine, so I came in to leave it on your bed. I saw the box at the side of your locker and I couldn't help myself. I'm so sorry.'

'Why didn't you tell me you had looked at it?'

'For feck sake, what did you want me to say? Here's your clean underpants and, by the way, you looked so handsome on your wedding day? I was just curious, you know. I wanted to see what Sharon looked like more than anything.'

'I would have shown you, you know. All you had to do was ask.'

'Would that not have been really weird for you, though?'

'Of course it would have been. No one wants to imagine sitting on a bed with their new girlfriend, showing them pictures of their dead wife.' He laughed without mirth.

She was caught up on the fact he had used the word 'girlfriend' for the first time. Nice one, Jen, he's talking about his dead wife and you are secretly delighted with your new label. She felt embarrassed.

'Ah Andy, I can only apologise. It was bad form to do that, but I swear I was here for just a few minutes and then gone again.'

'It's OK, Jen. I understand. I guess I would have been curious too. Now get into that bed, and get some rest. In future, if you're curious, just ask me.'

'I will.'

They drank their tea and got ready for bed. She set the alarm on her phone before curling up in his arms. It was the first time since she moved in that she had slept in this room. She knew they would tackle what was to come together.

Chapter 24

Jen's shoes clicked as she walked down the corridor in the hospital, a contrast to the squeaking shoes of the ward assistant power-walking in front of her. It was the usual scene. People talking in hushed tones, a nurse rattling a trolley, curtains pulled around beds and visitors laden down with grapes and flowers.

Reception had informed her of Tess's ward and room number.

She found her inside the door of the ward, on the left, and luckily she was in the end bed – it afforded a tiny bit of privacy. As well as that, the bed beside hers was empty, giving her some yards' distance from her neighbour. What was it about hospitals? Jen wondered. People tended to share their life stories with their fellow roommates, and no detail was spared. Tess had company. Another pale-faced inmate in a dressing gown, talking loudly about rectal exams and blood pressure. She had the good grace to excuse herself as Jen made her presence known.

'How are you today?' she asked as she laid the bag of clothes she had picked up at Tess's house at the side of the bed.

'I'm better today, Jen. I'm sore but I'm OK. I was pretty much out of it all day yesterday after the drugs.'

'I know. Your parents called me in the evening and I arranged to pick up these things for you. I rang the ward as well and they told me not to come in – you were asleep at that stage.'

'Thanks for looking after me the other night, Jen. You and Andy were amazing. I was a mess, and Doc was no help.'

Jen studied her friend for a moment. She was doing her usual thing, putting a brave face on it all, but she could see the devastation in her eyes.

'Has he been in touch, Tess?'

'Nope.'

What a complete asshole, Jen thought. 'He hasn't been in touch with any of us either, and up until an hour ago your parents hadn't seen or heard from him. Hugh is in great form though – they were up half the night last night watching movies in Dan's room. Andy has taken them down to the harbour today to fix the boat with him. He can stay as long as he likes with us, Tess. The joys of summer holidays.'

Tess lay back on the pillow and closed her eyes. Jen flicked through a magazine and knew her friend would speak when she was ready.

'The doctor came round this afternoon to speak to me.'

'And?'

'It was a bit more serious than I thought, Jen. I was lucky you found me when you did. It was the beginning of sepsis, caused by a urinary tract infection.'

'Oh Tess, you poor thing!'

'I had been feeling like crap for a couple of days, but said nothing. I really wanted to have a nice weekend with Doc so I didn't complain. It gets worse though.'

'Tell me, Tess.'

'The miscarriage was probably caused by the infection and

stress … that's what did the damage.' Her voice broke and she stared to sob. 'I didn't even know a bladder infection could cause a miscarriage!'

'Tess, honey. It's not your fault. You poor pet!'

'Jen, he cheated and stressed me out of my mind … and I can't help but wonder if the infection was his fault. He was sleeping with someone else so maybe he passed it on to me. I'm going to get tested for STIs – I'll have to after his bed-hopping! Goodness knows how many people he has slept with.' She was trying to speak but it all came out in breathless sobs.

Jen cried with her, and didn't know what to say. She held Tess's hand and tried to comfort her. What a surreal situation! 'Oh my God, Tess. That's horrendous. Maybe you should …' She thought better about continuing.

'I'm seeing one tomorrow.'

'What?'

'A counsellor – that's what you were about to say.'

'Tess, you have so much to deal with right now. A counsellor will help you, and so will we.'

Jen wanted to get into her car, go find Doc and punch him in the face. She felt like doing the same to Scott. He wasn't responsible for the affair of course, but he was responsible for driving Doc off the rails, plying him with drugs, and bringing that rotten cow to the house for the weekend.

'Scott came in to see me today.'

'What did he want? He has a lot to answer for, Tess.'

'He arrived in with flowers, and to see how I was. He has been trying to locate Doc for the last twenty-four hours – without success, I might add.'

Jen didn't believe that for a moment. Scott knew damn well where Doc was – they were probably partying together.

'He's going to look after the pub while I'm in here. Our business deal has gone ahead and the work is starting at the end of August, when the kids go back to school.'

'Are you sure that's wise, Tess? I mean, you don't really know him at the end of the day, and how much do you really trust him?'

'Funny, he said you might say that, all right.' Her voice had gone up a notch, and there was a quality to it Jen didn't like.

'Tess, all is not what it seems with Scott. Did he mention anything about Doc working for him?'

'What are you talking about, Jen? And why are you so down on Scott? He filled me in on quite the story here today.'

Jen knew she was angry now, and there was something really amiss.

'You knew about the affair, Jen, didn't you?'

'I had my suspicions after the party in my house, Tess. But I didn't know for sure.'

'Scott seems to think differently.'

'Scott can feck right off, Tess. He is a bad egg. He was the one that brought Clara there for the weekend, knowing full well Doc was cheating on you with her.'

'So are you denying you challenged Doc on Friday night about it?'

'No, I'm not denying it. I challenged him and he told me he was working everything out with you. He had made a promise to you and he wasn't going to fuck up again. This was all before the Clara one arrived.'

'I feel so betrayed by you. Jen. You should have told me that night. How can I trust a friend that keeps it all from me?'

'So you're telling me, on the strength of a conversation with Scott, that you're holding me accountable for this? Tess, that's really fucking unfair. And while we're on the subject, who do you think is plying Doc with cocaine every weekend? There is something going on there, Tess. Doc is out of control, but it's since Scott came on the scene. How can you not see that? And how can you be angry with me and not with Scott? He brought her to the house!'

Jen was furious at him. He had twisted the whole story and was implying she was in on it with them. She stood up to leave.

'Tess, we shouldn't be having this conversation now. You don't need to hear all this shit at the moment.'

'Perhaps if I had heard this 'shit' as you call it, sooner, I wouldn't be in this mess now.'

'Did Scott tell you what went on after we left the other night?'

'No, and to be honest I don't want to know.'

'Of course he didn't tell you. He filled your husband up with drink and drugs, and then let him off to follow his fancy woman. Scott knew all about the affair, and was sleeping with her as well. He only brought her to score off Doc. Doc is working for him, Tess, and it's something to do with drugs. He's probably blackmailing Doc. Can you not see any of this? Scott is a nutter, Tess. He tried to attack me in my kitchen a couple of weeks ago, and he implied he had something to do with Sharon's death. He also threatened to cancel Sal's exhibition in Dublin if I said a word. He was sleeping with Sal as well.'

'Jen, are you actually listening to yourself here? You are accusing Scott of being a drug-running rapist who killed his best friend's wife. He's blackmailing my husband and threatening you? You have one wild imagination. Are you really that obsessed with Andy? Scott is a very successful businessman, Jen, and he has his shit together. Are you so jealous of their friendship you would make up mad stories like that?'

Jen knew Tess wasn't herself, and was a bit out of it on all the drugs in her system, but her accusations stung. She hadn't told anyone about what happened in her kitchen until now, and Tess didn't believe her. He was a snake. He had got to Tess, and twisted everything. In her state she had fallen for it. Sal nearly had too. He was trying to destroy her, and drive a wedge between all of them. Andy was obviously next on his list. Would he poison his brain against her too?

'Tess, I don't want to talk about this any more. You need to concentrate on *you* at the moment, and we need to get you better. We will have this conversation again, but not here, and not now. You have known me a long time, Tess, and you know me well. I'm beyond disgusted you would even say something like that to me, but I'm not going to argue any more. You need to think about this though – every situation has Scott centre-stage.'

Jen looked at Tess, and she could see some of the fight go out of her. She would think about everything that was said, and Jen was sure she would see through his lies. Tess was a very shrewd woman, and as soon as she was feeling better she would see through all this bullshit.

'Now, I have been down to the pub – the gang are going to shift around the rota between them to cover over the next week. They have called in a couple of extra staff members, and if they are stuck, I told them to ring me – and of course you have just said you have Scott looking after things as well. Your house is still standing, I have fed the cat, there're bits in the bag for you and Hugh collected his toys. He wants to come in and see you tomorrow if that's OK.'

'How is he, Jen?'

Jen sat back down and squeezed her friend's hand.

'He's good, pet. He had a little cry last night, but I told him you had a bad tummy bug and the doctors were giving you medicine to make you better. He asked me about his dad, and I told him he was away working. I couldn't think of anything else to say.'

Tess started crying again. 'Whatever about not giving a shit about me, Jen, how could he leave Hugh like that? How could he do it?'

'I have no idea, Tess. I can't understand it either. He is struggling for sure. He'll be back soon enough, he'll have to.'

'His phone is still off. I never want to see him again. I hate him. He has humiliated me, cheated on me, and now this. He has betrayed both of us. I'll never forgive him for that, and that's why I rang my lawyer this morning. I want to divorce him.'

'Pet, I know you do and maybe that is the right thing to do, but you need to get yourself well again first. All that will be sorted in time.'

'Dad wanted to kill him stone dead yesterday. In spite of it all, it was so funny to see him like that. He actually reminded me of Scrappy-Doo. Then Mam was here, shocked at the language coming out of his mouth. Hilarious – you know Dad, he's so quiet usually.'

It was nice to hear her laugh. The whole situation was rotten, and her life had really changed that night. She was going to need her friends and family around.

'The bastard also took the car, Jen, as well as about sixty quid out of my purse.'

'Jesus, Tess, I never thought of the car. I had guessed about the money – I spotted your empty purse yesterday morning. What a complete rotter!'

'Rotter? Ha, Jen, I love the random shit you come out with when you're angry.' Tess was really laughing now. Part humour, part hysteria.

A bell rang in the distance, the signal for the visitors to leave. They ignored it.

'Tess, please don't worry about anything while you're in here. Everything is under control. I have taken a couple of weeks off from work, and Andy is not back out until next week. We'll hang on to Hugh, until he wants to go back to Nanny and Grandad. The pub will be grand as well – as you said, Scott is there too.'

'Jen, thanks for everything. We'll sort out our differences when I get out of this dump, but I would ask you to respect the fact Scott and I are in business together and, for my sake, if you see him around, you need to be polite.'

Jen didn't answer her. She was still really offended over it all, but today was about Tess and getting her better. She believed

Tess's attitude was all bravado and eventually the facade would fall to the ground. Then the real work would start. Poor Tess, she thought, what a terrible time for her!

'I'll get Hugh to give you a call tonight and, as I said, I'll bring him in tomorrow morning if that suits?'

'I would love that, Jen. I should be out in three or four days.' She pointed to the IV in her arm. 'Antibiotics. I have to finish the course before they'll let me out.'

'Look, Tess. You need to stay here, rest and get better. The hard shit starts when you get out of here and back to some semblance of normality, whatever that is. Try for the few days to just rest. If you need me, day or night, just ring me, OK?'

Tess cried again, and didn't answer her. A stern-faced nurse appeared at the door, pointing at her watch, and Jen knew no matter what she managed to say in the remaining minutes, it wouldn't stem the tide of tears. She gave Tess a hug and smoothed down the blankets, pushed the tissues and water glass within reach and made a beeline for the door.

Chapter 25

His head was pounding and he had the shakes, but that was the least of his worries. He tried to sit up in the bed and piece together what had happened. The reality was he didn't even know what day it was. The room stank of stale drink and cigarettes. *What have I done?* he asked himself. *What have I done?* The tears ran down his face and he felt sick with shame. *Tess. Tess. Tess.*

He was standing in front of the toilet trying to urinate when the contents of his stomach hit the back wall. Here he was, covered in his own vomit and piss, the sum of what his life had become.

The apartment was quiet. Scott wasn't back yet. Flashes of the previous day came back to him, leaving Weybridge coked out of his mind, and driving to Clara's apartment rather than the hospital. In a strange way, he thought he was doing the right thing by not going to the hospital in the state he was in. He vaguely remembered the journey and shuddered to think what would have happened if the Guards had pulled him over. He remembered the row that ensued between him and Clara, who had not entertained him for too long before turning him out onto the street. She lived in a pretty rough area, but in his state he didn't care. He went to the nearest early house. Memories of cheap whisky and drinking partners, and going back to a random dingy flat in the middle of the day, smoking joints and drinking warm cans. Anything to block out what was going on. *Tess. Tess. Tess.* He did remember that as soon as his stash of coke was gone, they were done with entertaining him, and showed him the door. Faceless people, people that he wouldn't generally give the time of day to.

Another vague memory of a taxi driver, reluctant to take him in his car, having to pay up before the journey even started. Luckily he remembered Scott's address – it was located close to the Clontarf Castle Hotel, his saving grace – luckier still, he had just caught Scott on the way out the door. He would give him a bed for the night. Not satisfied to go to bed at that stage, he ransacked the drinks cupboard and pushed himself further into oblivion with a bottle of Jack Daniels.

Was today Sunday or Monday?

The shower felt like tiny darts all over him, his throat was sore from the vomiting. What the fuck was he going to do? Where was Tess, and was she OK?

He vomited again, and watched the bile mix with the water on his feet.

You have hit rock bottom now, Doc. You lying, cheating bastard. You should be ashamed of yourself. Your wife and your son deserve better. Your baby is dead. It's all your fault.

He couldn't stop the train of thoughts coming.

Everything felt surreal. He went into the kitchen and put the kettle on. Even that was a chore. His hands didn't feel like his own – he couldn't stop the shaking. He thought about food, but that's as far as it went. Back to the bedroom he went, and threw on his stinking shirt and trousers. He had no recollection as to where his jacket was.

'My car. Where is the fucking car?' he asked the wall. He rifled through his pockets. Keys, phone, wallet – check. They were all there. Well, that's a bonus, he thought.

He turned on his phone, and waited. The messages started to come in, one after another after another. He was afraid to look but he had to. Out of nowhere, he started to cry. The fear had taken him over and he knew this was only the start of it. *Your game is up, Doc.*

Most of the messages were from Clara, and they were vile for the most part. He deserved it, he wasn't disputing that, but she was no lady. Notifications of three voice mails. Two of them were from Clara – he deleted them without listening to them. The other was from Jen. Simple and to the point, explaining to him his wife was still in hospital and his son was staying with them.

He sat with his head in his shaking hands. He knew now it was Monday evening. His wife had been in hospital since the early hours of Sunday morning and she hadn't bothered getting in touch with him to let him know what the story was. Nothing from her, not a thing. Was it any surprise that he was having an affair? She cut him out of everything. She didn't deserve him really.

His conscience had other ideas. Words like *cheat, bastard, deserving of everything that is thrown at you,* were flying around his head.

He couldn't stand the noise. He needed a drink.

The sober and logical part of his brain screamed at him: '*Get your act together, Doc! Get your car, and go home. Clean up the mess you have made and go see your wife. She's in the hospital for fuck sake!*'

He opened a shoulder of vodka, and poured it down his neck. His stomach went into spasm but he kept it in there. He just needed to think for a bit.

He sat down on the couch and reached for the television remote. The RTÉ news was on, meaning it was around six o'clock. The newscaster was droning on but his brain couldn't keep up with her.

'So, you found the vodka then?'

Doc leapt up off the couch and let a roar out of him.

'Scott! Are you trying to give me a heart attack, sneaking up on me like that?'

'I live here, Doc. I wasn't sneaking. If the damn TV wasn't so loud, you might have heard me.'

'Sorry, man.'

'You need to lay off the booze, Doc, and get your shit together.'

He really felt like shit now. Imposing on his friend, drinking all his booze, and it looked as though he had just worn out his welcome.

'Have you rung her yet, Doc? Your wife, I mean, not your bit of skirt.'

'No.'

'I went to see Tess today.'

Doc spun around on the couch and looked at him. 'Is she OK?'

'Of course she's not OK. She was pretty sick, she lost the baby and has a nasty infection.'

'Oh no!'

Scott didn't feel sorry for him. He had messed up, and got caught. If he hadn't got so out of it on Saturday night, it might have turned out differently. Doc was greedy when it came down to it, and his fondness for recreational substances was beginning to take him over. That suited Scott – as long as Doc had a want for it, he would need him. He only brought Clara to the party as he knew Doc was starting to have second thoughts about working for him. He needed a bit of leverage. Now, maybe this would all work out to his advantage. Doc couldn't live here of course – there could be no connection back to him – but he could set him up in a place and he would be really at his beck and call then.

'She will remain in the hospital for a few days, and then will go home,' he said. 'Jen seems to have everything under control. Hugh is with her, and she has sorted out staff for the pub. She was the one who broke the news to your parents-in-law about the affair, and losing the baby. You might have had some hope of fixing things with Tess if Jen wasn't on the scene, but she has really turned Tess against you now. You are fucked, man – home gone, wife gone, kid gone. As long as Hugh stays with Jen and her young lad, you won't have a hope of seeing him.'

Doc knew that Jen was a really loyal friend to Tess, and he knew he would be in for a roasting if he saw her, but the way Scott was describing her wasn't really right.

'Jen is just looking out for her friend, Scott. She's not that bad.'

'Well, according to your wife and your parents-in-law, Jen was the one that sealed the deal, and made Tess call a lawyer from her hospital bed, to initiate divorce proceedings.'

'Nah, man, you're getting it wrong about Jen. Tess is not that easily influenced. That would have been her call.'

'Why are you defending her, you stupid fool? I was there with your wife today. I have it from the horse's mouth. I tried to reason with her, and asked her to at least wait until she was feeling stronger before making any major decisions. She was having none of it.'

Doc didn't know what to think. Jen would be loyal to her friend and it wasn't in her nature to interfere like that, but why would Scott lie? Divorce proceedings – what the hell, he thought. His head was spinning. His mind went back to the conversation on Friday night: 'I'll blow the whistle, Doc.' Fucking bitch, Jen, you are a fucking bitch.

'I need to call Tess now.'

'No, you don't, you need to let her cool off. Send her a text, and tell her you're thinking of her and will be in touch soon. To be fair to you, she was the one that pushed you into Clara's arms. Your marriage was on the rocks anyway – this just sealed your fate.'

Doc really wanted to ring her. Just to speak to her and ask her if he could come down and talk to her. Even if she said no, at least she would know he had tried to make some form of contact.

'And whatever you do, don't ring Hugh. He is with Jen and she will not let you speak to him.'

'He's my son and Tess is my wife. I need to speak to them.'

'Look, do what you want. But if I were you, I would have another drink there to calm the nerves and then think about calling them. Are you hungry? Maybe we should go and get something to eat. Let the dust settle, man – you're in no state to go anywhere tonight. What if you ring her and she wants you to come to see her straight away? You can't. Clara texted by the way – your car is clamped outside her apartment.'

'Right, come on then. Let's go get some food and a beer.' He picked up his phone and dropped it into his pocket. 'I'll just get my shoes.'

Scott took out his phone and texted Tess.

Hi, Tess. I have tried to encourage Doc to give you and Hugh a call. He is a bit out of control at the moment, but is here and is alive. I will work on him. Get some rest and I'll call you tomorrow. Scott X

The response was swift.

Really appreciate it, Scott, but I couldn't care less. Chat tomorrow. T X

Chapter 26

'Looks like this weather is here to stay for a few days, Jen.' Sal was soaked to the skin, and the brown-paper bag that had been wrapped around the wine bottle had disintegrated. 'Is Andy due back in?'

'Here's a towel, Sal. Do you want to run upstairs and change into something of mine? You're drowned!'

'I have the PJ's here, I'll hop into them. So much for our balmy mid-August heatwave. *Pfff!* It's always the same.'

'Sal, quit with the weather talk, you sound like my mother. Dinner won't be long.'

Sal and Jen had organised a night in to have a proper catch-up.

'How is Tess doing, Jen?'

'She's OK. Came home from hospital a few days ago and is definitely on the mend. You know Tess, she's so strong. Just keeps ploughing on, and keeps it together. Little Hugh stayed here with us for the few days, while his nanny and grandpa kept vigil at her bedside. I don't think I have ever seen her dad so angry – the poor man will either kill Doc or have a heart attack. They only know half the story of course.'

'What do you mean, only half the story? I thought they knew about Clara?'

'Yeah, they do. It's complicated, Sal, and should be very private but it may have an effect on you, so I need to tell you.'

'What?' Sal looked distraught. 'Surely no-one thinks I knew about this?'

'No, nothing like that. Look, the short story is, Tess thinks that her infection may have been caused by something Doc passed on to her from Clara. She's getting tested for STIs. You might want to get checked if you were sleeping with Scott the same time as she was.'

'Oh for God's sake, I feel sick now! *Yeugh!* What kind of STI?'

'No, no, Sal, there's no actual evidence of an STI. The doctors put the miscarriage down to stress and the urinary tract infection – which could be just a normal occurrence. It's just that Tess has the notion that Doc might have given her the infection. All I'm saying is get it checked to be on the safe side.'

'OK – Jesus Christ, where will I get the time for a doctor's appointment? The exhibition launch is in a few days.'

'You are going to have to make time, Sal.'

Sal was pacing. 'I feel disgusted now. Why did I sleep with him? I'm dreading the launch – what if he's there?'

'You'll be fine, Sal. It's going to be a great evening for you, and even if he does show up, we will be there with you, so don't worry about it.'

'Actually, Livia called me this morning, just to let me know everything was fine, and I wasn't to worry about anything other than arriving on time to the event. She couldn't guarantee that he wouldn't be there, but she will, and will keep him in check – her words, not mine.'

'Well, that's good then.'

'And what about Tess, Jen? Has she seen or heard from Doc?'

'He finally sobered up and rang her. After a lot of grovelling and crying, she finally gave in and agreed to meet with him. Tomorrow.'

'You don't think …'

'Not a chance of them getting back together if that's what you were going to ask.'

Jen stood at the stove and stirred some fresh basil into the arrabbiata sauce. The garlic bread was in the oven, and they were having a big bowl of salad with it. Sal had splashed out and bought a really good bottle of Sancerre, a favourite of Jen's, even though she was predominately a red-wine woman.

Sal was really excited about the exhibition. She had spent the previous day in the gallery discussing everything and they too were excited. They kept reassuring her that her talent was really rare, and it stood out from the crowd. Sal wasn't convinced, but it made her feel proud anyway.

Jen poured the sauce over the rigatoni as Sal lit the candles. It looked pretty in the kitchen, but the place was now like a furnace from the heat of the stove. They were sweating – it was just as well the wine was chilled.

Jen put the pasta into a serving bowl, and the hot bread onto a board. She placed them in the centre of the table with serving spoons, plates and grated parmesan.

Jen broached the subject gently. She wanted to know about it, but knew Sal was still feeling the after-effects of the fall-out with Scott.

'Have you heard from him, Sal?'

'Nope.'

'Have you made contact with him?'

'Yep.'

'And?' Jen spooned pasta onto her plate, and didn't look at Sal while waiting for an answer.

Sal tore garlic bread in two. 'No response.'

'What did you say to him, Sal?'

'I just told him I appreciated what he had done as regards setting up the exhibition, but I would be grateful if he didn't come.'

'He won't show, don't worry.' Jen believed he would absolutely make a point of showing up, making everyone uncomfortable, and then he would leave. She wouldn't be surprised if he brought Doc and Clara along for the hell of it.

'Jen, the reason I asked you if we could hang out tonight was I wanted to apologise properly for being such a silly cow.'

'Apology accepted, Sal – now have some pasta.'

She heaped pasta onto Sal's plate and passed her the parmesan.

'Jen, I'm serious.'

'So am I, Sal.'

'He just really sucked me in. Did a real sales job on me. I feel like a total fool. We spent a lot of time together over the last couple of months and I felt like I was getting to know him. I really thought we had a connection, and that he cared about me.'

'Sal, we have all been blinded by men in the past. Don't beat yourself up too much about it. I just can't stand him and, to be totally honest, I'm a bit afraid of him now.'

'He wasn't happy about you and Andy getting together, that's for sure. He spoke a lot about Andy's wife, and how she kept him on such a short leash when Scott was around.'

'Is it any wonder his wife kept an eye on him, Sal? Look at the crap that went on with Doc. But . . . did he ever say anything else about Sharon? Anything about her accident?' Jen was on tenterhooks now. She wanted to tell Sal the whole story about what had happened in her house, what he had said to her and what his mother had said, but it might be dangerous to do so. She decided to keep quiet for now. She loved Sal but she wasn't totally sure whether she still held a candle for Scott.

'It's funny you should mention that. He passed a couple of

comments one night about it. We were in his place, having a few drinks, and he was talking about the night she died. He was fairly pissed, and he muttered something about her knowing it was going to happen. I thought he was just talking about the poor girl's mental state. That weirded me out a bit and I just changed the subject. He was a bit of a freak in other ways too, if you get me.' She threw a look at Jen.

'Sal, I think I can live without the details of your sex life with him.'

'I'm serious, Jen – I know we all have our preferences, but he was a bit much to be honest – he liked to get a bit heavy-handed. I told him that wasn't my thing, and he just called me a prude. I think he's a bit of a closet *50 Shades of Grey* fan.'

'Sal, please, *ewwww!* That's gross.'

'Ah Jen, you sound like a teenager!'

Sal was feeling a bit better about herself now, Jen could see. She needed to get stuff off her chest, and over a bottle of wine was the perfect time. Jen hoped she was sensible enough to steer clear of him, even if she did have any remaining feelings for him.

'Do you still like him, Sal?'

'Right at this moment, no, Jen. I think he's a total arse, but if he sauntered up to me when I was full of wine, I don't know if I could resist him. He's so hot, and about as charming as they come – you have to agree with me on that one, Jen.'

Jen didn't answer. He was hugely attractive, there was no denying that, but his character made him very ugly in her eyes. The more she thought about everything, the more convinced she was becoming that he might have killed Sharon. She almost laughed at the notion of sitting at her kitchen table, trying to figure out how to catch a killer. Maybe she had read too many James Patterson novels and her imagination had got the better of her. It was all crazy. His threats were real, but did that make him a murderer?

'Jen, why do you hate Scott so much?' Sal asked. 'I know he's been quite vile to you, and he did have some part to play in the whole mess with Tess and Doc, but I have never seen you like this with someone before.'

'He absolutely makes my skin crawl, Sal. From the first moment I laid eyes on him, I felt as though there was something amiss with him. I suppose, since the accident as a child, Mam always lived in a constant state of pre-empting any situation that could be dangerous.'

'Which you have continued with Danny.'

'Yes, I have, Sal, and it's something I will continue doing with him – the drills in case of fire or some other natural disaster, and the drills for if someone ever broke in or tried to harm us.' She laughed to herself as she thought about the last evening they were doing the safety drill.

'What's so funny, Mrs Health and Safety?'

'Last Thursday we did one of our drills, and it was for in case of a . . . ah Sal, I'm a bit embarrassed to admit this one.'

'You are going to have to now. I'm intrigued.'

'In case of a tsunami.'

Sal absolutely collapsed into a fit of laughter. 'Jen, that's the best one yet. We live in bloody Wexford. A flipping tsunami?'

'For your information, Sal, it has happened in Ireland. Go google the West Cork tsunami in 1755 if you don't believe me. A friend of mine from Cork told me all about it once, and they reckon it could happen again. Scary stuff.'

'Are you serious? A tsunami?'

'Yes, believe it or not.'

'And what's the drill then? You live on the beach, not a mountain in sight. How do we cope with a tidal wave here in the harbour?' Sal was sceptical.

'Grab the wine and kiss our arses goodbye, I suppose!' Jen retorted. 'It's just about giving him the skills to cope with something that might happen, Sal, instead of being paralysed with fear and fright. I don't think I'm doing any harm to him, and we always make it fun, rather than doomsday-prepper-type stuff. Mind you, the Zombie Apocalypse is on the cards for next week, so I need to source a bow and arrow.'

'Jen Harper!' Sal was about to go into one of her rants when she saw Jen's face crack up with mirth. 'I'm sure Andy would get a kick out of you dressed up as Lara Croft though!'

They howled laughing at the prospect of Andy finding them in full combat gear, sporting crossbows and rifles.

'Andy likes me just as I am, Sal. Scars and all.'

'And so he should, my lovely, and so he should. Has he mentioned any more about this trip of his at the end of the year?'

Jen winced at the thought of it. He hadn't spoken about it lately, but the ticket was booked and she overheard him on the phone the previous week speaking to a friend about it. He was still going. She had known that from the start, but it was starting to bother her. Danny would be back to school in a few short weeks, and before long Christmas would be upon them.

'As far as I know, he's still planning it, Sal.' She tried to sound light-hearted about it, but she knew Sal had seen through her. She also knew she wouldn't push the issue.

'A lot can happen in a few months, Jen – we don't know what's around the corner.'

'If you say to me "What's meant for you, won't pass you by" I might thump you, Sal.'

They both laughed at that.

'Do you love him, Jen?'

'Sally Pally Pee, the answer to that question is a resounding *yes*. I tried to pretend that I didn't, but I do. I have no expectations, I don't know where it's going to take us, but yes, I love him. And he's a total ride – that's always a bonus.'

They were both tipsy by now, but the wine had run out. Jen went to the drinks cabinet in the living room and got the bottle of Jameson. She also pulled a packet of cigarettes out from under the sink.

'Will we have an Irish coffee, doll?' she asked as she produced a carton of cream out of the fridge.

'Jen, I thought you'd never ask.'

'Ah here, Sal, don't bother going outside for a fag. Danny isn't here, so we can smoke. Just don't tell Andy. I told him I had given up again.'

While Jen set about making the coffee, Sal turned on the record player. As per usual, she pushed the coffee table out of the way – there would be dancing, there always was. Like clockwork, Jen would make the coffees, set them down and go upstairs to get into her pyjamas. Then the dancing would start.

'Sal, I'll just . . .'

'I know, Jen – PJs. Get them on you. It's time for a bit of Bruno Mars. My celeb crush. How you have him on vinyl is beyond me!'

'Amazon, Sal.'

They danced their little legs off. Jen's ankle was beginning to ache slightly, but Jameson was a good anaesthetic. They both danced all the worries and the sadness of the last few weeks right out of their system. For that moment in time, they were just two pals without a care in the world, having fun. They were caught up in their little happy dance, oblivious to the world that existed outside the walls.

Eventually they flopped on the couch and put the world to rights. Girl talk, into the wee hours. Sal was the first to start yawning, and they called it a night. She would sleep in Danny's bed, as usual. Same bed, just a different house.

They blew out candles, unplugged appliances, and even filled the ashtray with water.

They were so busy with the task of getting to bed that neither of them noticed the face looking in at them through the kitchen window. As they turned the last of the lights out, the person outside slipped away.

Chapter 27

Tess felt in control. After today, there would be no looking back. Physically, she was feeling stronger – mentally, she was in no place to wallow in self-pity. It was just her and Hugh now, and he needed her to be strong.

He had the good grace to ring the doorbell. She had wondered about that. Would he just walk in through the front door, or what would he do? She had put the chain on anyway, just to prove a point. He had lost all those liberties the day he cheated on her and his son.

He looked terrible – thin, drawn and sleep-deprived. A tiny part of her wanted to hug him and tell him it would be OK. Too late for that. She couldn't break now, she had been preparing for days. It was done. Time now for the arrangements. His eyes fell on the bags lined up in the hallway. Four of them, everything he owned.

'You have been busy.'

His tone was caustic, and she was having none of it.

'I will keep you on the doorstep, Doc, if you speak to me like that again. There is no room here for jibes and sarcasm. Your choice: watch your mouth or leave.'

He nodded and she led him inside.

She knew he had expected her to be a wreck when he arrived, begging him to stay and work things out. She had taken her time that morning getting ready for his arrival, carefully applying her make-up and of course wearing heels. The universal rituals and the female psyche, the tricks, the rules, the reinvention. Of course she had got a new haircut – it was therapy – cutting and slicing the old away, watching it fall to the floor in a swirl, before being gathered up by an over-enthusiastic heavily made-up young girl and lobbed into the bin. Good analogy for a broken marriage.

She had laid out cups and coffee, purposely choosing the smaller cafetière – she didn't want him here for too long.

She had placed the paperwork from the hospital beside the cafetière.

'We have a lot to talk about, Tess.'

'Actually we don't, Doc. The only thing that needs to be finalised is the divorce, and access to Hugh.'

'Please, Tess, don't be so cold to me. We can't just throw away our marriage like this – we owe it to each other to talk this out.'

He was keeping his voice calm and even – her threat at the front door had worked. She wanted to scream and shout at him about betrayal and hurt and heartbreak, but to what end? What was done was done.

'Doc, our marriage ended when you jumped into bed with your fancy woman. Our marriage went up in flames when you continued the affair for nearly two years, and any love or forgiveness in my heart turned to pure and simple hatred when I lost the baby.'

'Tess, please, it wasn't my fault about the baby. Everything else –'

'Oh but Doc, that's where you are wrong. It was wholly your

fault about the baby.' Her words punched the air like staccato notes. 'I contracted an infection and that's what killed the baby. For all I know it was from you and your dirty whore. You will burn in hell for that, and you should hang your head in shame. It's all in the paperwork in front of you there if you want to check, so don't even comment. You live with that now, Doc.'

He opened his mouth to speak and closed it again, his face ashen with shock.

'So, as you can appreciate, we are done. Nothing to talk about. O.V.E.R.'

She was beginning to enjoy this in a weird way. The cold rage and the hatred were too powerful for tears. She wouldn't break, at least not now. He had visibly shrunk in front of her eyes. The power had shifted, from him to her.

'Now. Here's how it's going to go from here on in. You will move out. You will pay half the mortgage, until there comes a time where I am in a position to sell – then we will split the proceeds. I don't really give two flying fucks where you get the money from. You will pay child support every week and you will see Hugh on alternate weekends, in your parents' house, here in the harbour. You will not bring him within spitting distance of that woman or your love nest.'

'You have it all figured out, don't you? Fucking control freak! It's no wonder I was having a fucking affair! A fucking bully is all you are – you pushed me into her arms, you silly bitch!' *Doc, stop. You know that she is right. This is your fault. Apologise. Give her that much.*

'Ah, hello, Mr Victim Mentality! Let me listen to your abuse about how I didn't understand you, and pushed you into her arms – in the hope you can justify your disgusting behaviour in your own head. All your drinking and whoring and drugging. Sure of course it's my fault!'

She was up in his face now, and she noticed drops of her own saliva on his face. He was staring at her, and she didn't recognise his face any more. Her Doc was long gone. She walked to the far side of the breakfast bar, to put some space between them.

'Get your bags, and get out of here. We are done.'

'Tess, please, I'm sorry. Can we try and figure something out? I'll go to rehab, I'll give up the music. I'll do anything it takes. You can't do this to me. What about Hugh? I own half this house – it's my home and I will not be thrown out like a dog on the street. Please, Tess, I'm not going.'

'You stupid big lumbering fool, it's too late for any of that! You will go – and I can make you – if you knew anything about the law you would know I'm within my rights to stay in the family home. Let's just leave it at that, will we? As a gesture of good will, you can keep the car – I have sorted something else – I have removed my name from your policy as well, so it's all yours. The bank account is empty, and I'm closing it.' She fired a roll of fifty-euro notes across the table at him. 'Unlike you, I'm not a cheat or a thief. That's half of what was left. Your parents were here yesterday. I will communicate with you via them. I have plenty of good friends and family around me. I don't need or want you here. You are some role model for your beautiful son! Did you give him any thought before you wrecked his family?' It was the only point in the conversation where her voice showed any hurt. 'I could learn to live with you shitting on me from a height, but for the way you have hurt him I'll never forgive you.'

'You like the sound of your own voice, don't you, Tess? All rehearsed, and everything squared away. Fucking Jen, egging you on of course, in your ear poisoning you, and pushing you to get rid of me!'

Doc, stop, don't do this. She's right – why are you saying all this shit?

'Jen is my friend, Doc. She is looking out for me and my son, something you are incapable of doing.'

'I'll choke the fucking interfering bitch! You mark my words, Tess. She will pay for this. I'm blaming her for all this shit you're spouting.'

'Sure you have to blame someone, don't you? None of this is your fault, is it, hon? Poor little Doc, you are so hard done by. Now get your bags, get out and go back to your fancy woman.'

He pulled the wedding ring off his finger and slammed it down on the breakfast bar.

She left him in the kitchen, walked down the hall and opened the front door. She went out and checked the car, making sure there was nothing belonging to her or her son in it.

When she returned to the house he was standing in the hall.

'Take the house keys off the fob, and go,' she said.

He fiddled with the fob for a few moments then threw two keys at her. He picked up the bags in one go, strode out, threw them in the boot and left without another word.

The house was quiet now. She returned to her cold coffee at the breakfast bar.

She looked at his wedding ring, too far gone to feel emotion. She looked at her own hand, and the pair of rings which hadn't left her finger in a decade. It was quite a job, but they came off. She fired all three of them into the back of the junk drawer. Game over.

She had a meeting with Scott scheduled for the afternoon. She needed him now more than ever, caught between a rock and a hard place on all counts.

Chapter 28

'Where's the visitors' book gone?' Sal asked Ruth the receptionist as she walked into the space.

Ruth smiled and answered her in gentle tones. 'Sal, you are starting to let your nerves get the better of you. The book is where it's supposed to be. Come into the back office and have a cup of tea with me – you have loads of time before anyone arrives. Your hair is perfect, and your dress is stunning. Breathe!'

'I feel sick with nerves and I can't stop going to the bathroom – if I have tea now, it will be the end of me. But thank you, you are really kind.'

'Sal, I have worked here for a long time. The thing I love about my job is that on a rare occasion we have an exhibitor who is really rare, and special. The magic ones. You are one of those rare gems, Sal.'

Sal blushed purple. 'Ah thank you, that's a lovely thing to say.' She probably feeds everyone that line, she thought, and then instantly felt bad – she was a nice woman.

'Tonight is the start of something very special, Sal. Just hold on to that thought when you feel yourself getting nervous. I'll get back to it here, and see you later. You have about thirty minutes before people start to arrive.'

Sal took one last look around the room. She couldn't believe it was her work on the walls of this mecca of the artistic world. Maybe she would even get a deposit or two put down this evening. The staff expected quite the crowd – new artists of note, as they called her, usually got a good response. All the heads would be in, and a group of her own friends and family were coming as well.

She ran through her speech in her head again. That was the bit she was dreading most. She hated doing public speaking, and she always got cotton mouth.

'Hi, Sal.'

'I thought I asked you not to come, Scott.' She kept her back to him, trying to control her breathing.

'You did, and that is why I came now. I wanted to apologise for what happened, and I wanted to wish you luck. The pieces really look amazing – you are very deserving of a place here.'

She turned to face him, and felt a pang in her stomach. He looked wonderful, in a royal-blue suit. Her resolve was waning, and she just wanted to jump on him, right there in the middle of the floor.

'I'm sorry for hurting you, Sal. You deserved better than that. I'm not proud of it.'

'It's fine, Scott. Water under the bridge. I can't be too mad with you really. If it wasn't for you, I wouldn't be here tonight.'

'I merely got you the audience. Your talent has you here tonight. Not me.'

She had never seen him so contrite, or genuine. They had been friends after all. It was her feelings that muddied the waters – he had never committed himself to her.

The first few people began to spill in through the door.

'Go do your best, Sal. Good luck.' He kissed her on the cheek.

'Stay, please?' She looked up at him, unsure of what was going on. She squared her shoulders, and floated over to her guests.

'May I have the bill, please?'

'Certainly, sir.'

'Thanks, Andy. That was a lovely treat.' Jen was feeling a tad merry. The wine had gone straight to her head.

'Come on then, Jen. We'd better get to the exhibition. I'm enjoying this date of ours!'

They walked round the corner, hand in hand. The restaurant was adjacent to the gallery, and they basked in the late August sun. Jen had been there earlier to drop off flowers from Tess.

Sal ran over to them as soon as they entered.

'I'm so glad you two are here.'

Her face was shining, and Jen felt so proud of her friend.

'I got the flowers from Tess. She's so good.'

'She did want to be here, Sal, but the last couple of weeks since she threw Doc out have been hard. She was right to take off on that little holiday with Hugh.'

'Sal, honey, I'm so delighted for you,' said Andy. 'The bloody place is packed. You look beautiful.'

'You don't look too bad yourself, Andy.'

'The dicky bow wasn't my idea – I feel like a twit.'

'Well, you look the part anyway.'

A waiter arrived with a tray of canapés and champagne.

Jen skipped the food and took a glass of bubbly.

'Cheers, Sal! To your success!'

Clink went the glasses.

'Go on and mingle, Sal.'

'It's showtime now, Jen. Time for the speech.'

The curator introduced her and after his speech it was her turn. Her speech was flawless. A number of questions about the pieces were asked and, all in all, the exhibition seemed to be going well.

Jen spotted Livia, looking incredibly beautiful and comfortable in her surroundings. They nodded to each other and smiled.

Then she saw him.

'What the feck is he doing here?' She looked at Andy. 'Did you know he was coming?'

'Of course I didn't know he was coming. Leave it alone. Just concentrate on our date night, OK?'

Jen could see him there, with Sal, introducing her to another suit. He was touching her arm and she was all smiles. She couldn't believe he had the cheek to show up, after what he had done to Sal and in general, but there was little she could do about it.

He saw her looking at him, and he smiled and waved over to them.

'I don't fucking believe it, he's coming over here!' she hissed, grabbing another glass from a passing tray.

'Jen! Andy! How are you?'

Sal had made a beeline over behind him, looking less than enthusiastic about the meeting.

Jen looked around frantically for Livia but couldn't see her.

Andy watched in disbelief as Jen drank the whole glass of champagne in one go.

'Steady on there, Jen dear,' Scott laughed. 'If you're not used to drinking champagne, it can go straight to your head.'

The sarcasm wasn't lost on Andy.

'Anything to make your presence tolerable, Scottie dear,' she replied.

'Now, darling, mind your manners and know your place,' he said with a smirk.

Scott was enjoying watching her get agitated. She knew it, and she was tired of saying nothing to him.

'This is Sal's night, dear, not yours,' Scott said, 'so let's all have a drink and be friends? Waiter! Here!'

'Yeah, Scott. Let's have a drink, and then you can tell us all how you took care of Sal.' Her voice was wobbly with wine, and she was beginning to get louder. A couple of disapproving glances were thrown in her direction. She knew she was being obnoxious, but she didn't care. She hated him, and everything he stood for.

'Jen, I asked him to stay,' said Sal. 'He came here earlier to apologise, an apology I have accepted, so let's just forget about it, OK?'

'Sal, are you mad? Please don't be a fool and let him bed you again. He's a creep!'

'OK, Jen, that's enough,' Andy said. 'Scott, I think you should go mingle with your friends over there.'

'Yeah, Scott. You go mingle with your friends and see what shit you can stir for them.'

Scott stood back and watched the show unfold.

'Jen, will you stop for God's sake? You're embarrassing me.' Sal was close to tears, and they had an audience.

'Is everything OK here, ladies?' Ruth, the nice receptionist, had arrived over to them. 'Sal, I think your friend has had quite enough to drink – perhaps it's time to call her a taxi?'

'*Excuse me?*' Jen turned on her. 'I am fine. I would be grateful if you would butt out of our conversation.'

'Right, that's it. Jen, we are leaving. *Now.*' Andy was furious. 'Ladies, I apologise. Sal, can you apologise to Scott for me as well. No need to call a taxi, the hotel is around the corner.'

'*Are you for real, Andy?*' Jen yelled. 'Don't you dare apologise on my behalf! You don't know the fucking half of it!'

'Thank you, sir, now remove her, please,' Ruth said. 'Sal, you need to go speak with your guests.'

Jen swung around and strode off, Andy practically running through the gallery trying to keep up with her. She stomped away ahead of him, like a bold child. She was mortified over the showdown, but couldn't stop herself. He was a monster and it was about time people started realising that.

She had to wait for Andy to let her back into the hotel room. He opened the door for her, and looked at her with a face of vengeance.

She was on a roll now, and headed straight for the minibar.

'Do you want a drink or not?' she asked. She poured the gin with such a force into the glass that half of it sloshed out over the side. She wanted to lick the damn liquor off the table.

Andy didn't like confrontation, she knew that, but she felt like shaking him. She was indignant over him apologising on her behalf.

'Yep, I'll have a drink, Jen, if it means less for you.'

'Jesus, are you implying that I'm an alco as well as a drama queen now?'

'What has got into you? For the love of all that is good, will you calm down? What the hell was that back there? You nearly ruined Sal's big night. Way to go, Jen!'

'Scott is a prick, Andy, and you are too blind to see it. Actually no, he's not a prick, he's an evil bastard. He has totally manipulated you and you are like a fucking lapdog around him.'

'Language, Jen.'

'Will you stop talking to me like I'm a fool? He's had it in for me since day one, and you are trying to defend him.'

He smirked at her, and raised an eyebrow.

'What are you laughing at?'

'You're funny when you're drunk.'

'Andy, don't laugh at me.'

'Jen, I love you, but my patience is wearing thin. Yes, Scott has behaved badly but he's my friend and has been very good to me over the years. You are just going to have to suck it up and get over it.'

'Get over it?' She was finding it difficult not to slur her words slightly – she should have eaten more at dinner but she had been too excited about the exhibition.

'Keep your voice down, Jen. Calm down, for fuck sake. What Scott did to Sal is really none of your business. She's a big girl, and she can fight her own battles. She asked him to stay there tonight, and it wasn't your place to kick off at either of them. You are rambling and talking shite. Let it go now, and let's just chill out.'

'Chill out? How the bloody hell can I chill out when I have a potential rapist-slash-murderer trying to get me out of the picture because he is obsessed with you, Andy?' Even she realised how crazy that sounded when the words had left her mouth.

'Oh for fuck sake, Jen! You are deluded. I would have never pegged you as the jealous type. Is this what all this is about, and now you are turning him into a monster? Who did he rape, Jen, who did he murder?'

'He tried to attack me in my kitchen one day and threatened to come back and rape me! Everything has gone to shit since he came on the scene. He has ruined my friendship with Tess, lying to her about me knowing everything! And all that shit with Clara, he did that for fun. Are you blind? Where does he get all his money, Andy? They are not that well off – you could see it in the house, the money isn't there. It's all a bloody show. He's up to his neck in drugs, and has dragged Doc into it all as well. Cokeheads, the pair of them! Who did he murder? You told me yourself you never really believed Sharon took her own life – she was afraid of heights – she would never have gone up that cliff on her own, in the dark! Well, Scott practically admitted to me that he murdered her!'

He said nothing. The silence was ominous.

She looked at him, waiting for a response.

Then he hissed: '*How dare you!* Stop this bullshit right now, and we will talk about all your crazy accusations when you are sober enough to make sense. How fucking dare you! Don't you *ever* bring my wife into a drunken rant again!'

'Your wife?'

'She's dead, but she's still my wife.'

His face was dark with emotion and she knew in that moment she had really messed up. He was disgusted with her, and everything she had said had gone over his head. He didn't believe her, it was that simple.

She hung her head and turned her back to him.

The bedroom door closed with a bang, and she was left alone.

Chapter 29

Andy slung himself up onto the bar stool and ordered a drink. He would go back up to her in a while when she calmed down a bit. He was furious with her for ranting shite at him. He actually couldn't remember the half of it now, but she had said some mad things about Scott. Yes, Scott had behaved badly in the Doc/Clara affair but that didn't excuse Jen attacking him in public, making a show of herself and wrecking the night for Sal.

But something was niggling at the back of his brain – he couldn't quite get a grasp on it – something about Sharon.

'I thought I might find you here – you are so predictable, mate.'

Scott had appeared at his elbow.

'Just in time too, I'm fresh out of Jameson here.'

'Waiter, two of those.'

'Scott, I'm sorry about tonight. Jen has been under a bit of pressure lately – you know what girls are like when it comes to their friends.'

'Apologising on her behalf, Andy? That's never a good way to be with a woman. Look, it's fine. Her sheer craziness tonight was admirable in a way. She's like a loyal dog – cute but aggressive at the back of it. No harm done.'

Andy didn't like the analogy, but he let it go. He'd had his fill of angry words for one night, and just wanted a quiet drink.

'How is Sal?' he said to change the subject.

'Oh, she's fine. We're all going to go have dinner a bit later. Do you want to come with us?'

'No, man. Thanks. I couldn't think of anything worse. Art talk and posh accents. No offence.'

'None taken.'

'How did you know where I was anyway?'

'I overheard you talking to Jen in the gallery. I know you better than you think, Andy. I knew you would end up sitting at the bar by yourself, waiting for the storm to pass. I thought I'd check in on you, make sure you were OK.'

'Cheers, Scott.'

'You're a good friend of mine, Andy. You know that. Come what may, I'll always have your back. I'd never let you down.'

Andy wasn't quite sure what to say to that. It was true. Scott was a really close friend, and he really enjoyed his company. He could see how he rubbed people up the wrong way but his heart was in the right place.

'Thanks.'

They spoke for an hour or so about all sorts, random small talk, and as the Jameson flowed Andy relaxed. They talked about the old college days, the night they had first met, the music debates and the girls.

'Andy, I've been doing a lot of thinking lately. I've got to the point in business where things are beginning to take care of themselves, and I have staff to do the donkey work for me. I think

I need a bit of time out. I've decided to book a ticket and come with you in January. For part of it at least. I have my own itinerary in my head but I'm sure we can overlap at times. See a bit of the world together, eh?'

Andy knew he wouldn't be going on that trip. It had been on his mind of late and, although he hadn't mentioned it to Jen, he didn't want to leave. Telling Scott would be tricky.

'Well, maybe. I've been giving this trip a bit of thought as well, and I'm starting to wonder if it's a good idea.'

'*What?* You can't be serious?'

'Well, I haven't decided for sure about going or staying, I just feel like I'm happy where I am for now.'

'What about all your talk about getting out of Dodge, and getting away from the small-town mentality? "The Tribe" as you called them, the "I was born in the village and I'll die in the village without ever owning a passport" people. Andy, what are you talking about here?'

Andy said nothing. The upcoming trip at the end of the year was losing its appeal.

'Ah, I get it now. It's because of her, isn't it? Has Jen tried to talk you out of it?'

'Yes, it is kind of to do with Jen, man, but no, she hasn't tried to talk me out of it.'

'Do you really want to be lumbered with a woman and someone else's kid, Andy? It was bad enough that the old bat forced you to stay there until the end of the year – she was bonkers anyway – but do you really want to live out your life in that hick town with all the hick people who don't know shit? Andy, you need to see the world and live life, not get stuck in that hole.'

'I'm going to let your comments about where I live and my neighbours and family wash over me, Scott. I will chalk that down to your arrogance. You would be surprised the lessons you might learn about etiquette and decorum if you spent any time in my community.'

'I would rather gouge out my own eyes than live that kind of life. Are you telling me she is worth throwing your life away for, and just getting stuck down there, until you are drooling on yourself and incontinent?'

'I love her, Scott.'

Scott was absolutely gobsmacked by the revelation. 'Andy, how long has it been since you started sleeping with her? Three or four months? Get a grip on yourself. She may be a good lay, but she's not marriage material. You need to remember that. She's not good enough or intelligent enough for you. Your life will never amount to anything with her. She's nice, but she's a plaything.'

'Scott, stop. I haven't made up my mind, but the thing is, it's my decision. No one else's. If I decide to stay, I will. End of.'

'Andy, don't make another mistake when it comes to being led by a woman. What is it with you and controlling women? She has probably been dropping suggestions all this time. I can't blame her for wanting to snare a man – it certainly makes life easy for her with a live-in lover – but she is bland, man, no offence.'

'Scott, fuck off, man. You *are* being offensive now.'

'OK, OK! I'm sorry. You're right, I crossed the line there. She is a nice girl – just don't rush into anything you might regret. Next thing she'll be announcing she's pregnant, and that's when your life is over for sure.'

They were both drunk at this point, and Andy was getting wound up by Scott's arrogance. 'Let's change the subject, and agree to disagree on this one, OK?'

'Fair enough, Andy. I just need to ask you one more question. I don't know how to say this really but …'

'Just get on with it.' Andy said.

'How do you know she feels the same way about you?'

'I don't, but I hope she does. We get on so well, and she makes me laugh. It's easy company. You know me, I'm not a big talker most of the time but I just feel myself in her company. She's kind, and she's genuine. Loyal too, you saw that for yourself tonight. She is just an all-round amazing girl.'

'Do you think she's trustworthy?'

'Yes, I'd like to think so anyway. Why do you ask?'

'Has she mentioned anything to you about me and her?'

'*What?*'

'No, no. Not like that. I'm not going to try and sleep with my best friend's woman, but I think I may have a bit of an idea as to why she dislikes me so much.'

'Go on, Scott. This better be good.'

'I called round one day to see you – I had forgotten you were out at sea. To cut a long story short, she made a bit of a pass at me. It wasn't anything too obvious, but I think it was there none the less. It was when you had just started seeing each other. Please don't say anything. I would feel like such a fool if I had misread the situation and caused trouble for her, but I think that's why she doesn't like me. Maybe she had a thing for me, and then you came along. Please don't think I'm being arrogant, mate. I'm just trying to protect you here.'

Andy felt like he had been slapped in the face. Scott has to have misread that, he thought. There's no way Jen would do that.

'She made a pass at you? Come on, Scott. Pull the other one. Not every woman in the world wants to fall into bed with you. Maybe that's why you don't get on – maybe *you* have a thing for *her*.'

'Andy, be serious. As I said, it was the most subtle of things, but it happened none the less.'

'OK then, Scott, you tell me exactly how she made a pass at you. Tell me. Making a pass at someone is just that – how can it be fucking subtle?'

'Andy, please don't get upset. I was asking her how things were going with you two, and how nice it was to see you happy. It's not like she threw herself at me, she simply insinuated that I could come down some night and she would show me how she liked to turn you on.'

You are a *liar*, Scott, Andy thought. You have always been a competitive prick when it came to women, just like in our old college days. He would ask Jen but for now he wasn't taking the bait.

'Now I've heard enough, Scott. Remind me again why we are friends. You think I'm a country bumpkin, with no mind of my own and every woman I have ever been with only has me because they can't have you. Your superiority astounds me. Ooh, are you surprised I could put a word like *superiority* into a sentence, Scott?'

Scott started to chuckle – a chuckle at first and then it turned into a big booming laugh.

'I love when you get indignant, Andy. It's quite the spectacle.'

'Well, stop winding me up with your nonsense then, and we'll be fine.'

Scott drained the last of his drink, and called for another.

'This had better be a nightcap, Scott – I'm wrecked.'

'Sure – actually, I really need to get back to Sal.'

The Jameson was served quickly. Andy got the impression the barman was trying to get rid of them – it was nearly closing time in the main bar.

'Are you and her back together?'

'Certainly not. I blew it when she found out about Clara, but I like angry make-up sex, so who knows? She is on a high tonight and might oblige.'

Andy just shook his head.

Scott drained his glass. 'OK, Andy. I must dash. We can hook up next week. I'll drop down to you?'

'Yeah, sure, just text me and we can arrange it. Thanks for dropping by tonight. I appreciate it.'

Scott gave him a hug and told him, not for the first time that night, that he was always there for him, no matter what happened.

'*Ciao*, Andy. See you soon.'

Andy sat at the bar and sipped on his whiskey. It had been an eventful night to say the least. He wouldn't mention to Jen he had spent the night at the bar with her nemesis. She had obviously fallen asleep shortly after he left. He had checked his phone a number of times and there was no message from her. She didn't surface in the bar either. It was so out of character for her to behave like that. All this drama with her friends had hit her harder than she was letting on. He wondered about the comment she had made, about Scott attacking her in the kitchen. Had she really made a pass at him, which backfired and now she was blaming him for it? No, she wasn't capable of that, or was she? There is no way Scott would make a pass at his girlfriend. It wouldn't happen, or would it? As for what she said about Sharon – well, just drunk, angry, horrible crap.

He would let it all go, and just see what she said in the sober light of day. He wanted to see her. He left the bar, and went back up to their room. When he let himself in, she was fast asleep on top of the bed, one shoe off and one shoe on.

Bless her, she's tiny really, he thought. It's no wonder she got drunk so quickly. He would have a chat with her in the morning, and all would be OK.

Fearing he would disturb her, he grabbed a couple of blankets from the wardrobe, and slept on the couch by the window.

Chapter 30

'What is it with me getting flowers from only women this week? Come on in, Jen – I'll get the kettle on.'

'Thanks, Sal.' Jen was feeing quite sheepish.

'Dan, do you want to go into the studio and draw me a picture? I'll get some water for Butch. Leave him outside, OK? He'll eat my brushes again.'

'OK, Sal. Mam still gives out about how much Butch cost her that day.'

They all laughed at that. Jen had been mortified over all Sal's new brushes being eaten by her pup on a visit, and had torn into town to replace them all. She had of course bought the most expensive ones in the shop. Six years later, Sal still had most of them.

Sal's kitchen smelled of fresh coffee and sandalwood. The little cottage was adorable and the owner's personality oozed from every brick.

'So, how was your head the other morning, Jen?'

'Really awful, Sal. Listen, about the other night –'

'Jen, it's OK. Honestly. I get it. I honestly do.'

'Did it go OK for you, after?'

'It was great. I sold three out of eight. Delighted with myself!'

'Sal, that's amazing. Well done. I'm so proud of you,'

'And look at this, a write-up in the *Indo*. *Whoop!*'

'Ah Sal, you are going to hit the big time. Don't forget me when you're famous.'

Sal made her way over to the kettle. 'So what happened with you and Andy when you left?'

Jen took a seat beside the little Aga, and shook her head.

'Sal, I was drunk and we had a massive row. I said a few things to him that I shouldn't have, and things have been really weird since. He has been really short with me. I don't know where he was after he left the room. He did come back that night, but he had been on the beer somewhere.'

'The Jameson actually. He was with Scott, Jen. I'll fill you in on that in a minute, but you need to tell me exactly what you said to Andy.'

'Why, Sal?'

'Because whatever it is you're thinking about what Scott is capable of, I'm beginning to think you're right. You were fishing for information about Scott the night I stayed in your place. Tell me, did you tell anyone about that night?'

'Sal, what is going on? You're scaring me now.'

'Jen, start at the beginning, and tell me everything.'

Jen didn't know where to start really. She filled her in about the night of the dinner party when he had threatened her on the patio, over the exhibition. She also told her about Tess, and the money for the pub. She told her about telling Tess some things in the hospital and that she didn't believe her.

'Don't mention any more of this to Tess, Jen. I don't think she can be trusted. She and Scott seem to be very close at the mo. Makes sense really if they are in business. OK, go on.'

She continued and told her everything. The day in the

kitchen, the threats, what Livia had said to her about Sharon and everything in between. The row with Andy and how she had blurted it all out to him.

Sal just shook her head when she was done. 'It's quite the tall tale, Jen. Sounds like a novel.'

'Please, Sal. You have to believe me. I'm starting to feel really scared of him. I feel like it's all coming to a head.'

'I believe every word you're telling me, Jen. All of it.'

Sal stood at the kettle in silence for a few moments and let the news sink in for both of them.

'I got to thinking after my night in your place, and the more I thought about it, the more it freaked me out. Things he had said about Sharon, the way he went out of his way to be horrible to you and to try and pickle my brain about you as a person. It was like he wanted you out of the way, and he wanted me and Andy all to himself, but I can't figure out why. I thought maybe he was in love with Andy, but no, that doesn't add up.'

'I know, I thought that too. I think he's just possessive of him, and doesn't want me or Danny around. I'm scared he's going to hurt us, Sal, and despite all that has happened Andy is totally blinded by him. It's fair to say he's almost brainwashed.' Jen was so relieved she could finally talk to Sal about this.

'The possessive thing I get – you should have seen him at the exhibition, he was like a guard dog with me – but I think it's more than that. When he came back from being with Andy the night of the exhibition, he was really agitated. He was too clever to come right out and say what was on his mind, but he seemed to be furious about Andy being in two minds about travelling in January.'

'What? Andy hasn't mentioned anything to me about that damn trip in January.'

'Scott is blaming you for getting your claws into him. He knew I was a bit pissed off with you, so he didn't hold back. He was pretty mental to be honest, and it all got a bit scary.'

'What happened, Sal? Please tell me he didn't hurt you?'

It was Sal's turn to look scared and upset. 'After dinner, we went back to his place. I was still on a bit of a high from the exhibition, and was having great fun. We had a few drinks. They were hopping off coke, and he was getting louder and more arrogant as the night went on. People got sick of listening to him – not his usual crowd, I expect.'

'Please tell me you left with them?'

'Well, no. But I did leave. The guys at the gallery had booked me a room in one of the hotels they use so I was safe enough, I knew I had somewhere to go.'

'So what happened?'

'He asked me to stay and have a nightcap which I did, and at this stage he was rambling about all sorts of shit. Doc, you, all of us, and Sharon too. I made my excuses and tried to leave, but he had other plans. He wouldn't have been capable of anything like, but he got a bit heavy-handed with me. Grabbed me, pushed me on to the couch and tried to get it on with me. I pushed him off and legged it. It would be funny really, if it hadn't been so serious. He was wasted, and all over the place – grabbed me hard enough to bruise me though.'

She slipped her cardigan off her shoulders and both her upper arms had black-and-blue marks.

'I believe you about the attack in the kitchen, Jen, and I believe he had the capacity and the desire to kill Sharon. I also think he has the same capacity to harm you. Jen, I'm frightened, and we need to do something.'

Part of Jen's brain had still been hoping she was being overly dramatic and wrong about how sinister he was. Now Sal was confirming all her feelings and she felt shaken.

'Tess can't be trusted, Jen. She and Scott are in contact all the time. He has her right where he wants her – her life is a mess, her marriage is over and I think he is pretty much blackmailing her with money. God knows, she needs it at the moment, but he has

260

taken advantage of that. He is absolutely loaded, Jen, and I believe that his money is coming from drugs.'

'He hasn't been down in a while though, has he?' Jen asked.

'Here's another thing that struck me as odd. He mentioned something in the apartment about you and I not being able to dance full of wine – "chavs in pajamas" he called us. I thought he was just talking about the weekend in his house, but now I think he was talking about the night you and I danced in your place. Did you tell him about that night?'

'Of course I didn't! I don't think I even went into detail with Andy about the fun we had. You don't think he was there?'

'That's exactly what I am thinking, Jen.'

'But Butch would have heard. Oh! Shit, he wasn't there.'

They were both completely freaked out by the idea he had been watching them. And it had been raining hard that night – what kind of a maniac would creep around a house in the dark and the rain?

'Jen, I think we need to go speak to Andy about this, and to the Guards.'

'But where would we even start if we went to the Guards, Sal? We have no proof of anything! As yet we only have suspicions. And a few threats. Besides, Andy has gone back to work. He won't be back till the day after tomorrow.'

'OK, well, maybe you and Danny should stay here for the couple of days until he is back? I have a meeting in Waterford this evening, but will be back for nine. You can just come down yourself later on.'

'Sal, are you sure we're not letting our imaginations run wild here?' But her gut was telling her otherwise.

'Maybe, but I would rather look like a fool than be a dead fool, Jen. Let's just play safe for a couple of days until you speak with Andy.'

'OK, let's do that.'

'Jen, I'm going to have to get going here. I can't get out of this meeting. Are you going to be OK?'

'I will. I have a lot of stuff to get done today, and I want to get over to see Mam and Dad. I'll text you later when I'm coming down.'

She gathered up her things, called Danny and went out to find Butch. Danny came out behind her, covered in paint.

'We'd better go home and get you changed before we go see Nanny, Dan.'

Sal texted a few hours later. She was delayed and wouldn't get home until after nine.

Sal. Don't worry. All is good. Dan wrecked so we will stay home. I'm fine. Hugs, and drive carefully. See you tomorrow X

K, hon. If you're sure. Hugs back to you X

Jen wondered if it would just be easier to call it a day with Andy. She knew she was in love with him, but that sometimes wasn't the be-all and end-all of things. Plenty of people in the world were meant to be together but for whatever reasons they couldn't. He was still leaving at the end of the year as far as she was aware – he hadn't mentioned to her he was in two minds about it so why not call it a day? Danny wouldn't be too affected by it. They slept in separate rooms when he was at home anyway, so he would be none the wiser.

It was all a big dramatic mess, and she felt that she had a big part to play in the making of said mess. Even if she did call it a day with Andy, her conscience wouldn't allow her to just forget everything. She would have to tell him about this. Then again, what proof did she have? For all she knew, she had added two and two together and got ten.

The wind had picked up considerably and she wondered how Andy was doing out on the high seas. Great – that's all I need now, she thought. Not only do I have being murdered in my bed to worry about, I'll spend the night worrying about him going overboard.

Her head was beginning to hurt. She needed to get out of her head and back into her evening. Dinner needed to be finished and she had only got half the house cleaned earlier. Or, she might just let the house go to rack and ruin for one more night, and watch Disney movies with her boy. Now that sounded like a plan.

She went into the living room and lit the fire, then went back to the kitchen. A big pot of stew sat on the stove, waiting to be reheated. Did she have anything for dessert? She opened the fridge.

'Ah, I don't believe this! Come on, Dan, we have to go out again. Jeepers tonight, will I ever get to sit down?'

'What's wrong, Mam?' he asked.

'I forgot to get milk and butter and we're all out.'

'Come on then, Mam. We can get treats for tonight.'

'That's the plan anyway, kid – treat night and DVD's. No treats until after dinner though, OK?'

'Deal. Mam, I really love you.'

'Aw, pet. I really love you too.'

Butch wanted in on the hugging action as well. He ran round then in circles and yapped until they gave him some love. She shooed him away and they ran out the door into the wind.

Chapter 31

'*Mary Rose*, do you not think I'm having enough woman-trouble at the moment, without you acting up? And now I'm talking out loud to myself again.'

It was just as well the old glitch with the trawler had reared its head and made them turn for home. The wind was moderate to rough and the sea was angry. There was a real fetch to the wind tonight, and he didn't like it. He'd had that uneasy feeling all day, as the weather began to freshen. Sometimes the most powerful tool a fisherman had was his gut. Fran had given him such a hard time about not casting off and he had never seen him so annoyed. He would have to get over it — surely now he too could feel the sea grinding under the belly of the boat. They would sleep on board tonight, and set sail at first light, if the pumps were fixed.

He sighed for no particular reason, and his thoughts went back to Jen. He had tried a couple of times to have a chat with her over the past few days, but the moment was never really right. He hated confrontation and he felt bad over his own behaviour. He had been weird with her.

He really wanted to have a talk about what she threw at him over Sharon's death. It was funny – most of the stuff she had said to him about Scott was a repeat of what his wife used to say.

'Mate, when we get back we're going for a few pints!' Fran called down to the engine room. 'You want to come?'

'Nah, man. I'm going to get the head down!' he shouted up the stairwell at the voice floating down.

'Your choice.'

Andy relaxed now that they were heading for home. He was looking forward to being on his own on the boat for a while. The reality was, he was at home on the boat – fishing was in his blood. He had tried to get away from it, but had come back.

On the other hand, it would to be good to go back to the house for the night. He wanted to text Jen but he was afraid to. Things had got intense all of a sudden, and he wondered would he be better off calling it a day? Part of him still wanted to travel and see the world but he had begun to think he'd prefer to stay here with her and Danny.

He picked up his phone. A message from earlier. He was disappointed. It was from Scott, not Jen.

Andy, great to catch up last Saturday. Really enjoyed the few pints. Hope everything is OK with you and your mignotta. Whatever happens, Andy, I will be there. I have your back. Chat soon and we can talk about the trip.

Scott and his Italian words! Andy didn't have a clue about the language, but something was familiar about that word. He had heard him use it before when speaking to him. Pretty weird text all in all.

He thought about the way Scott spoke to Jen. He could understand why she didn't like him. She accused him of being arrogant, which was true. She accused him of being possessive of him, also true. She accused him of trying to attack her in the kitchen. The lines in his brain started to blur. As each thought came, there was a crossover. He wasn't sure if it was Sharon speaking, or Jen. It played out in his mind, like a split screen, both women speaking, and saying the same thing at the same time: *He is obsessive – he wants to hurt me – I am afraid of him*.

History repeating itself.

Then the memory of where he had last heard that Italian word from Scott came back to him in high definition. It was as he sat on the beach with Sharon in his arms the morning they found her. Scott had found her. Jen's voice came back into his head: *You told me yourself you never really believed Sharon took her own life – she was afraid of heights – she would never have gone up that cliff on her own, in the dark!* The same thought he had himself, many nights as he sat with Scott and poured his heart out to him. Scott convinced him it was suicide.

Mignotta.

'Your little *mignotta* is gone. I'll never leave you. I will take care of you.'

He said it out loud, repeating the words Scott had said that morning on the beach, as they came back to him with absolute clarity. He punched the word into Google Translate, no longer thinking it was a term of endearment.

Enter Text: mignotta Translation: whore

Conversation after conversation flooded into his head. The way Scott was with people in general, the way he spoke to women, and treated them like possessions, using and abusing. The constant need for the high, be it through coke or drink. The superiority.

The rose-tinted glasses had suddenly fallen off and Andy was beginning to feel a real sense of dread.

He found Jen's number on his phone and rang her. No answer. He rang again, same thing, no answer.

Jen's voice pierced his thoughts: *A potential rapist-slash-murderer . . .*

267

Then Scott's voice: *She made a pass at me. Maybe she had a thing for me and then you came along.*

He knew now with certainty that Jen was telling the truth. She had so much baggage about her scars, there's no way she would make a pass at anyone. He needed to get home and fast.

Chapter 32

Danny bolted in the door in front of Jen and Butch went wild, welcoming him. She was glad to be back in the heat of the house. September my arse, she thought – it felt more like November. At least it was dry, but she wasn't sure if the rowan tree would take much more of a battering from the gale-force winds raging around the place. She locked the door and fired the keys into her bag, dropping it on the floor in the hallway.

'Dinner will be ready soon and then we'll stick on the movie.'

'OK, Mam. Can I have my ice cream now?'

'After dinner, you little monster! What did I say to you earlier?' She laughed to herself as she picked up his coat off the floor.

'OK. We're going to play Lego upstairs, Mam, while we're waiting.'

Danny and Butch scampered up the stairs.

She put the supplies into the fridge, and put the heat back on under the pot of stew.

'You really should get someone to change your locks, Jen. You wouldn't know who would let themselves in if they had a spare key. Under the flowerpot – how imaginative.'

Her heart stopped beating for a second, then she turned around to face him.

'What are you doing here?'

He was standing at the kitchen door, blocking her way into the hall.

'I just thought I would drop down and keep you company, seeing as Andy is working. Thought you might be lonely. I have locked the front door again for you – keep intruders out. Dinner smells great, what are you cooking?' He swung the spare keys around on his finger.

'Scott, my parents are on the way down now.' It was a lie, but she knew she was in real trouble. He was blocking the path between her and Danny. She had no way of getting to him.

'Your parents have their club tonight, do they not? If my memory serves me correctly, they never come down to you on Wednesday, as they go there. I think you are mistaken, my dear. No one is coming down tonight. Besides, you only have two settings on the table.'

'Scott, you need to leave. We are not friends, and I don't think we have anything to talk about.' Jen cursed herself for dumping her handbag as usual in the hallway. She couldn't get to her phone either. She needed to get him out of the house, and fast.

'Relax, Jen. Put the kettle on. Let's have a coffee and clear the air. Why don't I put an extra setting on the table? I will stay for dinner. That's a good idea, isn't it? We'll have dinner together, the three of us, and we can clear the air and be friends. Would you like that, Jen?'

'Honestly, Scott, I don't think that's a good idea. Danny is tired, and we just want a quiet night. I'll make you a coffee, but then I need you to go. I am happy to have a chat and clear the air. That sounds OK. I'll bring Danny up some dinner to his room and then we can talk.'

She was watching him like a hawk, and he was watching her. The thought of grabbing a knife out of the cupboard crossed her mind, but it wasn't a Hollywood movie playing out here, this was real life.

The monologue going on in her brain surprised her. *Just keep calm, Jen. Just keep calm. Don't rise him. Play him at his own game. Be charming. Diffuse the situation.*

'I would like to see Danny, Jen. He's a pleasant little chap – and, by the look of things here, quite the artist.'

He was flicking through Danny's drawing book, and she felt sick. She didn't want him next or near her boy or his things.

'Why don't you and I sit down and have something to eat, Scott? We can leave Danny where he is, and we can chat properly. You're right. We do need to clear the air and put things behind us, and why not do it now? Take a seat there, and I will get you a coffee.' She tried to plaster on a smile – it felt more like a grimace. How was she going to get him out of the house? 'I'll just pop up to Danny with some dinner.'

'No need to do that, Jen. He'll come down when he's hungry. I wouldn't want you trying to get out the window or anything up there now, would I, after coming all this way for a visit? Now, make the damn coffee and sit down.' That was an order, nothing pleasant in his tone of voice.

Her hands were shaking as she poured the coffee. She knew she was trapped here with him. Where had he put the spare keys? He must have slipped them into his pocket. The only way out was through the back door. She needed to get upstairs to Danny. For the first time ever, she prayed Danny wouldn't come down anytime soon.

'Jen, we have a lot to talk about here. Don't you agree? You're trying to paint quite the picture of me, are you not? Drug-running, murder, manipulation, all-round bad guy, isn't that right?' He was sitting bolt upright at the table, with his hands wrapped around the mug of coffee.

'I don't see you denying any of it, Scott.'

'Hmmm, let me see. Let's start at the top of the list, shall we? Drug-running. Yes, it's true, and it was all going swimmingly until you started to interfere. This is way bigger that you, my dear, and had started long before you came on the scene.'

'Tell me more, Scott? I'm intrigued.'

'Well, it all started a couple of years ago. Just after Sharon's death – I'll get to that in a minute. Doc and Tess were the perfect couple for it. They had their own business, and their marriage even then was on the rocks. Clara was a friend of mine, an old shag – she was working for me. The plan was for her to hook up with Doc, and get him onside. What I didn't envisage was they would actually have feelings for each other in the end.'

Jen couldn't believe what she was hearing. He was responsible for the affair; he had orchestrated the fucking thing.

'So anyway, Clara worked her magic on Doc, and Tess worked away in the pub. I could see that they were struggling, but I needed for her to be in desperate need of funds so she wouldn't ask too many questions. The time was right a few months ago. I had a lot of cash and I needed somewhere to dump it. My solicitor drew up the paperwork, and in her post-miscarriage heartbroken state, Tess didn't really read the small print. My solicitor works for me, so he made it all look above board. Job done. Nice income. Tess is unwittingly laundering drug money and her husband is the drug runner. Dig a bit deeper and the bogus paperwork leads nowhere near me. No connection.'

Jen felt sick to the stomach. It was becoming clearer by the minute he was a sociopath. She needed to get out. She knew she was in real danger.

'And that is where Andy comes in, dear, and I suppose Sharon. Andy is a fisherman at heart – with a brilliant brain. I met him in college, the friendship was genuine enough, it was just an added bonus that he was from a fishing family and worked at sea. I needed to get the stuff into the country under the radar. I needed a willing participant. Sharon was the driving force behind them – she was really ambitious and career-driven. In your defence, you are a much nicer girl, and a better match for Andy. So if the wife was out of the picture, it was a given gentle Andy would come home to his family. It worked. I knew he wouldn't partake in anything illegal, but his mate Fran was the perfect fit. It was all planned out, and the drugs were being picked up and brought in without Andy ever knowing.'

Had he just admitted to killing Sharon for drugs?

'Are you telling me you've been smuggling drugs into the country on Andy's trawler without him knowing, and you killed his wife just to get him back to the harbour, and onto the boats? Why did you need him? Why couldn't you have just picked a random fisherman to do your dirty work for you? Why Andy?'

'That's exactly what I'm telling you, Jen. Sharon was a cut-throat power-hungry bitch, so I was doing Andy a big favour by getting rid of her. Sure it's the romance of the century with you and Andy and, in effect, you should be grateful – I was doing you a massive favour as well. You are as shrewd as your Aunty Pat, Jen. You remind me of her. She knew what had happened with Sharon. I told her just before she died.'

'Scott, I have heard quite enough of this. I don't want to know any more, and I want you to get out.' She stood up from the table.

He stayed sitting. She made a dart for the door, but he grabbed her by the arm.

'Sit fucking down! You will listen to every word I have to say. Try a stunt like that again, and I will break your fucking legs.'

She sat back down and tried to figure out what to do. Her mind was going into overdrive, trying to come up with a plan. If she ran, she could lead him out of the house and away from Danny. All she cared about was keeping her little boy safe. But … afterwards … there would be nothing to prevent him from coming back to do as he pleased with her defenceless son.

'Where was I? Oh yes. So back to the list we go. Drug-running, murder, manipulation – you were right about it all. Everything was going fine until you stuck your little claws into Andy. Has he told you yet? Looks like he's not going on his trip – he has decided to stay here with you and your little brat. Fan-fucking-tastic. And they all live happily ever after. He loves ya, baby, scars and all!'

'How could you do that to your best friend, Scott? He thought the world of you. How could you destroy him like that?'

'It was all about the money, honey. I had to keep my suppliers sweet as well. You think I'm a bad boy? I'm a puppy dog in comparison to them. Swings and roundabouts, baby, swings and roundabouts.'

His sing-songy voice was grating on her nerves. Slowly but surely she could feel the adrenalin rise and a dark primitive rage grow from the pit of her stomach. Something had shifted in her head and her heart.

He will not hurt my boy.

'And where did Sal fit into your plan?'

'Nowhere. I just liked Sal. She is an incredibly talented girl. I actually could see myself settling down and retiring with someone like Sal. She was a sweetheart, and such a shame she found out about me shagging Clara. Even Mother Dear would have approved of Sal. She liked her, and you for that matter. I saw you talking the night you were there – no doubt she warned you about me. I told her about Sharon, you know. I wanted her to fucking suffer the consequences of her actions. She got herself pregnant with me all those years ago, just to trap my father, and then he ended up killing himself because of her. You are all the same – bastard women. Sal would have eventually done the same thing – used and abused for money.'

'Scott, you can put this right. You can get out now, and go somewhere. I will never breathe a word of what you have told me. You have the money – God knows, you have more than enough. Just disappear. What's keeping you here? You don't need to stay.'

'I want to stay for now, Jen. The trip with Andy was my retirement plan: leave the donkeys here to do my work for me, and I'm in the wind, travelling around the world. But you sure fucked that up on me, didn't you? You should have stayed away. He was my friend first, and all that fucking Sharon wanted was to separate us. She tried to come between me and Andy, and failed miserably. You are not going to come between us now. Andy will come on this trip. I just need an incentive for him to drop tools and go.'

She knew what was coming next, and she needed to stall him. Maybe someone would call round. She could hear Danny playing away in his room with the dog. Butch wouldn't recognise the menace in the situation – not unless Scott actually attacked her – after all, to him Scott was a visitor he was familiar with. He would just come down and lick him to death. She stole a glance at the clock. It was quarter to seven, and starting to get dark. The wind was still blowing a gale, so even if she ran out into the garden and started screaming no one would hear her. Her only option was to get Danny down here, and try and get him out the door at least. He would run straight to Sal's parents' place. It was part of the drill: if Mammy was in trouble, go get help either by ringing from home, or running to the house at the end of the lane. If only she could get him out the door.

'So what do you think of all that, my dear?' he said.

His tone was mocking but something in the way he was regarding her gave her a sudden insight. He wanted applause.

'Well, I think you're a genius, Scott. I had no idea you had such a complex plan afoot. You are actually amazing!'

He looked at her to see if she was mocking him, but she opened her eyes wide and made sure they were shining in admiration. He smiled at her, and shrugged his shoulders.

She knew he was covert in his narcissism but it was still there. He was a sociopath, a killer and a narcissist. The psychology lectures started to churn in her brain – psychopathy, narcissism, the traits and how to deal with them.

'How did you keep all that to yourself? If I had been clever enough to pull something like that off over the last few years, I would want the world to know. Oh my goodness! How did you ever think of all of it? You are unbelievable. And to get away with it, wow, I'm so impressed.'

She stood up from the table.

'What are you doing?' he asked.

'I was just about to get dinner. Would you like some?'

'Yes, thank you. Now Jen, how are we going to fix this?'

'I'll dump Andy. There's the incentive for him to pack up and go.'

'Now you're getting it. That's exactly what I want.'

She knew he was toying with her, and he had no intention of leaving the house with her still in one piece, but she could buy some time and become the manipulator for a little while.

She walked over to the kitchen door.

'Where are you going?' he asked.

'I need to call Danny down for dinner. I thought you wanted to say hello to him? He must be starving by now – we've been chatting for ages.'

He didn't try to stop her.

She called up the stairs. 'Danny darling, come down for your dinner! Now!'

She must play up to his obvious narcissism, try her best to come across as though she almost had a crush on him, was entranced by his brilliance. She wasn't religious, but right now she was praying to anyone who would listen. St Anthony and Mary were high on the list. It always worked for her father, she would learn by example.

He had relaxed further in the chair, but she needed Danny

here before she did anything.

'Hiya.'

Danny was looking at Scott. Jen knew by his face that he felt something was amiss. He was an intuitive little boy but, apart from that, Jen had let her mouth run away with itself when talking to Sal about Scott. Had Danny overheard some of that? Whatever the reason, Danny was on the defensive, she knew that, and she was delighted.

'Hello, Danny. How are you?'

'Fine,' he mumbled.

Under any other circumstances, Jen would have admonished him for his bad manners, but not tonight. Things just might be OK. She grabbed a jug of water and more cutlery from the press, and sat her son on the chair at the top of the table, closest to the patio door. Scott was sitting on the long side of the table, and Jen's place was at the end. Scott was between them, but it made no odds. She would strike when the time was right.

She could see he was beginning to get impatient at the lull in conversation, and she needed to get him back on track.

She brought the stew over to the table and served it into three bowls. She passed one to Danny and one to Scott.

'Scott, would you like a glass of wine with dinner? I think I have some here.'

'Certainly, yes.'

She got up and, trying to seem as relaxed as possible, fetched the wine and two glasses. She wasn't convinced he was falling for her act, but sensed he thought he had the situation under control – he had suggested dinner after all. She was formulating a plan and prayed it would work.

'If I had known you were coming, Scott, I would have made something a bit more suitable than peasant stew.' She poured the wine into a glass and put it down in front of him.

'Jen, dear, it's nice to have supper with the peasants now and then.'

He raised his glass but it hadn't reached his mouth when she hit him full force in the face with the wine bottle.

'*Run, Danny! Out the back!*'

Scott was stunned, and the leverage of her swing drove him off the chair. He hit the ground with a thud, and she burst into a run out the patio door, after her boy.

Danny had stopped running and was looking around for her.

'*Run, Danny!*'

She grabbed him by the arm, and ran full tilt through the orchard and in the direction of the beach. She didn't look behind her, she knew Scott was catching up. She was sprinting across stones in bare feet. They were on the beach, the wind throwing so much spray up from the ocean it felt like it was raining.

If they could just make it to Sal's parents' place they would be OK.

Danny was screaming, '*Faster, Mam! He's going to catch up!*'

She felt the rock connect with her back and she toppled forward, landing on Danny. He was on top of them before she could get back on her feet. He had her by the hair, and her son was clinging to her. He punched her in the face, but not hard enough to knock her out. She saw stars as he grabbed Danny by the scruff of the neck. She was now on the ground, he didn't even need to restrain her. He had her boy – she was going nowhere.

'Quite the little fucking actress there, aren't you? Good try, honey, but now you are well and truly fucked. You had some hope of someone calling to the house, but no one will be down here in the dark in the middle of a storm.'

It was at that point she noticed the hunting knife in his hand.

Chapter 33

Andy sprinted up the pier, trying Jen's number over and over. No answer. He tried Sal's phone and it was turned off. He felt the wave of panic rise again. He was going to call the Guards, but didn't know what to say. He might just find her and Danny on the couch, her not answering his calls on purpose.

He tried to attack her, and I didn't believe her. He killed my wife. *Rapist-slash-murderer* repeated over and over in his head. He was about to sprint down onto the beach and take the shortcut across the headland when he heard the van alongside him. He didn't need to turn around – he knew it was Brian, the Harbour Master out on his evening checks. Everyone knew him – he was a lifelong mate of Andy's.

'You're in a fierce hurry, lad – do you need a lift?' the familiar voice said.

'Quick, man, I need to get home. Jen and Danny are in danger!'

He didn't need to ask twice. The little white van took off at a speed of knots, and in the short few minutes it took to get there, Andy had given him the short pitch of the story. His shotgun was at home, Brian said. Andy was relieved by this fact. Brian and shotguns? Scary thought.

Jen's car was in the drive. No sign of anyone else. The lights were on, and all was quiet. Andy tried to slow his breathing and looked at Brian apologetically.

'No harm done,' Brian said. 'Better to be safe. I'll come in anyway – you have me worried now.'

Andy turned the key in the front door and there was no sign of life. Not a sound.

'Jen? Danny? You here, guys?'

Brian went upstairs. 'Hello? Anyone here?' He went into Andy's room. 'Andy, come quick!'

Andy got to the top of the stairs in three strides. His bedroom door was open and the place had been messed up. There was a smashed picture of him on his wedding day in the middle of the bed. Drawers were pulled out and some upended.

He reached up and ran his hand along the top shelf, searching for the hunting knife he had hidden at the back, away from Danny. It was gone.

Chapter 34

He was holding the knife against Danny's cheek.

'If you keep whining, you little brat,' he said, 'I'm going to gut you like a fucking fish!'

Danny stopped squirming. He continued to cry, but made no sound.

'Please, just let him go,' begged Jen. 'This is between you and me. Let my boy go.'

She was hoarse with fear, and this excited him.

Jen's eye had begun to swell shut, but she didn't break eye contact with him. Time had slowed down, and she could see the first drops of Danny's blood roll down the length of the hunting knife pressed to his face.

Her heart broke as she watched a damp patch spread down his jeans and over his feet.

'This is your mother's fault, you know, Danny. If she had just stayed out of it, everything would have been fine. But, oh no, the fucking whore had to spoil everything.'

Jen was close to hysteria. 'Please let him go! I'm begging you!'

'If you keep whimpering, Jen, I'll gut your little angel here. Or maybe I'll gut you first and make him watch.'

He laughed at his joke. The knife didn't move.

She needed to do something – no one knew they were down here and no one would come. It was them against him. She was Danny's only chance.

The wind had picked up again, and the sound of the waves crashing on the shore was deafening.

'All your safety plans never got you anywhere,' he said. 'You should have stayed away from me, Jen, but you couldn't help it, could you?'

'Please, let him go,' she pleaded. 'I'll do whatever you want. I'll give you whatever you want.'

'*Don't try and tell me what to do!*' he roared. The wind whipped the words from his mouth and flung them across at her. He was growing more agitated every time she spoke.

In the dunes right behind Scott, she caught sight of something but tried not to react.

'Danny, listen to me. I love you. It's going to be OK.' She had stopped crying.

'That's it, Jen, good girl. Say your goodbyes. I'll give you that much,' he said, as the smile left his face.

'Do you remember our game, Danny? Apart from me and your daddy, who loves you best in the whole wide world?'

She looked at him intently, willing him to give her the right answer. He looked in her eyes, and she saw a glimmer of hope in his.

'*Butch!*' he screamed, at the top of his little lungs.

The dog sprang from the dunes and went for Scott, sinking his teeth into his forearm.

The shock of the surprise attack was enough to make him loosen his grip around the boy's neck, as he tried to defend himself.

'*Run, Danny!*' she screamed as she wrapped her hand around a rock. Something primitive had taken the place of fear, and the adrenalin in her veins made her react at lightning speed.

Danny ran back in the direction of the house. He was gone.

She lunged at Scott, and smashed the rock into his face full force. She felt bone shatter under the weight of it, as his blood splattered over her arms and face.

'I'll kill you, you rotten bastard!' she shouted in his face as they fell to the ground wrapped in each other's arms. She glimpsed Butch beside them, knife in his belly, his eyes unseeing.

The blow to Scott's face had stunned him but it had not knocked him out. She clawed at his eyes and tried to swing the rock at his head.

He was on top of her, his blood dripping on her, and he was laughing.

'That's more like it, you little bitch. Now we can have some real fun. You like it rough, don't you?'

The punch to her face made her eyes swim, and deadened her senses. She was dazed. He stood up, grabbed her arm in a mighty grip and started to drag her over the stones. They were merciless, ripping at her skin and clothes. She felt her arm separate from her shoulder joint, and the pain made her vomit.

The waves shocked her back to reality, burned at her torn flesh, and the cold stabbed her all over. She couldn't catch her breath. She could hear him speaking but couldn't make out what he was saying. The waves pounded and pounded. They were relentless. She couldn't move, he was all over her. Was he laughing?

Danny was the only thing she was thinking about. He would be safe now: the game was the drill if someone ever tried to harm them. He knew what to do, and she was glad. The nausea and gagging was beginning to subside, but the burning in her lungs was immense. She couldn't feel her body any more, only the darkness that was enveloping her. She tried to focus on the lighthouse. As the light swept over the water towards her, she blacked out.

Danny ran back to the house as fast as his legs could carry him. He knew what he had to do, his mam had told him enough times. He had to ring the Guards and tell them the man was trying to harm his mammy, and then he would run down the lane to Sal's daddy. He tried to call Butch but the wind kept getting stuck in his mouth, and he couldn't really shout his name louder than the howling gusts.

The kitchen light was on. Now he felt scared that Scott was behind him. He ran into the house and slammed the back door and locked it.

'Jen, is that you?' Andy's boots made a real racket as he ran down the stairs.

Danny was bent over his mam's handbag and was rooting around.

'Danny, son, where's your mam? Are you OK?'

It was though he couldn't hear him. A second set of boots were on the stairs now, coming down.

'Danny. Talk to me, bud, what's going on?'

The touch of his hand on the boy's little shoulder made him jump. He looked at Andy, with blood on his face, and started to scream.

'Jesus Christ, Danny, where is your mother?'

'She's on the beach with *him*! He's trying to kill her, and me, like he killed Sharon!'

'Jesus! Danny stay here with Brian. Brian, ring the fucking Guards now. It's Scott.'

Andy saw the broken glass and half-eaten casserole as he ran through the kitchen and out the back door, pausing only for a second to run into the shed and grab the first thing to his hand. An axe – that would do. Not again – Scott wasn't going to take away the person he loved again.

He was on the beach within a minute. It was dark now. He thought he could hear Scott's voice, just audible over the thunder of the waves. He quietly made his way over that direction, and as his eyes adjusted to the waning light, he could see them. They were in the water. He was standing over her, and she was trying to get up while the waves crashed over her. She was alive, that was enough for him.

Scott saw him approach. He looked surprised.

'Scott, what are you doing?'

'What does it look like I'm doing, Andy? I'm cleaning up the mess.' His voice was high-pitched and manic. 'You arriving wasn't part of the plan.'

Jen was alive, but she wasn't moving away from him.

Scott put his foot on top of her head, and pushed her face into the water. 'I would put down that axe if I were you, Andy. I have your back, I told you. She needs to get out of the way.'

'OK, OK.' He threw the axe up the beach, and put his hands out, palms up.

Scott took his foot away and she surfaced, gasping for air.

'It was all going fine until she came along, Andy. She got her claws into you, her and her fucking rug rat, and everything changed. They are all the same, her, Sharon, my whore of a mother.'

'Scott, we can work this out – just let me take her out of the water.'

'Why are you defending her for fuck sake? She's ruining everything. Interfering. I couldn't protect him from Livia, but I made up for it with you. Sharon was bad, Andy, she would have ruined everything for you. She had to go. I made her go up on the cliff that night – after you two had quarrelled in the bathroom. She accused me of being a drug pusher and a bad influence on you. She had to go. I followed her out after she had a go at me, and I made her go up there. When we were far enough up, I pushed her. Her body wasn't supposed to wash up so quickly. I should have gone higher up the cliffs and made sure she went into deeper water.'

He was ranting. Screaming at the wind.

Jen was trying to drag herself away from him but the waves kept pulling her back.

Andy kept his eyes trained on Scott. 'Scott, you need help, man. It's done now. Let it go.' He was trying to keep his rage in check. He finally knew his wife hadn't taken her own life. His best friend had.

'No, it has to be this way, Andy. She has to go as well.'

He lunged for Jen, and Andy went for him. His full bodyweight slammed him into the water. Andy was bigger, but Scott was exceptionally strong, and high on adrenalin. He flipped him over, and got his hands around Andy's throat.

'You were my best friend. My only real friend, and you chose her over me. You did the same with Jen, and threw it all in my face again. You should have just –'

He slumped onto Andy's chest and a wave submerged them. Andy pushed him off and struggled to his feet as the wave receded.

He watched as Scott was dragged out to sea. And then he was gone.

Andy stared as another powerful wave raced in to shore. But it didn't bring Scott with it.

Jen dropped the rock and collapsed.

'Jen? Jen?'

There was no response.

'Jen, my darling, can you hear me?'

She was in his arms now, her face black and blue, her hair stuck to her forehead. He had held a woman like this before, his wife. It was all too much for him.

'Jen, I can't do this again. Please answer me.' He was rocking back and forth, rubbing at her arms. 'Jen, you're freezing, please wake up.'

Nothing.

'Jen? Oh God, Jen! No. Please God, please God. Don't let her be gone. I will do anything.'

Nothing.

He laid her down on the ground. He checked her neck for a pulse. It was there – faint, but there. She was breathing. Shallow breaths, but breathing. He could see from the shape of her shoulder that it was dislocated.

'I need to get you home.'

He picked her up and started back in the direction of their home. He held her bad arm close to her body, and she groaned when it moved.

'Jen, can you hear me? I love you, Jen.' He looked down at her, and she was trying to open her eyes. Thank you, God.

He could hear voices in the distance, and hear sirens.

'What the fuck? Jen? Is she OK?' Sal ran across the beach with Brian.

'Don't touch her – we need to get her to the house. Where's Danny?'

'He's fine. My parents are there,' Sal said. 'We rang for the Guards and an ambulance. She was in my house today. She knew this was going to happen.'

'Brian, you need to check the beach,' Andy said. 'He was pulled out to sea. You need to get the boats out here too.'

'I'm on it.' Brian took the torch from Sal, and his phone out of his pocket. He would first call his crew and then the lifeboat. A search would be on the water within minutes.

'Be careful. There's an axe on the beach – find it and take it with you!' Andy shouted over his shoulder.

They got into the house and a minute later the police were banging on the front door. Another two came round the back.

'The ambulance is en route – is she breathing?'

'Yes, thank God,' Andy said. 'You need to go down the beach and find him. He went into the water. The trawlers will be out there soon.'

They were local Guards, they knew the drill. But they rang in to request the lifeboat launch anyway. Protocol. The crew would be well on their way by now.

'Rescue 117 has been deployed. If he's in the water, they'll find him.'

Jen was starting to come round, but was in agony.

She was saying something but Andy couldn't make out what it was. Scott had really given her a going over. Her bottom lip was split and swollen and her eye had ballooned.

''Any …'

'What are you trying to say, love?' Andy said. '*Shhh*, it's OK, the ambulance is on its way. It's OK, you're safe.'

'Danny. She's looking for Danny.' Sal was beside him.

Danny was in the kitchen with the Guards and Sal's parents. Sal called him.

He stood at the door and Sal explained that Mam needed a little kiss, and not to be scared. Her face was really sore, but she would be all better when the doctor came. He ran straight to her.

'I love you, Mammy. Your lips are purple, but I did like you asked. Our game worked. Butch is not here though. He'll be back soon. The doctor is coming.' He planted a big kiss on her face, and stood back. He started to cry.

'Come on, champ, we'll go get some tea.' Sal took him out of the room.

Jen squeezed Andy's hand as a tear fell off her cheek. 'Mind him until I get home,' she mumbled.

Two men in green uniforms with grab bags arrived into the sitting room and in minutes had her in the back of the ambulance and en route to the hospital. Sal had called her parents and they were going straight there.

Andy marvelled once more at how a rural community behaves in times of crisis. Already the house was full of neighbours with trays of food. The women always convened as soon as the alarm for the search party was raised. As wives and mothers of fishermen, they were used to the procedure. Three women were in the kitchen, setting up a station for the volunteers who came in their droves to join the search party. Men of all ages, ready to help, and to support their own. Andy had changed and was putting on his jacket to join the search, but the local Guard wouldn't let him.

'Andy, I can't let you join the search. You know that.'

'I'm going out there, *now*. Come on, you would do the same. Don't do this.'

'Aye, I would do the same, and I know what I would do if I found the cretin. That's exactly why you're not going. You'll be more help to us here. The big fellas from town are on their way out, and they'll be wanting to talk with ya, lad. Your father has just come in. Go talk to him, son, he needs to hear this from you.'

Tess had arrived with Hugh, and the two children were curled up together on the couch watching a movie. It was only eleven o'clock but it felt like the middle of the night. Sal and Tess hugged as they both stood on the patio, smoking.

'I had to stay here with Danny, the poor little angel is terrified. I couldn't go to the hospital. I was so glad to see you and Hugh coming. How have you been, hon?'

'I have been better. Better than Jen though. What's the news?'

'Her mam just called. They're keeping her in tonight. Dislocated shoulder and a lot of bruising. They are monitoring her for fluid in her lungs. All going well, she will be home tomorrow. It all feels so weird, Tess. He tried to kill her and Danny too.'

'Little did I think she would be the next one of us in the hospital, Sal. She told me about her suspicions, and I accused her of being crazy. She was right all along. He's the crazy one. I have been the worst friend.'

'Why did he do this to her, Tess?' Sal was in tears.

'Because he's a psycho, Sal, that's why. Is it true he killed Sharon? Poor Andy, it's all so crazy.'

'And we were all sucked in by him – none of us listened to her. We're all responsible for this, Tess. All of us.' Sal's voice broke, and she tried to swallow. 'We let her down and he nearly killed her.'

'He used us all, Sal. Now we have to pick up the pieces. I don't know how Andy is going to deal with all of this, and what about poor little Danny? He's only a baby.'

'What about Doc, Tess, where is he?'

'I have no idea.'

'Oh, we have to ring Will – he can't hear about his through anyone else. I fecking forgot about him. I have no number for him.'

'Andy probably does. Are you OK to tell Will, Sal?'

'Yeah, I'll tell him.'

Sal reluctantly knocked on the sitting-room door, and went in to Andy and his parents.

The wind had died slightly, to the point where it wouldn't impede the search on the water. The lights of the fishing vessels could be seen from the patio, illuminating the black ink as they searched in formation, the area dictated by tides and prevailing wind.

There was a bizarre feeling in the house. Like a funeral, except that people were mourning for a woman in the hospital and a woman who was long dead and buried. The kettle was turned on every time someone arrived. Women talked in hushed tones about the attacker and, as Andy crumpled into his father's arms, a woman cried.

Chapter 35

'Dad, stop fussing. I'm OK.' Jen pulled herself out of the car.

Her dad ignored her request. 'Jen, you heard the doctors – you need to take it easy.'

Andy opened the front door and Danny ran out to meet her. He threw his arms around her and she tried not to wince.

The house was quiet enough when she went in. Andy took her into the sitting room. The fire was crackling and the TV was on.

'Sit down there, love. I'll get you a cup of tea. Sal and Tess are in the kitchen, and Will is outside.'

He didn't want her to go into the kitchen or the garden where she could see that the trawlers were still out, as were the volunteers. Scott still hadn't been found. Teams had been walking the headland and the beach from first light.

'Would you like a sandwich?'

'I'm not hungry, but thanks. I'm just going to go upstairs and tidy myself up.'

'Right. I'll make the tea.'

Andy left and a moment later Will stuck his head round the door. When he saw her, all his pent-up anger dissipated. He hugged her tight and told her everything was going to be OK. She cried and apologised to him, over and over.

'You saved him,' he said. 'He's OK thanks to you.'

He didn't have the heart to tell her that he and Andy had buried Butch at first light. The Guards had confiscated the knife and left them to bury the little animal. They put him under the rowan tree, with Pat's ashes. Danny kept asking for Butch, and Will didn't know how to tell him his little best friend was gone. Will suggested he would take him for a couple of days. Jen agreed it was the right thing.

'Right, I'll go find him and pack a few things for him.'

'Thanks, Will.'

In the kitchen Sal and Tess were sweeping and mopping. They had decided it would be best for the volunteers to be fed and watered in Sal's home place. They were trying to get Jen back to some semblance of normality, whatever the hell that was.

'*The three of ye have a lot to answer for, I tell ye!*' The sound of Jen's gentle Dad shouting at them stopped them in their tracks. 'She came to all of you, and told you what she thought and you fobbed her off. She didn't come to me, and 'tis a shame because this would never have happened. I would have believed her, I wouldn't have a reason not to!'

'Mr Harper –' Tess said.

'Don't you "Mr Harper" me, Tess! God knows you have your own burdens at the minute, but you know my girl well. She has a heart of gold, and always sees the good in all around her. Something was amiss with that lad, and she knew it. And you did nothing. And for what, I ask you, for a few bob to keep that bar afloat for the Dubs? Shocking.'

'Ah come on, John, that's not fair,' Sal said. 'He lied and cheated all of us.'

'Don't you tell me what's fair, young Sal! You weren't much better. Sure didn't you get swept up in his charm altogether? Did he try to kill *you*, ha? Did he?'

'Dad, that's enough.' Jen walked into the kitchen.

'Is it, Jen? It isn't nearly enough. He nearly killed you and my grandson.' His voice was thick with emotion, and his eyes were filling up. 'Andy, you and I will be talking as well. Soon. It's not the time or the place here now, but we will be talking. This is some way to find out about the two of you courting.'

He disguised the catch in his voice with a cough, and went out to the garden.

'It hit him hard, don't take what he said to heart,' Jen said. He's right, she thought. None of them listened.

'Sit down there, Jen – I'll make tea,' Sal and Tess chimed in unison. They nearly fell over each other getting to the kettle, both really hurt by what had just been said – the truth.

'Any word from the search, Andy?'

'Nothing, Jen. No sign.'

'He's still alive, guys.'

'Jen, he was unconscious when he went in. I saw the water take him – the tide was going out and the waves were powerful. He didn't surface, he wasn't washed back in – I would have seen him. He was pulled out to sea.' He was looking in the direction of the sea, and added almost as though he was making a wish, 'I'm certain he was swept out.'

'Just like you were certain of everything else, Andy?' she retorted.

He hung his head and didn't say anything else.

'I'm sorry, that wasn't fair,' she said. 'How long does it take for a body to wash up?'

'It depends on a number of things. Look, the boys out there know what they're doing.' He was in work mode now.

'Unfortunately, it's not new to any of us, a search operation like this – tides, currents, winds and other factors will be taken into account – but they will know where to look, and they will find him.'

Jen's Dad had come back into the kitchen.

'Andy is right, Jen. If he went into the water, he won't be coming back out. He's gone, darling. It's only a matter of time before they find him. Don't worry – those lads will find his body. Rest now, child. I'm going to head off home for a while. Just ring me if you need anything.'

The warmth in his hug made her feel like a little girl.

'Thanks, Dad. For everything. I love you.' She spoke into the crook of his neck, and she didn't want to let go.

'Right then, sure I'll be seeing all of you soon no doubt. I was a bit hard on you – just mind her for me.' He didn't wait for a response but left.

'Do you feel like chatting for a while, Jen? We could all go in to the fire, and just talk.'

'Thanks, Sal, I'd like that. You all need to hear this story.'

She told the story like a sequence of facts. Funny how the brain can remember every last detail of all the things a person would rather forget. As she came to the end of the tale, they all felt like victims and survivors in equal measure, albeit their experiences came in varying degrees of catastrophe. They all knew that as survivors they would pick their way through the rubble, blinking in the sunshine. The wounds would heal, but the scars would always be there. Their relationships had changed, dramatically, but they had survived, unlike the man who through his own deluded mind had inflicted all the wounds in the first place.

'Jen, you look shattered,' Sal said. 'I'm going to go now, but I'll be back over in the morning, OK?'

'I'm going to leave as well, Jen,' Tess said. 'Try and get some rest for yourself. Andy will take care of you.' She looked at her friend and was sad. She knew things had changed between them.

'Thanks, girls. We're going to be OK. We'll get through this, and I'll relax once I know he's been found. The shrink will help too.' She tried to make it sound upbeat, but it sounded more like a plea.

'Of course you'll be OK, Jen.' Tess hovered at the end of the couch.

They hugged her one after another, careful not to hurt her. She looked frail sitting on the couch beside Andy.

Sal and Tess saw themselves out.

'Andy, what if he comes back? What if he is never found?' She reached for her phone, to text Will. 'I just want to check if Danny is OK – I should have kept him here.' She was struggling with one-handed texting, and her shoulder was throbbing.

'Let me write the text for you. Danny is safe with his dad, and he's probably spoiling him right now.'

'Poor little Butch, Andy. The poor little fella saved us, and now he's dead.'

The dam burst. She was on her feet, and hysterical with fear, shock and sadness. Everything tumbled out of her mouth, all the parts she hadn't told the girls.

'I'm terrified, Andy. What if he comes back or worse again if he is never found? Could that happen? How likely is that? The detectives in the hospital said that could happen. What if I never know? What if I can never go anywhere again without looking over my shoulder for him? I'll never be able to let Danny out of my sight. I'll have to tell the school.'

She was starting to panic, and every time she moved she made the pain in her arm worse. She started to tug at her neck, where the sling was rubbing. It jolted her arm and she cried out in pain.

'Jen, whoa! You need to slow down. Sit down here, please. Just slow down, pet. We will answer those questions, one by one. It's OK to be frightened, but I swear on my life I will never let anyone hurt you or Danny again. I swear to you, Jen. I love you.'

'How are you going to do that, Andy? You can't be with me 24/7.'

'I'll do whatever it takes, Jen.'

'I'm so sorry, Andy. I'm so sorry about Sharon. It's so fucking awful. I wish I had never moved in here, I wish you didn't know me.'

'Jen, my darling, *shhh*. Now I know the truth. The horrible truth, but now I know. Now I can come to terms with it too. She is gone, Jen. Maybe now we can all rest in peace.'

The words saddened him, she could see it, and as much as she was in pain for what happened to her and her boy, she was heartbroken for him too. He was mourning the loss of his wife all over again, and she didn't know how to help him. She was afraid for them too, and if this would be the end of what they had. And then, she just felt selfish for thinking like that.

'Let's try and get some sleep, my love,' Andy said. 'We'll start afresh in the morning, and just figure stuff out as it comes, OK? Now, it's time for painkillers and medicine. I'll get you some water.'

He went to walk out to the kitchen, but she followed him. She had done that a couple of times over the course of the evening. She was too scared to be on her own.

She let him take care of her that night, and didn't object as he carried her up the stairs, much like he had taken care of Tess that time.

She felt anger towards Tess – she had sold out to him – but equally she felt sorry for her. She could be in real trouble with the pub now with Scott gone.

'Andy, I'm sorry for everything.' The codeine was making her sleepy. She was feeling comfortable in the bed. Andy had propped her up from all angles with pillows and her arm was well supported. He was sitting on the bed, trying to figure out how he would get in there without disturbing her or the pillows. It just wasn't going to happen.

'Jen. I'm not going to fit in there tonight.'

'Please don't leave me, Andy. I'm scared.'

'I have no intentions of leaving you, Jen. Now, or ever. Just sit tight for a minute. I'll be back.'

He came back into the room, dragging his mattress with him. He made a bed on the floor between her and the door, close enough to be able to hold her hand.

'Now we are sorted.'

A gentle snore was the response.

He didn't sleep that night, he was too frightened. Every noise and groan from the house made him jump, and he nearly lost his life a couple of times when she cried out in her sleep. But she slept. Tomorrow was a new day, and they would take everything as it came. Hopefully they would have news regarding the search, but he was beginning to have his doubts.

Chapter 36

She lit a candle in the window and looked out onto the dark land. It was the Winter Solstice, December 21st, the shortest day of the year. It was one of her favourite days. The day her ancestors celebrated the returning of the light to the land, after the longest night. As she laid the holly and the candle in the window, she recited the old Irish blessing in her head:

'May peace and plenty be the first to lift the latch on your door,
And happiness be guided to your home by the candle of Christmas.
In the New Year, may your right hand always be stretched out in friendship,
And never in want.'

She had no idea whether the blessing was authentic or good old paddywhackery. Ever since she had read the verse on one of Danny's homemade Christmas cards from school one year, she had made it part of her own solstice ritual – a new Harper tradition.

She could see the reflection of the Christmas-tree lights in the window, and the house smelled of cinnamon.

'Solstice Blessings to you, Andy.'

'*Winter is here*, Jen,' he replied in his best attempt at a foreboding voice.

'*The night is dark, and full of crazy people,*' she added before they both cracked up laughing. They were making up their own lines from *Game of Thrones*, a regular thing.

'Mam, can you give me a hand here?'

'Hand of King Andy, Dan?' Andy asked.

More laughter.

'What are you on about, Mam?'

Jen felt light-hearted. Laughter had been scarce in the house of late, but something had started to shift. The counselling was of real benefit to both herself and Danny. The little boy had been distraught when Jen and Will told him about Butch. A couple of weeks later, his dad had arrived down to the house with a new pup, Mr Cassidy, a little black-and-white Jack Russell, a rescue pup. Danny had cried and ignored him at first, saying he would never take the place of Butch, but the adorable little yapping and playful nature of Mr Cassidy had won him over. Jen knew things would be OK when Danny gave the pup Butch's favourite toy. Then Andy overheard the child talking to the pup one evening, telling him that Butch was a Superhero and had saved his life, and if he wanted to take his place he would have to be very clever and look after his family.

Andy had dealt with everything in his own way, but that too was working. They were coping well.

'Right, come on then, you two. Your dad will kill me if you're late,' Andy said, and picked up the keys. 'Dan, don't forget the present. Are you ready, Jen?'

Danny ran ahead out to the car, excited about going to a proper party in a hotel.

'No, not really, Andy.'

'It will be OK – you have us with you, and it's your parents' wedding anniversary – you'll be among friends.' He squeezed her hand.

'I know, I know, I just haven't been out much as you know, and everyone will be home for Christmas. I just feel like they'll be all talking about it.'

It was true, and he knew it. She hadn't really been outside the door of the house save for school-related things in the last few months. She was afraid of what people were saying behind her back, she was afraid of what they would say to her face.

'Jen, we will stick together, and it will be fine. No doubt they will have something else to talk about by the end of the night anyway.'

'You're right. Come on so, before I change my mind.'

She knew her mam wouldn't relax until she saw her walk through the door of the function room, and sure enough, when she saw the three of them walk in, her face was a picture of relief.

'Happy 40th Wedding Anniversary, Nanny!' said Danny as he handed over the present. He had insisted on wrapping it himself, and it looked as though it had been left out in a storm. His nanny loved it. It was a memory box. Andy had made the wooden box, and Danny had painted it in all the colours of the rainbow. There was even a Lego *Mr and Mrs* stuck to the lid. He had spent hours drawing pictures and putting together photos to put inside for his grandparents.

Jen's dad and Andy were in cahoots about something but it all seemed positive. It had taken a bit of time for her father to warm to the idea they were together but, once he did, he and Andy were good pals.

'I'll get the drinks in, Jen. Back in a minute,' said Andy and he weaved through the crowd.

The whole village was there in the local hotel, and everyone was having a great time. The two-piece band were letting rip with a Hozier song, and already the dance floor was filled with neighbours and friends. Danny was off with two of his little chums from school. Everyone knew everyone.

Jen was still apprehensive. There were a number of faces dotted around the room that were back for the holidays, and more than one was looking in her direction. She wasn't sure if she was being paranoid, or if that horrible Elizabeth was actually pointing and laughing. Another nut-job – the village Poison Ivy.

'Come on out of that nutter's eye-line, doll,' Sal said. 'You are giving her ammo by looking so nervous. I have a drink waiting for you.' She steered Jen over to the reserved table, but not before giving the village gossip the evil eye. 'Silly cow, she always had a thing for Andy anyway. You all right, Jen?'

'I'm better now that I'm sitting down with you, Sal. I was expecting a bit of this anyway.'

'They'll be grand, feck them. They'll have something else to gossip about soon enough. Don't you dare let them ruin your night! Ah Jen, your parents are just the picture of romance. Forty years, can you imagine?'

They looked so sweet together, totally in tune with each other and they had always seemed to be so in love. Her dad of course wasn't the most romantic man in the world, but he showed his true colours when they needed to be seen. Such a loving, loyal man. Her mother always told her she knew from the moment Pat had introduced them that they were meant to be together. And so it was. Forty years and still going strong. He was even taking her on a second honeymoon in a few weeks.

'So, how have you been, Jen? How is the counselling going?'

'It's actually of real benefit to me, Sal. I'm coping and not as bad as I was when they first called off the search. I have come to terms with the fact he is not coming back, even though they didn't find him.'

Sal was glad to hear this. When the search was first called off, Jen nearly lost her mind. She was convinced he was still alive and was going to come back and finish what he had started. But Sal had certainly seen a change over the last few weeks. Christmas was a good distraction. Santa would be arriving in a few nights and Danny was hyper.

'Have you seen Tess?'

'Ah Sal, I wanted to go see her when Doc got arrested, but to be honest I couldn't be dealing with someone else's drama at that moment. And I don't know if she has really got over the fact I didn't warn her about the affair.' Jen took a swig from her wine. She could smell the food being prepared in the background. She was starving. The finger food wasn't due to be served for another little while – she would have to make do with the nuts on the table.

'Evening, fair maidens.' Andy hopped in on the tail-end of the conversation. He nearly spilled Jen's drink in the process.

He was a bit highly strung, and it made Jen uneasy.

Sal and Andy exchanged glances.

'What's up, guys?' Jen asked.

'Fine, fine,' they both said and started to laugh.

Sal and Andy had got quite close after that night, and the three of them spent a lot of their evenings together.

'What were you two whispering about anyway?' Andy said.

'Doc and Tess.'

'It's an unreal situation. What a mess.'

Doc had been pulled over in the car a few weeks previously, on suspicion of drink driving. The Guards had searched the car and found five kilos of cocaine stashed in the boot. He had been on his way to Dublin with it, and now was on remand in Clover Hill, awaiting sentencing.

They saw Hugh before they saw Tess. Jen was happy she had come down – it would be nice to see her.

Tess made her way over to Jen's parents and, being the gentleman he was, he walked her over to them.

The girls embraced but it was strained. Jen could see she had lost weight – her friend had always been plump but the stress of it all now made her face look drawn.

'Now Poison Ivy will have two of us to talk about.' Tess waved over in Elizabeth's direction as she took a seat.

They all laughed.

'It's good to see you all.'

'You too, Tess. I'm glad you came. How are you?'

'Living on my nerves, Jen. Waiting for that knock on the door of the pub. The money is gone, and the reality is I don't know where it came from. It's only a matter of time before someone comes a-knocking. But anyway, it's just one of the many shit things at the moment. I made my bed and now I have to lie in it.'

Jen didn't know how to respond to that.

'But enough about the crap stuff, Jen. Let's just have a few drinks and a laugh tonight.' Tess hugged her again, and changed the subject.

'They're bringing the food out now. Brilliant. I'll get some drinks, ladies, as long as you three sort out my food.' Andy was gone again.

'He's just acting weird tonight, girls. Have either of you noticed that?' Jen was beginning to get a bit worried – was all the pressure of baby-sitting her getting to him?

'No more than usual!' Sal said with a giggle.

The band took their break as the food came out, and the room was suddenly quiet. Everyone was sitting down and eating. There were about eighty people there, all friends of Jen and her parents, all from the community. A number of her father's work colleagues were there too, and all in all there was a lovely vibe in the room.

Sal and Jen had come down to the hotel that morning and dressed the tables with candles and flowers. The place looked so pretty. Jen had put a collage together of pictures of her parents on their wedding day and every anniversary since. It was a lovely thing to see, and how they looked as happy now as they had on this day forty years ago.

As the staff cleared the tables, Jen's father took his place in front of the mic. He thanked everyone for joining them on their special evening. He spoke of life, and ups and downs, and the importance of love. There was more laughter than tears in the room as he spoke, but there wasn't a dry eye in the place by the time he started to wrap it up. His wife then said a few words, and thanked the community for showing the family the level of support they had, over the last while. The New Year was less than a couple of weeks away and a time for a fresh start.

Then, before Mr Harper stepped down, he invited Andy to the stage to say a few words.

Jen was startled and not too pleased. Presumably Andy also wanted to thank the community for their support of Jen and, frankly, she wished the subject could be dropped.

Andy walked over, shook hands with Mr Harper and prepared to speak.

Sal was beaming at the table, and Tess couldn't help but smile. She hadn't been privy to what was about to happen, but she could guess.

'Em, folks. I won't keep you long, I'm not much of a public speaker.' His voice was brittle with nerves. 'I just wanted to take this opportunity to mirror what has been said, and thank you all for your support over the last few months. It has been difficult and we would have never got through it without the community behind us. We are looking forward to the new year, and a new beginning.'

The round of applause erupting gave him a moment to pause and gather his thoughts.

'But, before I go, I would like to ask Jen something.'

Jen glared at him. She couldn't believe he was doing this to her. She was going to give him a piece of her mind for drawing attention to her like this.

She looked at Sal and saw she was in tears, and slowly but surely the penny started to drop. Danny was with her parents,

Will and his partner, and they were all up out of their seats in excitement. Andy's parents were there too.

'She's going to be mortified that I've put her on the spot like this, but it couldn't wait. Jen, can you come here, please?'

She reluctantly walked over to where he was and turned her back to the crowd. Danny walked over to Andy and handed him something.

'What in blue blazes are you two up to?' she asked.

'Jen Harper. I love you, and I want to be with you, today and always.'

He dropped to one knee, and everyone was on their feet, scarcely breathing with anticipation.

'Jen, will you marry me?'

She didn't have to be asked twice. She nodded her head, and burst into tears. The whole place erupted into cheers and applause. He put the ring on her finger, and she recognised it straight away – her grandmother's. Her parents had been in on the whole thing. The band started to play through the flurry of handshakes and hugs. The phone cameras were out in force, taking pictures of the happy couple, arm in arm. Everyone who needed to know was there, and before long the Facebook notifications began to fly in from the tagged shots.

'Dad! You knew about this?'

'Of course I did, Jen. Andy came to me a couple of weeks ago, and asked my permission. I suggested he do it tonight. He didn't want to hijack our night, but I insisted. I'm happy for you, love – he's a good man.'

'Thanks, Dad.'

She hugged her parents. Danny arrived for a hug as well.

'Mam, I knew all about it too! I was the very first person in the world Andy told. He wanted to know if it was OK with me.'

'And is it, Dan?'

'Yeah, Mam, he's cool, and he told me I'd get to help him organise everything.'

Andy was absolutely beaming with pride and love. He ruffled Danny's hair and planted a kiss on Jen's cheek. From behind them, they heard the distinct pop of a champagne bottle. It was Sal and Tess, with a bucket, tray and glasses.

'You two knew as well, I suppose?' she enquired.

'I did,' said Sal.

'I didn't – but I guessed,' said Tess. 'Congrats to you both, I'm really happy for you.'

She looked happy for her friends, but Jen could hear the weight of sadness in her voice. Understandable, she supposed.

The night passed so quickly. There was lots of dancing and fun and Jen for the first time in a long time felt at peace and happy. She knew it was quick, they had only been together for a short time, but they were very close. Everything that had happened in the last few months had only brought them closer. She felt a heaviness in her heart as she thought about Sharon, and how she must have felt the night he asked her. They had set her free, and cleared her name of the suggestion of suicide. And despite the horrific nature of what had been uncovered, it had been a huge relief for her parents that their daughter hadn't killed herself in despair. Andy had visited them when the news broke first, and they had spoken for a long time. The anger and the hurt began to lift, and finally he felt as though he had their permission to move on.

The light was beginning to return for sure. The longest night was here, but in the darkness something beautiful had begun to shine. Love and hope. Jen could start thinking about the future, as a family.

CODA

Andy carried Danny up the stairs and laid him in his bed. He had fallen asleep in the car on the way home, gone from chatting the ears off them to snoring in minutes.

Jen made tea, and the two of them panned out on the bed drinking it, fully dressed. Both were fairly sober, but lightheaded from the excitement.

'Are you happy, Jen?'

'Yes, very. Are you, Andy? Are you sure this is what you want?'

'I have never been so sure of anything in my life, my darling. The last few weeks, as I came to terms with it all, I realised life is too short to wait around, and be afraid of letting things happen.'

'What about your trip? Are you still going to go on that? I don't mind, you know. You don't have to cancel.'

'Well, I am going on a trip. But with you and Danny.'

'What?'

'That's the other part of the present tonight. We are all going to Disneyworld in January, and we're going to meet my sister and her family out there.'

'Oh Andy, Danny is going to be over the moon!' She was really excited. Andy's sisters had all come home after he told them about Sharon. It had been a short visit but she had got on with them all like a house on fire.

'I love you, Mr McClean.'

'I love you too, Miss Harper, soon to be Mrs McClean.'

She picked up her phone and had a look on Facebook. 'Oh, look at this!' Several of her friends had tagged her in pictures. She was chuffed with all the likes, and the lovely comments. It seemed like the whole world was delighted for her. She kept looking at the ring on her finger, and she felt like the luckiest woman in the world.

'Oh, by the way,' he said, 'Sal left something under the bed for you. She knows what you're like, and wanted to get you something straight away.'

'Please tell me it's not something dirty? That would just be wrong. You grab it there – I have a couple of voice mails.'

Andy produced a beautiful box, tied with a big red ribbon, from under the bed.

Jen dialled her voicemail, hit loudspeaker and opened the present.

It was a box full of bridal magazines. Jen laughed out loud when she found hi-lighters, and post-its. There were a dozen publications in the box. Sal had known this would give her a good laugh, and let her get planning straight away.

The first voicemail was from Andy's sister. She was so delighted to welcome Jen to the family and she couldn't wait to see her in the New Year.

The second was from all her workmates. None of them could make it, as it was one of the busiest nights of the year in work, but they had a staff party planned for her in between Christmas and New Year. They all sang and whooped down the phone, and Jen thought she would burst with excitement.

Then the final voicemail started.

'*Congrats, guys, you look amazing in the pictures. So happy for you – aren't you the perfect couple?*'

The air was sucked out of the room, both of them frozen in a sea of bridal magazines.

Andy grabbed her hand.

'*Guess who?*' his voice said. '*I'm in Europe. It pays to have contacts and friends in the right places, when you want to get out of the country in a hurry. But know this, Jen, I'm watching. I'll always be watching. I told you on the beach I would gut you and your little boy. My time will come.*'

Neither of them spoke. Words were futile. The looks that passed between them said enough. Scott had won.

The weeks of therapy and healing had been for nothing. The

happy ending and the romance were lost. He had inflicted a mortal wound and won the war. They should have known – he was too clever for all of them. He had the last laugh and had got away with murder. First Sharon and now he would kill her too – one way or another.

Time slowed as her feet reluctantly shuffled towards the bedroom window. Despair hung heavy in the air like fog and even the comforting glow of the lighthouse beam couldn't compete with the darkness surrounding her. Death had been invited, and it would eventually arrive.

She could hear music but couldn't tell if it was in her head or rolling in on the sea. It was the tune to a childhood rhyme – she remembered it from her playground days. The words formed in her head.

Ring-a-ring o' Roses,
A pocket full of posies,
A-tishoo! A-tishoo!
We all fall down!

Jen's heart broke in two. She sank to her knees as the last flame of optimism died.

Andy went to her and held her as she cried.

In that moment, he vowed never to let any harm come to her or Danny, ever again. He would protect them no matter what the cost. The war wasn't over and Scott would never win.

Scott had brought them to their knees, but they would not fall down.

THE END